BL
R
C
C000049082

ALSO BY DYLAN YOUNG

The Silent Girls

BLOOD RUNS COLD

DYLAN YOUNG

bookouture

Published by Bookouture in 2018

An imprint of StoryFire Ltd.

Carmelite House
50 Victoria Embankment
London EC4Y 0DZ

www.bookouture.com

Copyright © Dylan Young, 2018

Dylan Young has asserted his right to be identified
as the author of this work.

All rights reserved. No part of this publication may be reproduced,
stored in any retrieval system, or transmitted, in any form or by
any means, electronic, mechanical, photocopying, recording or
otherwise, without the prior written permission of the publishers.

ISBN: 978-1-78681-403-6
eBook ISBN: 978-1-78681-402-9

This book is a work of fiction. Names, characters, businesses,
organizations, places and events other than those clearly in the
public domain, are either the product of the author's imagination
or are used fictitiously. Any resemblance to actual persons, living or
dead, events or locales is entirely coincidental.

CHAPTER ONE

It was hot for June. Sweltering for Scotland. The meteorologists called it a plume. Mediterranean air from southern Europe billowed up across the Channel, sending temperatures soaring. Suddenly men were in T-shirts and shorts, girls in denim cut-offs and flouncy tops, their pale northern thighs and chests blotched from the sudden exposure to rarely experienced levels of UV.

Thirteen-year-old Kirsty Smeaton told her eleven-year-old sister Blair she was taking her to the shop on Market Street for an ice cream. But really it was because their mother wanted half an hour's quiet to smoke and watch the soaps on catch-up.

Blair dawdled beside Kirsty, concentrating on the Twister dripping sticky green and yellow tracks onto her fingers. Heat seemed to flow up in waves from the pavement. They'd crossed back over the Esk and Kirsty had demolished half of her Solero already, struggling not to get any gunk onto her phone. Her friend Marie had just sent her a Snapchat of her kid brother, Charlie, in a paddling pool with a rubber ring on his head, and she was texting a thumbs-up emoji in reply as she walked along the park path. She didn't notice the dog until it emerged from behind the white van and they almost walked into it – a gorgeous, wonderful, floppy-eared German Shepherd puppy.

'Careful now,' said a voice.

The van stood parked at the kerb in the lay-by on Station Road, opposite the print works. A man followed the dog onto the pavement, clutching a long lead.

'You need to look where you're going, ladies,' said the man, 'in case you trip over Banshee, here.'

'Banshee, is that his name?'

'Her name. Cos she makes a noise like a banshee when she says hello.'

The dog looked longingly up at the girls' lollipops, straining at the lead. The yellow and black jacket strapped around her chest said, 'Guide dog puppy in training.'

'Awww,' cooed Kirsty.

'Can we pet her?' Blair asked.

The man frowned. 'Well. You shouldn't. Not really. Not while she's being walked. But let me put her back in her crate and then we'll see.'

The man picked the dog up and walked to the rear of the white van, opened the doors and put Banshee into a mesh cage. Both girls followed their progress, leaning in to touch the dog through the grille. Banshee was now in a tail-wagging frenzy, trying to lick as many bits of their flesh as she could.

'Are you teaching her?' asked Kirsty, grinning.

'Oh yes. She's a quick learner, too,' said the man, adjusting the rear door inwards a little, shielding the dog from the street. He unclipped something from his belt. Something black and cylindrical that looked like a torch. He reached forwards casually as if he was going to shine it into the van, keeping it at shoulder level. Kirsty followed his hand. It moved slowly, non-threateningly, the man smiling as he noticed her curious gaze, tilting the object almost as if offering it to her. As if he was about to explain.

Blair was too preoccupied with Banshee to notice. But Kirsty frowned, her instincts alerted, blinked once and looked up into the man's face just before he thrust the prongs towards her T-shirt and hit the skin behind it.

She jerked away, but not before the stun gun sent 800,000 volts pulsing through her with an accompanying crackle and buzz. Kirsty clattered against the van's rear plastic bumper, her knees folding under her. Pain erupted as her muscles went into spasm and she collapsed against the inside of the rear door. She tried to scream, to breathe, but nothing, for several long seconds, emerged from her locked-up body. The very last thing she remembered before being thrown into the rear next to the yelping Banshee was seeing Blair's lolly tumble from her hands.

One eyewitness on the other side of the bridge later said they saw a dog handler talking to two girls. The older girl seemed to slump and needed assistance getting into the back of the van. The witness had been too far away to see the make or model. Too far away to see a number plate. The driver, she reported, closed the rear doors, walked calmly around and drove away.

They found Kirsty eight hours later, stumbling, disorientated, in a field in Pennycuick with a stolen German Shepherd puppy at her side. She could add nothing to the accounts other than describing a man dressed in a brown short-sleeved shirt and cargo pants, wearing sunglasses under a green baseball cap. His shirt had looked a little bit too large for him, he spoke in a calm and steady voice that she didn't recognise and, through her tears, she could think of nothing that made him stand out.

Despite a huge search, house to house on the streets surrounding where it had happened and a Police Scotland city-wide sweep that day, there was no sign of Blair Smeaton anywhere.

CHAPTER TWO

The staff nurse was new. He'd seen her a couple of times on shifts, her face blooming pink with adrenaline, her dark hair tied back. She was young, still keen.

'Dr Hawley, Dr Hawley!' Her voice cut through the war-zone noises; clattering trolleys, someone vomiting in an adjacent cubicle, an elderly patient pleading to go home, her confused begging forlornly hushed by a relative. Hawley didn't reply immediately. He was busy turning over black instrument boxes on a shelf, searching for an ophthalmoscope. He needed it to examine a stroke patient's retinas but the one he liked, the one with the least dust on the lens, wasn't where it should have been. He preferred the wall-units, the rechargeable type. They, at least, never went walkabout.

'Dr Hawley.'

He felt a hand on his elbow and turned, flicking his gaze down to her name badge. Kelly Mann. The noise of an ambulance siren slowly getting louder in its approach from the city centre drew her attention for a moment and she glanced towards the entrance. More patients on the way.

'Motorcycle accident according to Charge nurse. Multiple injuries. No idea where we'll put them.' Kelly shrugged and proffered a sanguine smile.

'We'll find somewhere. He's a magician.'

Kelly let out a small sigh. She hadn't quite developed the thick skin you needed to work the Friday night six to two shift. Maybe she never would. Every training NHS doctor and nurse did a stint in A and E. It was more than a bit like conscription given that every day in every hospital in the country felt like a battle. But this wasn't Syria, this was Bath in June. Not many trainees stayed after their mandatory stint. Only the brave, or the very foolish. Hawley knew to which category he belonged.

'What can I do for you, Kelly?'

Someone, probably an anaesthetist judging by the green theatre scrubs, ran towards the resuscitation room. Through the open door, Hawley counted at least eight staff working on a forty-six-year-old cardiac arrest.

Kelly said, 'I know it's not yours, but I have a six-year-old who fell off a swing. Goran was dealing with it but he's been in there,' she nodded towards the resus room, 'for twenty minutes and I just need someone to take a quick look and sign a form so that we can get the poor little thing to X-ray. Do you mind?'

He wanted to suggest she ask someone else but one glance told him there was no one. They'd had the usual slew of drunks and minor traumas, but the evening had been compounded by a collapsed stage at an agricultural show. No fatalities, but they could have done without the extra dozen cuts and scrapes that needed dressings and sutures.

With someone a little more experienced he might have suggested she fill the form in and he'd simply sign it, job done. But Kelly was new. It wouldn't be fair to ask her to stretch the rules she was still learning.

'Please?' She let her chin fall and batted her lashes. He hesitated and her lips morphed into a flickering smile of confusion. That would have been his chance. There, with that little flicker. He could have told her why he hesitated and why he couldn't help. But a paramedic pushed through between them, brusquely excusing himself, and Hawley's chance evaporated, the moment lost. He was caught now with no way out. Despite all the promises he'd made to himself and stuck to for years, he heard himself say, 'OK.'

Kelly beamed. 'Oh, thanks. I know I'm being a pain, but she's such a sweetie.'

She was already turning, leading the way across the frantic department, towards the paediatric cubicles. He heard a name as Kelly turned to deliver it, but only vaguely. The noise of shouted orders and bleeping alarms competed with the dull buzz in Hawley's ears. He felt a prickling in his fingers and clutched his cold hands together. They crossed a corridor and the noise changed. The volume dropped away and instead of cacophony, here were muffled voices and the miserable wailing of a sick baby. Kelly pulled back a curtain and smiled brightly.

'Hi, Ashlee.'

A student nurse in lilac scrubs stood sentinel at the bedside, the relief at Kelly's return obvious in her anxious face. The little girl looked tiny on the trolley, her dark skin stark against the yellow sheets. A grey sling held her right arm flexed. Kelly kept eye contact, her dazzling smile not faltering for a second.

'Where's Mummy, Ashlee?'

'She's taken Efren to the toilet.'

'Poor Efren,' she made a joke of it, dropping her voice in a conspiratorial whisper. 'Look, I've brought Dr Hawley to make you better.'

Ashlee whimpered.

Kelly turned to the student. 'Lucy, pop to the loo and tell Ashlee's mum the doctor's here.

Lucy nodded and hurried off.

'I want Mummy,' Ashlee said.

'No, it's OK, Ashlee. All Dr Hawley wants to do is look. All he's going to do is look at your poorly arm.'

Hawley watched the exchange from the foot of the bed.

'Will you let him have a peep if I hold your hand, Ashlee?'

Ashlee gave a solemn nod.

Hawley didn't move. He looked at the little girl. She was scared and vulnerable. He felt saliva pooling on the root of his tongue. He tried swallowing, but his throat felt tight and narrow, forcing a noisy gulp.

'Hi Ashlee,' he said, his voice cracking.

Ashlee said nothing.

'Show me,' Hawley said. He moved to the side opposite the sling. Kelly, confused, waited.

'Just lift the sling a little,' Hawley ordered.

Ashlee's arm was resting on her abdomen. Carefully, Kelly lifted the bandage. Hawley leaned forwards and peered. The swelling above the wrist looked like a barn door diagnosis. He'd put money on it being a Colles' fracture.

'Yeah, that needs an X-ray.'

'Good. I'll get the form…' she froze with one hand raised and sent him a manic smile, 'which I've left on the desk. I'll be two seconds.' Before Hawley could respond, she swept the curtain back and exited, leaving him alone with the little girl.

He turned back to look at her.

She watched him, her eyes huge, brow furrowing, sensing at last that something was off-kilter.

He almost laughed at the thought. Off-kilter was putting it mildly.

Hawley forced a breath, steadying himself. He ought to say something. Reassure his patient. But he didn't trust Ashlee. More importantly, he didn't trust himself. That was why he avoided seeing children whenever he could. It was difficult. Sometimes impossible. And when it became absolutely essential and unavoidable he would. But always with a nurse present and with a parent. There was good reason. That was the sort of world it was these days. Hawley knew that only too well.

It was why he never saw children alone, like *this*. It provided far too many opportunities for misunderstandings.

He didn't say anything to Ashlee. He merely turned away and swept out of the cubicle, not wanting to let thoughts, dark thoughts, crowd in on him again.

He almost collided with Kelly, beetling back around the corner.

'Dr Hawley?' Concern tipped the last vowel of his name up an octave.

He held out a palm, willing her to stop and be quiet as he recovered.

Kelly ignored him. 'What's wrong? Is it Ashlee?'

She brushed past him, opened the curtains. Hawley heard her voice, in control, soothing. 'Hello sweetie. Won't be a minute. You OK?'

Hawley waited until Kelly emerged from behind the curtain.

'Whatever's the matter?'

Hawley was shaking his head. 'You should never…' he blew out air. 'Never leave a kid that age unchaperoned.' He sucked in a breath through his nose. 'Never alone…'

Not with me.

Kelly stared at him. 'I only went to get the X-ray form.'

Hawley squeezed his eyes shut and then opened them. 'Never.' He shook his head.

'But you were—'

'Never.' It came out through gritted teeth and made her flinch. 'Never fucking ever…'

Kelly flushed.

Hawley closed his eyes again, knowing he was going way too far. This girl wasn't responsible for his baggage. Baggage that had fallen open again here in this busy A and E, spilling out all its dirty laundry for her to see. But she had to know. That much she had to realise. He picked up a clipboard from a desk and grunted. 'Give me the form.'

Kelly handed him the slip. He filled it in, signed it, gave it back, not meeting her gaze when he said, 'Get someone else to look at the X-ray.'

She took it and said to his departing back, 'Have I done something wrong?'

He stopped, half turned. 'Kids are… You can't be too careful. Get Goran to review her.'

Kelly nodded, tight-lipped. 'You sure you're alright?'

In his head, he could hear a shrill voice laughing maniacally. He was far from alright. He quelled the voice and said, 'Fine.'

As he walked away, he could sense her eyes on him.

Sometime during this shift, she would speak to Goran about him. He had a good idea of how that conversation would go. Goran would sigh and explain how it was such a shame. That Hawley was a good doctor, an asset to the unit whenever he did a shift. But that there was something no one could quite put a finger on. And when Goran would ask why Kelly wanted to know, she'd explain about Ashlee, and Goran would bare his teeth in a grimace of pained understanding. Dr Hawley avoided kids. Would swap the crappiest file, even see to a constantly retching food poisoning case or debride a putrid gangrenous foot, anything so long as he didn't have to see any kids. The other staff were only too happy to help him out. And Kelly would ask why. And Goran would reply with a faraway look and explain that no one really knew but it must have been something bad. Maybe he'd lost one along the way. A meningitis, or an Addison's. Something that had left deep and unhealed wounds. And Kelly would nod and look sympathetic and feel sorry for him.

Hawley went to the bathroom. Sweat had beaded on his clean-shaven top lip. He splashed water over his face and let it run over his wrists before sucking up a mouthful in his scooped hands. He glared at his reflection in response to what had just happened, and his own eyes looked back at him accusingly. There were easier ways to earn a living, but the crisis in recruitment in emergency medicine and the government's targets of four-hour waits ensured that he, with his qualifications, could pick and choose his shifts in almost any unit in the country. But that still didn't explain why he worked the worst of them: the Friday and Saturday nights, the bank holidays. What did explain it was the fact that they *were* the worst. He gobbled them up, relishing the constant mayhem. Alcohol-related injuries made up four out of every five emergency episodes during the weekends. That meant lots of fights. Lots of blood. Hardly any kids. No one in their right mind who wanted any semblance of work–life balance would ever choose to do the job.

He let out a wry exhalation on hearing his thoughts form the words 'right mind'. What did that make him? Not right? Not normal?

He dried his face and hands and tried to clear his mind before pulling open the bathroom door. There was work to be done.

CHAPTER THREE

It was DI Anna Gwynne's second week back at work and at last, at long last, she was beginning to feel normal again. It had taken a while. She'd made the most of it though, especially the last few weeks. She'd eaten well, thrown herself around the gym, swum lengths in the pool, made sure she was as fit as she could be. The dark circles under her hazel eyes had finally faded, though it had taken four of the six months she'd been off work before they disappeared completely. The pain from the stab wounds and the bruising around her windpipe had long gone, too, but there were other scars that would take far longer to heal.

Her attacker, a serial killer and rapist called Charles Willis, had been sentenced, but he'd only been caught after he'd killed four people and very nearly killed her on a chilly November day just over six months ago. In the slow weeks of recovery Anna decided she'd no one else to blame for him almost succeeding but herself. She'd finally seen through Willis's clever subterfuge and had exposed his years of sexual assaults, tying him to several murders. For that she'd been lauded. But her procrastination, her self-doubt, had almost got her killed. There was a lesson to be learned there.

She gave evidence at his trial before her return to work. Willis was charged with four counts of murder, one of attempted murder and eighteen counts of rape or attempted rape. Anna described how Willis tracked her on one of her fitness runs, shot her with a veterinary dart laced with a powerful opiate and tried to kill her. She'd sat as Willis's barrister, on the question of premeditation, cross-examined her. How could she be certain murder had been his client's intent?

Anna fixed him with a cold stare and said, 'I can't be certain. But unlike his other victims, I was aware of what he was capable of. Perhaps he'd only make that final decision once he'd finished stabbing me.'

She'd found it an interesting position to be in, trying to be as professionally objective as possible to bring Willis to book while having a very personal need for justice and closure. The Crown Prosecution Service's barrister was anticipating an indefinite term with no option of parole at sentencing. Anna would drink to that.

Anna got up from her desk and went to the window. The way she held herself made her look taller than the five seven that she was. Her dark suit jacket was draped on the chair back, and her shirt – one of several of the white or light blue she usually wore to work – was new and still had crease lines from how it had been packaged. She'd cut her hair back-to-work short and her skin was a healthy colour from the hours of running she'd done over the last month.

Outside the office in Avon and Somerset Police's HQ, the summer sun was already warming the morning air, trying to make life just a little more tolerable on the western side of Britain. A blue-sky day with the promise of long light, tanned limbs and long drinks outside in the streets. Not the sort of day for contemplating mistakes or regret.

Though it was now possible for her to go a day or two without dwelling on the attack, still a shadow lurked. A reptilian skin of memory that she thought she'd shed. And there was the paradox. Anna dealt with the sins of others like a butcher deals with cuts of meat. And, just as a butcher would, inevitably, get blood on his hands, she was tainted by the mental stains left by dealing with criminality. Yet they were nothing a good glass of Riesling and half an hour's dreamy Pink Floyd, or pastoral folk ballads from Zeppelin, could not ease away. A trick taught to her by her dad.

But since Willis had put his hands upon her, his shadow was always there in the background, like spilled port on a white carpet, resisting all her efforts at scrubbing him out.

Because of him and what he'd done, for a while Anna had doubted the wisdom of the road she walked. Perhaps not quite an existential crisis, it had still involved a stepping back, a sensible weighing up of her options. She'd chosen her job because it challenged her and she was good at it. The possibility of closing a case, of helping a victim, of relieving a family of the pain of not knowing drove her on in some way that was difficult to deny. And what other job was there that allowed her to be her stubborn, driven, analytical self and encourage her to use those traits? She couldn't think of one. Slowly, as the weeks of recovery passed, her doubts had faded until, at last, she'd got the all-clear from the medics and here she was.

In early as always, she turned from the window in the open-plan office of the south-west Major Crimes Review Task Force, and sat, hip on a desk, looking at the whiteboard and the pinned photographs from the reactivated cold cases the team had been pursuing while she was away. Set up, as with many forces, in response to advancements in DNA techniques, the team was tasked with seeing if fresh eyes and technology could solve some of the region's unsolved cases. Murder and rape were high on the agenda; and these had become Anna's bitter bread and butter.

One such case was the rape of a young woman in 1983 near the racecourse on the outskirts of Bath. Lucy Bright survived, but her life had been blighted ever since. She'd never married and was not in a steady relationship. The attacker's violations had left, as so often happened, the kind of deep and irreparable psychological damage that some victims were simply unable to overcome. Justice meant a lot to these people – offering a chance for them to draw a line in the sand from where they might start again – and its absence festered like an open wound.

At the time of the attack on Lucy Bright a significant amount of evidence and samples had been collected, including the attacker's semen, but little had been made of those at the time. Analysis of these samples would not have included DNA. But with the establishment of the National DNA database in the early 1990s, samples in historically unsolved cases could be reanalysed and compared with newly acquired data. The samples from Lucy Bright's case were logged but yielded no results initially because the perpetrator's DNA was not in that database for a match to be made. For years, her attacker remained at large, dodging justice's bullet.

But bullets could ricochet.

In March 2017, a DNA sample from a drink-driving offence was loaded onto the system and threw up a partial match of sixteen alleles out of a possible twenty-four tested. Callum Morton, aged nineteen, had not been alive at the time of the rape in 1983, but the match was close enough to suggest that a relative of his could have been involved. Anna's team was alerted, the cold case their responsibility, and two men were now suspects: Morton's father, Peter, a fifty-three-year-old paramedic, and his fifty-five-year-old uncle Dominick, a businessman with several properties abroad. Neither man was aware that familial tracing was slowly closing a ring around them.

Justin Holder and Ryia Khosa, the squad's DCs, had worked up the case in exemplary fashion in Anna's absence. They had enough evidence to question both men, but Superintendent Rainsford, Anna's commander, was wary. If they interviewed the wrong man, there was a chance he might alert his brother. Rainsford did not want this to turn into a messy international manhunt involving Europol.

Typically, the squad had at least three cases running, each member of the team involved to varying degrees with tails on half a dozen more needing to be tied off. But all would be at different degrees of maturity with one usually dominating, according to the progress it was making.

The second case was much more challenging and a stark contrast to the evidence-rich case of Lucy Bright.

Rosie Dawson had been abducted and murdered in 2008 at just ten years old. The image pinned to the board, a posed school photograph taken a few months before her life was so brutally ended, revealed a happy little girl with missing front teeth, oblivious to everything except the need to show the world how big her smile was. Rosie wore glasses to treat a squint, a red V-neck school sweater and a tie knotted tightly at the collar of her white school blouse. Anna couldn't help but smile when she looked at it, but within seconds a flood of anger would follow. But that was OK. Anger was good. She could channel that mental energy. And that was one of the things she could gladly give these innocents. Her energy.

Even so, Rosie's case was proving to be exceptionally challenging. Anna stared at the image, feeling the dull anger pulse, absorbing it and letting it direct her thoughts.

Child abductions were on the rise in the UK. Stranger abductions made up about 40%. Almost fifty abductions, or attempted abductions, took place every year and were inevitably sexually motivated. Three-quarters of them failed; kids were wary. Every child knew the watchwords Stranger Danger, and yet being forced or invited into cars was still the commonest method.

Thankfully, the high-profile cases were still rare but fifty cases a year meant four a month. And this month was no exception. Just that morning Anna got up to find every news bulletin showing another horror story. Young Blair Smeaton from Edinburgh, taken and still missing. She knew they had a separate word for it up there: abduction of under twelves was known as plagium. It was on the books as a defined common-law offence. Today was day two of Blair's abduction, and she didn't envy Police Scotland the task. They'd have the paedophile unit on-board and would be liaising with child-protection to make sure Blair wasn't on any of their lists. They'd have queried the Police National Computer for known offenders, using extended search terms to link to the MO. Press appeals had already gone out for anyone with any information. They'd have a POLSA, a police search advisor, coordinating the search and bodies on the ground doing house to house. It was protocol. What Avon and Somerset would have done when Rosie went missing.

Rosie's photo had been up for only a few days, posted on the whiteboard by Trisha Spedding, the squad's civilian analyst, and already her face was haunting Anna's dreams. The unsolved murder had been plucked from the cold case files at Superintendent Rainsford's request. Some new information had come to light. The force's Hi-Tech unit thought they might have a lead from some images located on a computer file found by Belgian police. But, like all cold cases, it was taking a while to get to grips with it. They'd been frustrated by bureaucracy already, waiting for paper files to come from the force's offsite storage facility. Whoever had carried out the last review had managed to split the file and the Records Management team were having a hard time pulling things together.

Had she lived, Rosie would now be a teenager, pining no doubt for some boy band member, working out what she was going to do with the rest of her life. All of that had been stolen from her by a monster who had grabbed her cruelly from the very arms of her family and ended her life in the most brutal way.

And to top it all, this investigation had an added wrinkle. A new team member was doing the work-up at Rainsford's insistence. Detective Sergeant Dave Woakes had joined three weeks before Anna's return and appeared to have found his feet quickly. Rainsford had taken one look at Anna on her first day back and used words like, 'Ease back into the swing of things,' and, 'Let someone else take the weight,' with a look in his eye that said this was an order rather than a suggestion.

But Anna was finding it very difficult. Taking a back seat had never been her forte. Plus, they'd yet to get to grips with understanding the significance of the image the Belgian police had found. It was a combustible mixture that drove her exasperation level up from a slow simmer to a low boil over the last couple of days. Her easing-back-in period was well and truly over. The tricky bit would be not treading on too many toes.

Anna's approach to any cold case, taught to her by her old boss, Ted Shipwright, was to treat each one as if it had happened yesterday. It needed enthusiasm and urgency and fresh eyes, and a soupçon of anger did no harm either. She had no difficulty bringing a barrow load of all that back to the team.

By eight the squad room was full. Holder called out a cheery hello, looking like a twelve-year-old with large-framed glasses, a clean shave and close-cropped hair. He wore a suit half a size too small for him, as was the fashion. Khosa, her dark hair glossy and sharply cut, like her suit, went straight to her desk and dumped a large handbag onto it. It jangled as it settled.

'What have you got in there, Ryia?' Anna said.

'Just the basics, ma'am. Plus, I've had another set of keys cut for my brother, who is staying with me for a week.'

'No,' said Holder, pulling out a front pocket wallet and a phone. 'These are the basics. I picked your bag up the other day. It's like four kilos.'

Anna grinned. 'Your brother on holiday?'

'No. Off to uni in October. Just visiting his big sis.'

'How's it going?'

'Really well. He's drunk all the milk already and doesn't know what a washing machine is.' She sat, giving both Holder and Anna a forced, over-bright smile.

Trisha Spedding arrived a minute later. An attractive forty-something in a business suit and three-inch heels, she was the civilian analyst on Anna's team. Immediately she sat down, took off her heels and put on a pair of Nikes. She'd told Anna that on average she walked 5 kilometres a day at work and might as well do it in comfort.

Anna smiled. This was her team.

Before Trisha's laces were done up, DS Woakes came in through the door backwards, a cardboard tray of coffees in one hand. Not as tall as Holder, Woakes was compact and fit with a football player's quick reactions. He'd come to the squad from Leicester, where he'd worked drugs and serious crimes, but he was an Essex man by origin and the flat words, the 'mates' and the 'yeahs' peppered his sentences when he got excited. This was his first sergeant's post and everything about him suggested a kind of suppressed energy, like a shaken bottle of Dr Pepper with the top still on, ready to froth up with one twist. He was quick to smile and just as quick to lose it if he thought you weren't looking. Anna had heard he was good at his job, but she wasn't sure how good he was with people.

'Right, ma'am, Americano with one sweetener; Justin flat white with one sugar; Trisha tea, milk only; and Ryia, espresso, no sugar. Bosh.' Woakes entered the squad room with a big smile.

'None for you, Dave?' Anna asked when the drinks were distributed.

'Nah, try not to. Sends me a bit twitchy does caffeine. Just water while I'm training for the Ironman.'

'Ah, yes,' Anna remembered. Woakes was one of those. No longer playing competitive sports, he competed with himself in punishing training regimens and even more punishing endurance competitions like Tough Mudder and Ironman. The modern-day equivalent of self-flagellation.

Anna stood at the end of the squad room, next to the whiteboard and her office, a small glass box that had been Ted Shipwright's up until a few months ago. She was still having problems coming to terms with the fact that it was now hers. Rainsford made her promotion permanent as soon as she'd arrived back from sick leave.

'OK,' Anna called everyone to order. 'Let's start with Lucy Bright.'

Khosa and Holder exchanged glances, Holder shrugged, Khosa stood up.

'Trisha's checked with the golf club, ma'am. Dominick Morton's booked in with a foursome teeing off at nine.'

On Saturday mornings, Dominick Morton, the businessman brother, played golf at a club in Nailsea. Anna knew only one sure way of finding out which man was the perpetrator, and if they were careful enough, they could do it without either of them knowing.

Anna nodded. 'And how did you manage it without arousing too much suspicion?'

'Trisha?' Khosa looked towards the analyst, who coloured immediately.

'Said I'd found a personalised golf club cover and asked if a D. Morton was playing there this weekend so I could bring it in. They were very accommodating.'

Anna smiled and nodded. Trisha was a gem.

'So, what's the plan?' Woakes said.

'We're going for lunch,' Khosa said. 'Morton usually has a sandwich and a pint after a round. We'll watch when he goes out for a cigarette. Justin will follow him out for a vape.'

'Do you vape?' Anna asked Holder.

'No, ma'am. But my cousin does and he's got me some nicotine-free juice.'

'So then?'

'With a bit of luck, we'll get the stub Morton has smoked and—'

'Do you want me there?' Woakes cut in.

'No, it'll be fine, sarge,' Holder said.

'Happy to come along,' Woakes persisted.

Anna shook her head. 'No need to baby them, Dave. Besides, I can only swing overtime for two. And I trust them.'

Woakes nodded. He looked a little disappointed.

Keen, this one.

'Thanks, Ryia,' Anna said. 'Dave, you're up. Tell us about Rosie Dawson.'

Trisha said, 'You'll be glad to know we finally got the files late yesterday afternoon and I emailed a summary over to Sergeant Woakes. I've got copies here.' She handed out some folders.

Woakes stood. He'd taken off his jacket and his shirt was open at the collar, his ID badge hanging on a navy lanyard. In his hand was a blue plastic folder. From this he took several photographs and began pinning them up on the board under Rosie's happy face.

'June 6 2008. Ten-year-old Rosie and her grandmother, Grace Dawson, were walking home from school through a park in Clevedon, not more than seven miles from where we sit. It was about four thirty, the park wasn't busy. On the way home, they took the woods path behind Highdale Avenue.'

Woakes put up a large schematic. 'This is at the rear of houses but is not overlooked. Someone came up on Grace's blind side and struck her from behind. The blow was severe enough to knock her out. She fell and suffered a facial fracture from contact with the ground. She was dragged behind bushes and we assume Rosie was abducted at that point. No one saw anything there but witnesses described a man in army fatigues leaving the park with a very large rucksack, exiting on Highdale Avenue near the church a short time later.' He pointed to the label 'Christchurch'. 'From there, we have no further sightings.'

Anna, one ear open to Woakes' voice, sat thumbing through her copy of the file, already thickening from the addition of her own notes. What Woakes hadn't said was that Rosie's grandmother always picked her up from school, and because it was summer, she preferred to walk if the weather was good. Rosie liked seeing the squirrels and sometimes went to the play area in the park. Small details that were probably irrelevant. Except that small details were sometimes the most important in cases like these. They were the threads which would pull the patchwork together.

Woakes pinned another image up on the board. Bones, small and white, arranged at the bottom of a black plastic bag, the skull on top. All that was left of Rosie Dawson.

'Fourteen months later, some walkers found a plastic bag containing human remains beside a path near Charterhouse in the Mendips, twenty miles from where she was abducted. Dental DNA testing threw up a match for Rosie Dawson. The bones were bleached, with strong traces of hypochlorite. Forensics said they were also boiled. So, there's the abduction site and the discovery of remains site. But no crime scene otherwise. The remains yielded sod all forensic information other than traces of Rosie's DNA, handsaw marks on the vertebrae and knife marks around the long joints where the head was removed and the long bones separated. Probably for ease of disposal.'

Khosa looked troubled. 'I don't want to ask but I presume this was all done post-mortem?'

Woakes nodded. 'They were specific about that. No ancillary cut marks around the vertebrae like you might get with movement if the victim was struggling and alive. Knife marks on the long bones suggest that the flesh was cut through to the bone before the saw was used to sever the joints.'

'It's butchery,' Holder said.

Woakes nodded.

'But nothing that tells us how she was killed?'

Woakes shook his head.

Anna said, 'OK. He kills Rosie, dismembers her, boils the remains to strip the flesh, then uses the bleach, the hypochlorite, to destroy any DNA traces he'd left rather than to try and hide who Rosie was. Her DNA would still be in her marrow and inside the teeth. He must have known that. It suggests that he was not expecting anyone to find them, but if they were found, he'd not leave any evidence. So, he's careful and very methodical.'

Holder said, 'So we don't know when she died?'

Woakes shook his head again. 'We don't know how or when. The bag was black plastic, like you'd find lining a million bins. Sold in two of the big four supermarkets across the country. No fingerprints. As for when, you know the stats on child abductions. Usually, if the victims are killed immediately they're found within a five-mile radius. If the killing isn't immediate, then they're usually kept alive for twenty-four hours maximum. The child becomes a liability. They're too difficult to keep under control.'

'So, because she was found twenty miles from the location of the abduction we can assume she was kept alive somewhere for longer. That's irregular…' Holder exhaled loudly.

'Exactly. That's the kicker. The other thing that stands out is the fact that Rosie had Down's syndrome,' Woakes added.

Anna broke her silence. 'So, do we think Rosie was targeted because of it, or is it irrelevant? Must be something the investigating team looked at? Other Down's syndrome victims. But it's worth looking again.' She turned to Trisha and said, 'We'll need to run that through HOLMES,' before standing and walking towards the whiteboard to stand with arms folded. 'And the fact that the bones were left near a well-walked path is particularly odd.'

Trisha nodded. They'd use indexers to input data into the Home Office Large and Major Enquiry System, but Trisha's role as an actions coordinator meant that she would have a handle on what everyone was doing, gather up their reports and ensure they were indexed.

'It could suggest the killer wanted them found,' Khosa said

Anna nodded. 'Or that they were discarded in a panic. And why this particular path? I think it's worth a visit. But Justin's right, it means he must have kept Rosie somewhere. Maybe when she was alive, but certainly for her disposal. If he was boiling body parts, he'd need something big enough to use for that too.'

Trisha had gone very pale.

'He must have had somewhere safe, somewhere he wouldn't be disturbed to hide her, to do that sort of thing with the body,' Holder said.

'God, is this a man or an ogre?' Khosa said.

Woakes nodded. Anna turned back to look at the rest of the team. Khosa was busy making notes, Trisha was shaking her head slowly. But Holder could only nod. He kept on nodding for several seconds, his eyes focused on the pen in his fingers. He could get a job with the manufacturers testing the longevity of the spring in the retractable mechanism the way he kept pressing again and again. Anna knew that look. These were difficult cases for her young team to deal with and did not make for easy listening. It wasn't their first murder and it would not be their last. But child murders, and especially ones with this degree of planning and execution, were mercifully rare. She broke the uneasy silence in the room to bring them back to focus. 'What about the recent input?'

Khosa sat up. 'You already know that our Hi-Tech unit got flagged by the Belgian police. They carried out a raid on an illegal pornography site administrator a couple of months ago. They run everything child-related through new facial recognition software now and they got a hit on Rosie. Hi-Tech have now sent that image over, ma'am.'

Holder's eyes snapped up and Trisha frowned.

Khosa shook her head and reassured them. 'No, don't worry, it's not even category C, but they're pretty certain it is Rosie.'

Sexual Offences Definitive Guidelines had been in existence since 2014 and related to indecent images of children. Categories A and B were the worst. Category C were often non-overt, so Khosa's reassurance was a very welcome clarification.

Khosa punched her keyboard and rotated the screen for the others to see. It showed a little girl sitting on a blanket in a grubby vest, her tear-streaked face smeared with dirt, staring into the camera. Khosa was right, there was nothing at all suggestive about the image, but that did not make it any less disturbing. The lost and desperate look in Rosie's eyes was difficult to look at. Anna concentrated on the accessory details. A concrete floor and an unplastered drywall, bottles of water and, in the corner, a bucket. Black plastic with a wooden handle.

'Is this where he kept her?' Trisha asked.

'Probably,' Woakes said.

On the image, a caption read, 'PPV – Soon.'

'What's PPV?' Holder asked.

'Pay per view,' Khosa said. 'That's what Hi-Tech said.'

Something cold and unpleasant uncoiled inside Anna.

'We need the tech guys to help us with this and pronto,' Anna said to Khosa.

'Yes, ma'am.'

'Meanwhile, let's see if there's anything that gives us a clue as to location, any branding on the water bottles, a sales tag on the bucket. Was Rosie wearing the same clothes as when she was taken? Anything that might help.' Anna turned to Trisha. 'Get everyone a copy.'

Trisha nodded.

Anna sighed. 'So, minimal forensics. No time of death. No clue as to where she was kept until now. And no one was arrested or interviewed?'

'Lots of people interviewed. The dad, uncles, vicar at the church she went to, oh, and a doctor she'd seen. The one they thought was a nonce.'

Anna registered Woakes' slang. Nonce was a prison term for a pariah within the prison community. A child abuser or a grass. Her preferred term was known sex offender, but she let it slide.

'What about the family?'

'Small family unit. Mother, father and grandmother. Rosie had a sister who was seven at the time. No interfering uncles or neighbours. Everyone was interviewed and checked out. CCTV at the school showed her teachers leaving and they were all traced.'

'Father?'

'Worked in the bearings factory. Day shift. They had to go and fetch him when they found out what had happened. Clean as a whistle.'

'What about this suspect with the rucksack?' she asked.

Woakes nodded. 'Rosie was 47.5 inches tall. She weighed 33 kilos. A big rucksack can have a 150-litre capacity.' He put an open laptop on the nearest desk and clicked a few keys.

Anna watched as a 4-foot replica dummy – folded, knees bent, arms restricted across the chest, mouth and eyes taped – was fitted into the huge backpack with ease. They threw in 30 kilos of weight, and the uniform in the demo lifted the pack onto his back and started walking. It looked heavy. But it also looked very plausible.

No one spoke as the film ran.

'So, he was fit enough to be able to carry one of those with a 33-kilo load,' Khosa said.

Woakes killed the video.

Anna opted for magnanimity. Rainsford would be proud. 'OK, Dave, lines of enquiry?'

Woakes had a checklist and copied it to the board. 'Divvy up the reports: witness statements, interviews, etcetera. Go down to the abduction site and the discovery site, and see them for ourselves. Re-run what little forensics there are. See if any of the new tech can squeeze anything from the few samples they had. The plastic bag or the bones. And get Hi-Tech to tell us what they know about the images.'

Anna nodded, but it all felt a little rushed and insubstantial. Almost as if he knew this would lead nowhere.

'Worth asking anyone any more questions?' Khosa said. 'There is a witness list. People came forward after the appeal. Two people said they'd seen a man carrying the rucksack leave the park. Two others said they saw either him getting into a van or a van leaving the area at that time, and an off-duty special constable confirmed the sighting.

Anna nodded. Direction of travel for a perpetrator was always useful. 'See if anyone is still around.'

Khosa nodded. 'Trisha's already started tracing them, ma'am.'

Cold cases suffered from the real possibility that witnesses had moved away. Sometimes even abroad after this length of time.

'I've traced one so far,' Trisha said.

Anna nodded. 'Great, I'll take that. Oh, and can you find out if the special who saw the car is still on the force?'

Trisha nodded.

Woakes, realising he'd dropped the ball, chipped in. 'Yeah, of course. Tick all the boxes.'

Holder said, 'What about reinterviewing the family?'

The frown lines on Woakes' head deepened. 'I'd stay away from them for now. We don't have anything new to talk to them about and I don't think showing them the Belgian images would help. If something comes up, we'll get a FLO to link up.'

Anna nodded. A family liaison officer was always needed in these instances.

'But given this new image evidence, I reckon this doctor the previous team interviewed might be worth a shout.' Woakes looked down at the file. 'Name of Hawley.'

Anna narrowed her eyes. 'In what way worth a shout?'

'Pretty obvious, isn't it? Whoever did this is no fool. She was taken on her route home – he knew where Rosie went to school. Knew how big a rucksack he'd need. The other suspects all had tight alibis accounting for their whereabouts at the time of the abduction. But his was iffy. Claimed to be asleep in his room after a night shift with no witnesses. I'm a great believer in low-hanging fruit, ma'am. Especially when it's easy to shake the tree to see what falls off. Bish bosh.'

Anna could spot a scattergun when she saw it. Woakes had his finger on the trigger of one here and it grated. It wasn't her style to make assumptions. Apart from reviewing what already existed, the one concrete piece of new evidence was the image found by the Belgian police. The logical thing to do was prioritise that and analyse the outcome.

But Rainsford's words rang in her ears. She didn't want to be accused of not letting her team take the weight. It was also useful to reinterview suspects – as long as it didn't scare them off.

'OK. Set it up for Monday,' she said, already regretting it. Something told her that Woakes' 'bish bosh' approach was going to lead to trouble.

'But we also need to start doing the legwork. Once we've interviewed this Dr Hawley, you and I need to visit where all this started, Dave. Get a feel for the case.'

Anna took the contact details for the witness Trisha had given her and went back to her office. She sat at her desk and dialled the one confirmed number next to a name.

Valerie Cobain had been walking her dog on the afternoon Rosie was abducted, and she reported seeing a man dressed in army fatigue trousers, a green army T-shirt, sunglasses and a hat emerge and cross the road. She'd been walking away from the man, but when her dog paused to relieve itself, Valerie had glanced back from 100 yards. The man's quick and purposeful stride, and the fact that the backpack looked very heavy, struck her before she'd reached down to scoop her dog's poop into a plastic bag. Valerie had been sixty-five at the time.

Valerie answered Anna's call immediately and listened while it was explained to her how Avon and Somerset were looking again at the case. Her account tallied exactly with the witness report Anna had in front of her. The man, Valerie explained, walked purposefully, leaning forwards because of the weight of the rucksack. He had not looked up but she remembered he'd worn sunglasses and a camouflaged floppy hat. A bush hat.

'Of course, we lost poor Roxy two years ago,' Valerie said.

'Roxy?'

'Our Lab. The one I was walking.'

'Sorry to hear that. Valerie, do you remember seeing him get into a car?'

'No. But he must have because one minute he was walking up the hill, the next he'd gone. He must have got into one of the parked cars. But I don't know which one. I didn't see.'

'Were there many cars parked on the street?'

'Quite a few if I remember rightly. Always are there. People using the park, you know.'

'Notice any vans?'

'Not really. I wasn't looking, if you know what I mean. There might have been.'

'And this was,' she scanned the notes, 'about four forty in the afternoon?'

'Yes. I used to take Roxy out after her tea.'

Anna made a note. Always useful to have someone who was a creature of habit when it came to drawing up a timeline.

'Does this mean you know who it is?' Valerie asked, her voice hushed.

'We're following up on some new information. Cases like Rosie's are never completely forgotten.'

'I hope you do catch him. Terrible it was. The whole town was shocked that it could happen to one of our own. In Clevedon of all places.'

'Valerie, if you remember anything else at all, here's the number to get in touch with.'

'Let me get my pen.'

Anna repeated the number twice.

And so it begins, she thought.

CHAPTER FOUR

Blair had stopped crying. For now anyway.

The cave smelled funny. Old, like the toadstools under the wet wood in Haugh Park where she sometimes went for walks with Kirsty. The dog man had left her a little lamp and told her to leave it on all the time and if it went out there was another one and another one. A miniature fridge hummed in one corner, containing milk and water. There was no window in the cave and the walls were too smooth and it was dead quiet. Quieter than when you hid under the bedclothes in the dark because you'd heard something on the creaky landing at home. It didn't help that she'd lost her hearing aid.

She'd wrapped herself in the duvet because the cave was cool, though she wasn't cold now. She thought about everything that had happened but it was hard because her thoughts were coming all at once, jumbling and mixing her up. The policeman had noticed her T-shirt. Maroon with a 'G' in yellow letters. He said it was the right thing to have worn because where they were going was magical, just like Hogwarts. He told her how Kirsty had collapsed and had to go to hospital and that was why he'd let her out of the van. He said there were bad people after them and that one of them cursed Kirsty and that was why she'd got all funny and twitched. He told her how he had to take her, Blair, away from the bad people, the ordinary people because, just like in books, she was special. A good witch. Blair witch. He'd laughed then.

The dog man said he had to take her because the bad, ordinary people wanted to hurt her. They didn't understand how special she was. He'd fetched her because they had a really big, scary adventure to get through before she could go back and tell Kirsty all about it. Tell her who she really was.

She'd wanted to believe him. He wore a kind of uniform and he had Banshee too. But a part of her remembered Kirsty twitching on the floor of the van. A part of her, deep inside, cowered, terrified, because Kirsty had told her things. About bad men who wanted to steal you into their cars. Kirsty told her if it ever happened to scream and run away. She had screamed and the man put tape over her mouth as well as Kirsty's. And he hadn't left Kirsty for the ambulance, he'd just thrown her out of the van in a field with poor little Banshee. And then he'd driven the van into a bigger lorry and driven her to the cave.

A part of her knew this wasn't real, not the magic part anyway. But the rest of it was. The bucket in the corner where she was supposed to go to the toilet was. The smell, the duvet, they were all real. Not having her mum was real. Not knowing if Kirsty was OK was real.

After a while, Blair got up and picked up the lantern. The room wasn't big but the shadows in the corners were dark and deep. She ran her hands over the walls. They were smooth, but the floor felt rough and stony. At the end of the room she saw a big, round, flat stone. It looked heavy. She tried to shift it and it moved, just an inch, but it did move. The light from the lantern wouldn't shine into the gap, but it was dark in there and it felt deep, she could tell that much.

She went back to her duvet and waited, wondering if Kirsty was OK. Hoping that she was. Wondering if the dog man was coming back. She felt the tears coming again but she forced herself not to cry.

CHAPTER FIVE

If they weren't out interviewing or otherwise engaged, Superintendent Mark Rainsford, commanding officer of the MCRTF, liked to 'have a chat' with Anna on Friday afternoons. He probably would have preferred the word debrief, but he was doing his best to shrug off his military background. Chat definitely had a warmer feel to it.

Tall, slim, white-shirted always, straight back on pain of death, Rainsford had, at least, also taken off his jacket on what had turned into a stifling afternoon. First time ever she'd seen him jacketless. Anna looked forward to the evening news headlines. It wasn't every day that hell froze over.

'What?' Rainsford asked, seeing her smile.

'Nothing, sir. Just wondering why, in this country of four seasons in every day, we're not geared up for the extremes, that's all. A heatwave has us sweltering, a bit of snow closes all the airports.'

'The foibles of a maritime climate, Anna. But we wouldn't have it any other way, now would we?'

'No, sir.'

'How do things stand?'

'Justin and Ryia are moving forward on the Bright rape case, sir. We're going to attempt to obtain some DNA for elimination testing. We want to make sure we approach the right suspect. Dave has just briefed us on the Dawson case.'

'How's he shaping up?'

'He's keen, I'll give him that. Unorthodox, certainly.'

'You two should get on well then.'

Anna gave him her best inscrutable look.

Rainsford sighed. 'He's still on a probationary period here. He'll want to try and impress.'

'I don't want to be impressed, sir. But I'm happy to be fair. See what his approach leads to. And the Dawson case will be a good test. As far as I can see, evidence was, and is, thin on the ground.'

'What direction does he want to take it?'

'Revisit the scene, review forensics and reinterview a suspect. See what we can glean from this new image.'

'He did some very good work in the Midlands.'

'Serious crimes, wasn't it, sir?'

Rainsford nodded. 'Exposed a nasty drug-trafficking ring. But it doesn't mean he's cut out for what we do here, I appreciate that. Plus, he's ambitious. He's the type of bloke who'll be watching you, too. Seeing how you got up the ladder.'

'So long as it doesn't get in the way of how we work, he can watch what he likes. I'll keep you up to speed, sir.' She got up to leave but Rainsford's pained expression stopped her.

'I've been avoiding this, Anna, but I can't any longer. Hector Shaw wants to see you. Or rather he wants you to be available for another… expedition. He said the weather was now warm enough.'

She kept eye contact with Rainsford, though the desire to squeeze her own eyes shut and grind her teeth almost overwhelmed her. He read the stare with sympathy.

'You're under no obligation. No one would blame you. I want to make that absolutely clear.'

She nodded. Rainsford did earnest employer exceptionally well. *What a military training at Sandhurst did for you*, she supposed.

Stop it.

She wasn't being fair. Not to Rainsford, nor the regional commander nor the chief constable. Every one of them said exactly what Rainsford had just repeated when they found out what Shaw had done. Meddled with an investigation and manipulated Anna in a dangerous and Machiavellian way. Anna still found it difficult to believe that a man in a maximum-security prison serving an indeterminate sentence for multiple murders could exert any influence on events outside. But this wasn't any man; this was Hector Shaw.

Interviewed by Anna seven months ago as part of a cold case investigation when his DNA lit up the board thanks to advanced analysis techniques, Shaw became the prime suspect in the rape and abduction of a girl called Tanya Cromer. It had been Anna's job to try to get his confession. If she could get Shaw to admit his involvement, Anna'd hoped she'd be able to give Tanya's family the closure they needed, to confirm her murder and put her body to rest. But Shaw'd had other ideas.

He hadn't confessed, but he'd led Anna and her team to Tanya's body, and to those of another man. The man Shaw claimed was her true attacker. The DNA evidence from the scene that flagged Shaw's presence also confirmed that a second man was there. A man called Petran, whom Shaw admitted to burying alive.

Had Shaw killed him? And had he killed Tanya? Shaw had also promised Anna more 'buried treasure' – his euphemistic term for interred bodies. And it was this veiled promise that Rainsford alluded to now. Yet, sitting in front of a man who could have committed these crimes wasn't the only, nor the worst, aspect of her involvement with Shaw. What she could not have anticipated was for Shaw to develop a liking for her. Something she had not encouraged in the slightest.

Anna had been working on Charles Willis's case at the same time as reinterviewing Shaw. Believing in Anna's ability to find Willis, Shaw had somehow used his connections both inside and outside prison to bring Willis out of hiding and into a direct confrontation with her. He'd even managed to expose her address to the world, and to Willis in particular. It had been, in Shaw's words, 'a test'. One that she'd passed, but which had put her in mortal danger in the process.

Though it was a sunny Friday afternoon, the shadows under Rainsford's desk cast by the slanting sun felt suddenly and unaccountably chilly on Anna's legs.

'I haven't drawn a line under the Tanya Cromer case yet, sir, we both know that. What he wants to see me about now may be related to that. It may be something else. All I know is that he insisted on it being summer. When it was warm,' Anna said.

I want to be able to smell your perfume, or your nervous musky sweat.

'I know he's been sending you emails. I've shown some to cybercrime, by the way. They're looking into it.' Rainsford looked suddenly like he'd bitten into something disgusting. 'Shaw's poison, we all know that. Pure rat bait.'

'But just like rat bait he's useful, too.'

Rainsford waited.

Anna sighed, her mind made up. 'Shaw and I have unfinished business. I've been putting it off because… because I felt I needed to be stronger. But I'm ready now.'

Really?

Rainsford nodded. 'I hate myself for even talking about—'

Anna interrupted him. 'He knows things, sir. I wouldn't be doing my duty if I didn't…' she searched for the right word and settled on, 're-engage. Petran's death needs investigating. Shaw refuses to talk to the team who've been looking into it. He may well be wanting to talk to me about that.'

A tight little smile softened Rainsford's expression. 'Petran is, or rather was, on the watch list in at least three force areas for sexual harassment, theft and petty crime.'

Anna nodded. 'That all ties in with Shaw's story, sir.'

Rainsford looked at her appraisingly. She found it mildly disconcerting. 'Shipwright was right about you, Anna.'

It broke the tension. Mention of Ted Shipwright, ex-DCI on her cold case team and her mentor, had that effect.

'Have you spoken to him recently, sir? Last I heard he was taking up painting.'

Rainsford shook his head. 'The ACC wants us to write to retired DCIs, see if any of them want to come back part-time to solve this bloody recruitment crisis. There is no substitute for experience, Anna.'

Her heart quickened. Having Shipwright back would be—

Rainsford dashed her hopes with a held-up hand. 'Of course, I wouldn't dream of it. I value my intestines, and Mrs Shipwright assures me she'd have mine as a pair of garters if I so much as suggested it.'

A balloon deflated in Anna's chest. Her old boss had come through a heart attack alive and well. She had no right to expect anything of him, other than the odd word of advice. He'd done his time and taught her well. She mentally rewound the tape and replayed the snippet that brought Shipwright into the conversation in the first place.

'How is he right, sir? DCI Shipwright, I mean.'

'Fishing, Anna?'

'I never fish, sir, but a little validation is always welcome.'

Rainsford held her gaze, laser-like. 'Ted said that I should trust your judgement when it comes to Shaw. And, in his opinion, everything else.'

Anna nodded, the subtext, like a wayward ventriloquist's dummy, screaming to be heard from its locked box. Giving Anna Gwynne her head had already almost got her killed. But it also led to the closure of one of the biggest cases in Avon and Somerset's history.

'Thank you, sir.'

'And you? Are you OK, Anna?'

'Shipshape, sir.'

'OK. Well, I've said it once and I'll say it again. It's good to have you back. I'm here if you need me.' Rainsford smiled. It lasted three seconds before he put on his serious, down-to-business face again. 'Shall I set up Shaw for Monday afternoon?'

CHAPTER SIX

SATURDAY

Some weekends, Anna made the journey back to her sister Kate's house for a Sunday lunch with her mother, her brother-in-law Rob and their two kids. Sometimes they'd go large and have Rob's parents over, too. But today Kate was coming over to Bristol for the afternoon and evening and Anna had all sorts of plans to clean up the flat. Essentials needed doing: laundry, show the hoover around the floor, catch up on paperwork and chill.

That idea lasted until mid-morning when she finally gave in to that part of her brain that would not stop thinking about Rosie Dawson. She fetched the file from her briefcase and, dressed in a pair of shorts, a strappy vest and flip-flops, took her coffee outside. Trisha had made summaries and photocopies of crime scene photos that had no right being looked at on a furnace-hot day with the sky untroubled by a whisper of cloud above. She read the reports but, as always with cold cases, had no feel for it yet. One of the difficulties she always encountered was getting a handle on the geography. She'd only ever been to Clevedon, the town where Rosie was abducted, to walk on the pier. Didn't know what *sort* of place it was. It soon became too hot to sit out, and after twenty minutes Anna could feel her skin tingling. It matched the frustration she felt for the need to get on with things.

Though the plan was for them to visit the abduction site after speaking to the doctor that Woakes had the hots for on Monday,

Anna gave in to her need to act. It had dawned on her early on in her career that at some point in any investigation she would need to be alone at the scene. Take in what the photographs didn't show. Smells, noises, things that the perpetrator and the victim would have been aware of. She changed into jeans, kept the strappy top on, and a little before midday, eased herself into the greenhouse her car had become and hoped that it wouldn't take too long for the air con to kick in as she headed, ironically, back towards her place of work.

Clevedon sat almost halfway between Bristol and Weston-Super-Mare on the estuary. Victorian in design, with its renowned pier, Clevedon looked across the Bristol Channel at industrial Wales. This was a leafy haven where kids could go to a seaweed-striped beach to kayak and crab, while Dad did the half-hour commute into Bristol. It was not a place where people got murdered or kids stolen. Everyone knew that. Yet the estate agents couldn't emblazon those facts all over their brochures in big bold letters because they'd be had up by advertising standards. Bad things could happen anywhere, even in Clevedon. And what had made it so much worse was how it had taken place under Avon and Somerset's very noses. Clevedon was only six miles from police HQ in Portishead. You could walk it. Indeed, the point of abduction had been no more than two hundred yards from the old Clevedon nick on Sunnyside Road as the final, crowning insult. People had taken it very hard.

She parked in the new station at Castlewood and walked towards the path where Rosie had been taken, stood on a mini roundabout and stared at the trees in the wood. Fir wood. Odd name; most of the trees looked deciduous to her. No one had seen anyone in combat fatigues enter the area in 2008. She looked at her map. Up to her right was the B3124 and stretching to the east, Court Wood, a much bigger area, full of leafy paths and narrow trails. Plenty of room for someone to wait and cross over at the narrowest point. At All Saints Lane, perhaps?

She took the path behind the houses on Highdale Avenue, noting the marked section; a bend just behind St Nicholas's school. When she arrived there, she looked around. The perpetrator had chosen well. A quiet spot. Not overlooked by the nearby gardens, at a point where the bend in the path hid walkers from other users in both directions. This was a very devious and very planned attack by someone who'd scoped the area and bided his time. He was *organised*. May even have waited for the ideal moment over the course of more than one day. What did that tell her about him? That he was local? Unemployed? That he wouldn't have been missed from work on a sunny afternoon at around 4 p.m.?

From the abduction point she walked the path again, leaving at the Hill Road end. It took her ten minutes to reach the point where they believed he'd parked his car. She walked back, fetched her own car and drove back to the same place on Hill Road. From there, it was a five-minute drive around the town over a couple of roundabouts to the M5 junction, and a major motorway that stretched from Birmingham to Exeter. A corridor running north–south through countryside and cities where someone could hide a small girl in any one of thousands of locations.

But Anna needed to find just one.

In all the time she'd been in Clevedon, she'd passed only a half-dozen people. Sleepy wasn't the word for it. And on a weekday, the only people around at the time Rosie was taken would have been parents and children. Whoever had done this would know that and planned it very carefully. This was not an opportunistic crime. The abductor knew his entry and leaving points and had a quick and clean exit strategy. Anna felt the tingle that had driven her out of the flat that morning kick up a notch.

She looked through her windscreen at the quiet road, knowing that something heinous had taken place here nine years ago. People who took children did so to feed a need. An urge. And that urge was rarely assuaged by doing so only once. Reoffending rates amongst child sex offenders was high with almost 20% doing so within a year. It wasn't unreasonable to assume that whoever had done this to Rosie may well have done it to someone else. That thought alone was more than enough incentive to fuel her conviction that this murderer needed to be caught.

Anna gunned the engine, pleased with her morning's work and feeling, for the first time in weeks, the satisfaction of knowing she was back in the hunt.

CHAPTER SEVEN

Khosa was sipping a lime and soda, Holder half a shandy. The sandwiches were home-made, but they'd skimped on the pickle in the ploughman's. Khosa looked around at the decor, unimpressed. Framed photographs of team captains stared down from the walls. Above Holder's head, a glass case containing a club presented by someone called Jacklin took pride of place. There were wheel-back chairs and round wooden tables. In a bar next door, lots of men in brightly coloured sweaters sat talking loudly and laughing in leather club chairs. The waitress who'd brought their food was a pasty-faced seventeen-year-old string of beans with acne. Behind the bar, a ruddy-faced husband-and-wife team ran the ship.

'So, this is golf, then.' Khosa said.

'Don't know,' Holder replied. 'I've only ever been in one other club. That was with my dad at a municipal course down in Devon. This is a private club. In fact, I'm surprised they let you in.'

Khosa's eyes flashed.

Holder laughed. 'Women and golf clubs. Didn't I read somewhere that some club or other in Scotland has only just voted to let women in?'

'Oh good. Pass me the application form.' Khosa made big eyes at the ceiling.

It was one thirty-five in the afternoon and they'd been sitting in the lounge bar of Camber Hill Golf Club for thirty minutes. They'd chosen a table near to the players' bar so they could watch Dominick Morton walk in from the eighteenth hole and were now waiting for him to appear. They might even have to buy another drink each. Holder was contemplating suggesting it when Khosa said, 'Your three o'clock,' and dropped her gaze.

Morton walked into the bar with three other men. All portly, all dressed in chinos and polo shirts, tanned from hours spent outside searching for balls in the rough. Morton ordered a round of beers and took the tray over to sit with his fellow foursome to dissect the round.

Khosa and Holder couldn't hear what was being said, but the occasional peel of raucous laughter spelled banter. Ten minutes after he'd walked into the bar, Morton got up and walked through the lounge towards a bifold door leading out to a patio with wicker chairs under umbrellas. Holder followed, reaching into his pocket for his prop e-cigarette.

Morton climbed down some steps to talk to a fellow smoker while Holder stayed on the patio, watching. To the left, a cylindrical metal refuse bin stood against the wall, its lid open to the elements and filled with sand. A dozen stubbed-out cigarette butts were already buried end on. Holder stood, watching a young kid practise putting, merrily vaping up his apple-flavoured concoction, pretending to contemplate the golfing world at his feet and taking very little notice of the players who sauntered up to the putting green. Seeing, but not registering, the man in the lime-green golf sweater, Nike hat and sunglasses with his back towards him who seemed preoccupied with his set-up over the ball in readiness for a putt.

Morton smoked aggressively, occasionally laughing at something said or possibly his own joke, the laugh segueing into a thick, chesty cough. The other smoker walked off. Six minutes after walking out, Morton took one long, final drag, blew out the smoke, exchanged a quip with one of the players on the putting green and stubbed out the cigarette. Holder noted its position, trying not to stare. There was a brief moment when Morton's eyes and his met, but it was fleeting and meaningless. Holder waited until Morton had gone inside, then he stepped down off the patio and turned towards the litter bin, only to find the man in the lime-green sweater and sunglasses already there, leaning over it, peering at the butts.

'Excuse me,' said Holder in a harsh whisper.

The man looked up and over his shoulder, smiling. He was wearing golf gloves and had a plastic evidence bag in his hand. At the bottom of the bag was a cigarette stub. Holder looked from the bag to the face, confusion rendering him momentarily speechless. He felt a hand on his elbow and the man walked him away from the patio.

'Good round?'

'What?'

Three steps and his elbow released, Holder watched as the sunglasses were whipped off to reveal Woakes under the hat.

'Sarge?' Holder stepped away, blinking, befuddled.

'Sorry, Justin, mate. You won't believe it but an old mate of mine plays up here. So I thought, why not? Help out, you know. Borrowed the kit and, Robert's your father's brother.'

Holder looked at the evidence bag. 'You're sure you've got the right one?'

'Of course. I was watching him all the time.'

Holder exhaled. 'Sorry, it's just that DI Gwynne said—'

'I know. I didn't want to steal your thunder, Justin. Not trying to pull rank either. It was too good a chance to miss, is all.'

Holder looked distinctly unconvinced.

'Look, I'm not trying to make you look a mug, honest. At the end of the day we've got a result, yeah? Bish bosh. And Gwynne would have wanted me to make sure, you know?'

Holder blinked. He didn't know.

'Great, now, come on. Where's Ryia?'

'She's inside waiting for me.'

'Right. It's my round. We should do shots?'

Holder's face was a picture.

'Only kidding, Justin. Come on, let's give her the good news.'

CHAPTER EIGHT

That evening, Kate dragged Anna into the Milk Thistle. At a little after eight, it was still early for a Saturday night and the cocktails weren't cheap, two good reasons why they succeeded in grabbing a corner table in the first-floor bar with low, opulent, green leather chairs. The crowd was noisy, young and not bothered by the prices. Oak-panelled walls, weird rabbit portraits and a speakeasy vibe, by ten it would be heaving. But for now, it was still manageable and they could at least hear each other speak.

They'd met for a rare afternoon out. Rare in that no children were involved and it was as much an indulgence for Kate as it was a 'treat' for Anna. Rob, Kate's husband, now running the family haulage business, was over networking at a commercial vehicle shindig and they'd caught the train. Rob had gone to play with trucks, and Kate, having offloaded both of her children with their grandmother back in Wales, met Anna in town for an afternoon of shopping, which usually meant Kate daring Anna to try on clothes she'd never consider for herself normally and then telling her how fantastic she looked in them. Some shoes, a cocktail dress and a sale handbag were the result. Kate had come away with plenty more swag, none of which was from a sale. Rob was doing well.

They'd dined at the bar in the Riverstation on Harbourside early. Kate wasn't staying overnight – that would have been too much to ask of their mother – and Rob had arranged to meet her at ten to nine at Temple Meads to catch the return to Cardiff.

'We've got ages, yet, babe,' Kate said as they taxied back into town. Anna knew there'd be no point arguing. Kate was nothing if not determined when it came to having a good time.

The Milk Thistle's daisy fizz was a heady mix of pear syrup, Tanqueray gin and some sort of bubbly. And even though there'd been wine with the meal, these were slipping down way too easily. Kate looked totally at ease, as if she did this sort of thing regularly. Anna knew she didn't unless she had a doppelgänger who looked after her two toddlers while the real Kate hit the town. But this was Kate's sort of place, not Anna's. If asked, Anna would be hard pressed to tell anyone where her sort of place truly was.

Anna glanced around. The bar sparkled with groups of people. Some couples, but mainly groups. Young women dressed – barely – in whatever fashion the current crop of reality show vixens were sponsored to wear, seated at the tables. The men, all gym-trimmed, tanned, white shirts and too tight jackets at the bar. This was how the evening courtship ritual started. Both groups ever hopeful.

'Anything there you fancy? You've got to get back on that 'orse, girl.' Kate delivered the statement in an exaggerated valleys, dropped 'h's accent that drew a few looks from the nearest group of men.

'Stop it,' Anna warned. Kate's teasing barbs about Anna's paltry dating history were a running theme. Whereas Kate, married with two children and still drawing stares, thrived in these environments, Anna found them barely tolerable, and then for only short periods. Relationships were not on Anna's current agenda. People in general, come to that.

Kate giggled. 'Oh, God, remember when we sneaked out to Simon's eighteenth at the rugby club?'

'You sneaked out. I had an invite.'

'Yeah, but we were both underage.'

'I was underage by six months; you were only fifteen.'

'Dad went ballistic.'

Anna smiled. Ballistic, as applied to their father, was hyperbole of the nth degree. It had not been in Tom Gwynne's nature to be ballistic. From what Anna could remember, he'd given them both a stern talking to, despite the fact that Anna's only motivation had been to see and hear a local band that Simon had hired for the gig. Their mother, on the other hand, launched into a vehement and sustained dressing-down, ending up with the dread and dire warning that they would not be welcome in the house if they ever got pregnant.

'Mum was the one who went ballistic,' Anna corrected her.

'Mum was always going ballistic. What about that time I lost a flip-flop out of the window of the car in north Wales. I thought she was going to have a stroke.' Kate began giggling.

'You were twenty-two at the time,' Anna said.

'Shut up. I was seven.'

'She made Dad turn the car around and fetch it.'

Kate doubled up. After several intakes of breath and in between groans she managed to say, 'She was such a witch.'

Is such a witch.

'It's a wonder she didn't take a wand out and shout "*Accio* flip-flop".'

Kate's laughter erupted, loud and sustained. Anna watched her and joined in. Subdued but genuine. Kate caught it. 'It's so good to see you smile, Anna. We really should do more of this.'

Anna nodded. She was right. It had been a long slog after her attack. And though she got some relief from imagining that the pink rubber thing she kept in the bottom drawer of her bedside table might actually belong to one of several hot bodies she could see on screen in any of her favourite films, it wasn't quite enough.

'Hey, Anna, I wasn't expecting to see you here.'

The voice came from behind her. She saw Kate's eyes flick up and then down, her eyebrows raised in puzzled surprise. The club chair made it awkward to swivel but then the man who'd spoken walked around to Anna's line of sight.

Woakes held a glass in his hand. Fizzy water, Anna guessed.

'Dave? What are you doing here?'

Woakes shrugged. 'I've arranged to meet an old mate.'

'Oh, this is Kate, my sister. Dave Woakes, our new detective sergeant.'

He leaned over to shake Kate's hand. An aroma oozed off him. Notes of leather and bergamot.

'How long have you been with the squad?' Kate asked.

Anna heard the emphasis Kate placed on the word 'you' and chose to ignore it. It might have simply been her accent, but then the flirting genes in the Gwynne pool had mostly settled in her sister.

'Few days. Still finding my feet. You live in Bristol?'

'No, I am here on a mission to get my sister back into the world of the living. I myself am the mother of two small children in that other place over the water.'

'Wow, you don't look like—' Woakes caught himself. 'That sounded all wrong.'

'I take them where I find them,' Kate said, grinning.

Woakes turned his attention back to Anna. 'This a regular watering hole for you, then?'

'Never been here before in my life.'

'S'nice. Pricey but nice. Can I get you two another round?'

Anna glanced at her watch and held it up to Kate. It was after eight thirty.

Kate nodded with a turned-down mouth.

Anna said, 'No, thanks anyway. I have to get my sister to the station for nine, otherwise she turns into a pumpkin.'

'OK, well, later, if you change your mind, you know where I am.'

Woakes drifted away. Kate called an Uber and Anna gathered up their shopping. Five minutes later they were on their way to Temple Meads in a Toyota Prius.

Kate stayed surprisingly quiet for all of three minutes until she said, 'So, is Dave attached?'

'No, Kate, don't.'

'Oh, come on, Anna. Clean, fit-looking, nicely dressed – you could do a lot worse. And I saw the way he looked at your legs. Plus, you're a genuine departmental hero.'

'I work with him.'

'So it's not a definite no, then?'

'It is. Definitely. Not my type.'

'Oh yes, your type. Still waiting for the memo on that one.'

'Kate, please.'

'All I'm saying is that he's there in that bar and has offered to buy you a drink. What's wrong with that?'

'Nothing. But if it went beyond a drink, that wouldn't be good because I have to see him every day and probably give him a bollocking now and again.'

'Maybe you could do with a bollocking now and again. In a way of speaking.' Kate grinned.

'Don't be so disgusting.'

Kate shook her head, still grinning. 'Come on, Anna. You've had a really rough time. I know you're looking forward to burying yourself in work again, but there is life outside Avon and bloody Somerset. And not everyone is a villain. Don't dismiss Dave,' she made her eyes huge, 'out of hand, that's all I'm saying.'

Rob was waiting for them in the station, flushed from a little too much lager. Anna hugged them both and waved them off as they walked arm in arm towards their platform.

Woakes and the Milk Thistle were a ten-minute ride away. Home, Netflix and an already opened bottle of wine in a one-bed flat in Horfield twenty minutes in the other direction.

She got in a cab, pushing her parcels in front of her. 'Horfield, please.'

Anna didn't believe in mixing business with pleasure. In fact, she had a problem with pleasure full stop.

At home, she did the sensible thing and drank a pint of water, keeping the Riesling corked for another evening. She knew she'd drunk a little too much and was glad she hadn't drunk anymore. She wasn't used to it, that was a fact. She switched on the TV, searching for something noir enough to get her teeth into. By eleven, she'd fallen asleep on the settee.

Her dream began as an all too familiar one. She was running through the woods and something was chasing her. Whenever she'd turn and look there'd be nothing there. Nothing to see. But she sensed a presence. An invisible threat. She kept on running.

Most of the time, she got away.

Sometimes, she didn't.

When that happened, she'd jerk awake, sweating, disorientated, full of dread, aware that no matter what time it was, she would not sleep again that night.

But on this Saturday night, her dream changed. This time she ran out of the woods, out into the open air and onto the moorland, empty and vast. She knew that this was an older place, the foothills of the black mountains where she'd hiked with her sister and her father so many times before.

She trod a winding path with vistas beyond, and in the distance she glimpsed a building, a church with a spire on the edge of a cluster of buildings. Generic markers in her dream world, dragged up from recent memory, and one of the few real pieces of evidence from the files she'd pored over that morning. The place where Rosie's remains had been found. A place modified and twisted by her subconscious into this desolate landscape. She stopped walking and looked around. All was still and quiet except for a thin wind that blew consistently. And on that moaning wind there came a whispered voice.

'Here, Anna. I'm here.'

She turned, trying to locate the source.

'Find me, Anna, I'm here.'

She started running again, her eyes darting, seeing nothing until, at last, she came to the edge of a cliff, to a stuttering stop where she looked down from a precipitous height. And there, below her on a vast plateau she saw where the voices came from. A strange arrangement of potholes and sinkholes arranged in the shape of a flattened skull.

'Here, Anna, here…'

She woke fully at six. Something in what she'd read and seen already about Rosie Dawson's case was tugging at her, demanding to be digested and absorbed.

When she'd worked with Shipwright, she'd been his deputy, learning, watching. She'd always kept her intuitive glimpses, these unformed convictions that plagued her sleep, to herself. She knew she'd revisit them and make the connections, but only in retrospect. As always, the peeling apart of these subconscious thoughts would reveal a pattern, a truth that she'd chosen to ignore.

She'd dreamed of Charles Willis's first victim half-buried in the earth when she'd been involved in his case. In her dream his first victim had risen and held out one hand, staring at Anna with dead, blind eyes. Seeing where it was impossible to see. It was Willis's supposed blindness that had kept him hidden from the police for so long, and Anna couldn't stop wondering if she should have spotted this. If in her dream her subconscious had tried to tell her.

A degree in criminology and psychology had taught her that dreams were a way of assimilating and integrating new information, nothing more. But now, after Willis, she was more prepared to take notice and accept that this part of her process was as valid as knocking on doors and trawling through files.

There might come a time when she'd make a leap, join a link that had always been there to join. Nothing mysterious, nothing supernatural, just the way her brain worked. Shipwright saw it. Encouraged it. And so had Hector Shaw, though in his case he'd needed to test her abilities in the most devious and almost fatal way. He'd taken a liking to her introversion, her need to be paradoxically analytical, to be detail-oriented. Seen how it might be a weakness, but also how it gave her an edge in her job.

And now, Rosie Dawson needed her to do that job.

CHAPTER NINE

SUNDAY

By way of penance, and as a distraction to her Milk Thistle-induced headache, after breakfast Anna did all the chores she should have done the day before. This was the same flat Hector Shaw had somehow managed to show to the world. Most people would have ended up traumatised by such an event. Some might have wanted to leave the flat, the neighbourhood, the city even. Certainly, that would have been a normal reaction.

Normal. Not a word Anna considered applicable as she splashed water on her face and glanced up at her reflection in the bathroom mirror that morning. Other descriptors were available. Stubborn, hates crowds, mixes on her own terms, happy to be in her own head. She looked at her frown lines. Still there. A tad deeper if anything. The little muscles under her eyes still bunched in a way that made it look like she was smiling a lot of the time, even when she wasn't. Her face seemed puffy from the previous evening's alcohol, but her skin was good and she didn't need to tie her hair back anymore. During her recovery from the attack, as the stab wounds on her breasts healed and the neck bruises faded, Kate convinced her to cut it short and go the full platinum-white.

'On trend,' Kate called it. 'Very *House of Cards*. And when your roots start showing you'll look dirty enough to mingle perfectly undercover with the addicts down in St Paul's.'

Bruised and battered in her hospital bed, Anna had wondered, not for the first time, how this ebullient extrovert could possibly be her sister. Perhaps she'd been swapped at birth. Now, several weeks later, Anna still wasn't sure about the hair. Kate called it unicorn-white. Who on earth would call a hair colour after a mythological horse?

Restless and always in work mode, when her work phone rang with Holder's number as the caller, she answered right away, keen to see how yesterday had gone with Morton.

'Morning, ma'am.'

She picked up on the downbeat tone right away.

'What's wrong, Justin?'

'Don't you know?'

It was a little after eleven thirty and she'd made herself a coffee and wandered into the garden. The Nespresso machine was a present from Kate and Rob and had become a three a day vice. Outside, the sun was blazing. She'd bought a cheap wooden bistro set from B&Q and put it in a sunny corner. No one else used the garden, and the landlord had wisely used Cotswold chippings and flagstones in lieu of a lawn. Anna had added a few pots and done some planting, which she watered religiously. But something in Holder's voice made her stop, put the coffee down on the table and concentrate.

'Know what?'

'I thought Sergeant Woakes would have—'

'What's Dave got to do with it?'

'He said you'd sanctioned it.'

'Justin, you are making no sense at all. Did you have a rough night?'

'No.' Holder sounded angry. Not like him. He caught himself and said, in a more measured way, 'No, ma'am. Just a very confused one.'

'I'm listening.'

Holder sighed. 'Me and Ryia were ready to take the sample yesterday. It all worked out fine. I followed Morton out, watched him have a smoke. I was about to nick the stub when Sergeant Woakes turns up in full golf gear and nabs it in an evidence bag.'

'*What?*'

'You didn't know?'

'No, I did not know. What's more, I saw him last night and he never mentioned any of this.'

'You were with Dave Woakes last night?'

'I was with my sister,' Anna said, very carefully, 'and we bumped into him in a bar. He said nothing about it.'

'This is doing my head in.'

'Not half as much as it's doing in mine. Did he say why he was at the golf club?'

'He was togged up. Said he was meeting a friend there.'

Another friend?

'Justin, I didn't sanction anything. It is possible that Dave was indeed at the golf club and wanted to lend a hand. But I did not send him. I know you and Ryia are more than capable.'

'Thanks for that, ma'am. That's a relief. Ryia was well cheesed off.'

'I'm sure she was. Still, you did get the evidence?'

'Yes.'

'OK. Good. Then no harm done. I'll see you tomorrow, Justin. Enjoy the rest of your day.'

Anna picked up her coffee and sipped, but Holder didn't ring off. Static crackled between them. Did he want to say something else?

'Justin?'

'Ma'am?'

'Come on, spit it out.'

'It's just… since he arrived… things aren't the same. And the way he was dressed at the golf club, it wasn't subtle. I was worried that…' He tailed off.

'Right. I'll speak to Dave about this—'

Holder interrupted her. 'So worried that I convinced Ryia we ought to follow Morton and get another sample. We did. He usually has a final cigarette when he gets out of his car at home. Uses an old bucket inside the front gate as his ashtray.'

Anna smiled. Holder had done his homework in this case.

'And I know it's technically theft, but I got a friend of mind in Forensics to run the DNA sample today. She's been threatening to show me how she does DNA extraction and the new Rapidspot tech. Ninety minutes from loading the sample to accessing the NDNA database, she said. And she was right. It's amazing. She's always banging on about enzyme buffers and resins to stop DNA degradation and vortexing the elution and stuff…' he paused, realising he was rabbiting. 'Anyway, I got her to show me on Morton's fag-end sample.'

Anna was shocked. If they'd taken evidence from Morton's property, it would not be admissible. But it had never been meant for the courts. This was for elimination and she hadn't heard Holder as anxious as this ever before.

'And?'

'The DNA on the cigarette from Morton's garden is a familial match, but not the one found at the rape scene. So, it's not the golfer we're after, ma'am; it's his brother, the paramedic.'

'What?'

'I know. So, Riya suggested we check in on Peter Morton and here's the thing: his wife had just been on the phone with Trinity reporting him missing. He didn't come home after his shift yesterday. She thought we'd called in to talk about that.'

Anna sat down at the little table. She kept quiet, giving Holder the floor.

'We've just come back from visiting Dominick, the golfer whose DNA we now have. He has properties in Benidorm as you know. He spoke with his brother yesterday evening. Joked with him that someone at the golf club had been sniffing around nicking cigarette stubs. His golf partners thought it might be drugs related.'

'So, someone saw Woakes pick up the cigarette butt?'

'Yes, ma'am.'

'And now our suspect has flown the nest?'

'Yes, ma'am. Looks like it.'

Heat rose in Anna's face.

Shit.

'Right, first thing tomorrow, get on to the Border Agency, see if Peter Morton's actually left the country. If he has, talk to the National Crime Agency. He's no longer just a person of interest, he's wanted on suspicion. That way they can get in touch with the Spanish Police's Fugitive Unit and they can find him for us if that's where he's gone.'

'Yes, ma'am.' She heard the instant change in mood in Holder's voice.

'What a balls-up,' Anna said.

'Yes, ma'am.'

She killed the call, exhaled loudly and immediately rang Woakes' number. He didn't pick up. She left a message for him to call her back and paced.

The call from Holder had left her confused. What was Woakes playing at? Was this a genuine helping hand, a question of being coincidentally in the right place at the right time, or was Woakes collecting badges in the hope of a gold bloody star?

Angry, Anna did what she always did when she needed to vent: put on some running gear, tied the laces of her trainers, slid on her backpack and left the flat.

After what she'd been through with the Willis case, the normal reaction would have been to at least choose a different route to the one where she was attacked and almost killed. But that was not Anna's way. She jogged across the common, busy with late-morning walkers, relishing the sun's caress on her neck, hit the pavements and ran exactly the route she'd taken the morning when Charles Willis shot her with a tranquilliser dart. Her only concession was to have her PAVA spray and telescopic baton in her backpack. She'd also taken some extra classes with the physical instructors at HQ. All a little after the horse had bolted admittedly, but in her line of work, she knew with absolute certainty there would be other wild horses.

She ran until the sweat blocked her vision. Quite apart from the physical benefits, running for her was a tool. With her body distracted, her mind had free reign. Frustrations and problems were turned over in the background of her consciousness, dissected and, more often than not, some kind of decision reached. If she'd been an author, plots would have been resolved on her runs, or characters devised, the muse invoked. Today, her mind flitted between what Holder had told her, seeing Woakes in the Milk Thistle and a sunny park in Clevedon, but frustratingly, she didn't know what to make of any of it. So much so that when she reached Horfield Common on her return, she paused to take on some fluid and rang Woakes again.

Still no answer.

Annoyed, she rang off just as a BBC news alert came up on her phone and distracted her. Another North Korean missile test dominated headlines as it had done for weeks and she flicked across to read the feed. The abduction of Blair Smeaton appeared halfway down. She called it up and a video clip of Blair's mother's appeal for information played. Anna watched it all the way through. It was depressingly familiar. Another vivid echo of the Willis case. Anna was never sure how much media appeals helped. They hadn't helped the young girl Willis had taken then, and they were unlikely to help Blair Smeaton. Yet many people would see the video she'd just seen and empathise with Blair's mother's dread. The exact same dread Rosie Dawson's mother would have felt nine years before.

Sympathy and empathy were all very well, but they would not help catch the people who had done these terrible things. It was harrowing viewing made all the worse by knowing one could do very little. A frustration shared by the majority of the millions of readers and viewers.

But Anna was not one of that majority.

She could and had done something about catching these killers.

CHAPTER TEN

Blair heard the door opening above her. A trapdoor into the cave. She looked up and saw the dog man standing there.

'Hello, Blair.'

She thought she heard her name but she wasn't sure. She couldn't hear properly without her aid. But it didn't matter. He was a bad man, like Kirsty had told her. And though there was nowhere to run to, like Kirsty had told her, she found somewhere to hide. The man couldn't move fast in the small cave, and the steps up to the doorway were narrow. She knew she had time.

Blair grabbed the duvet and scuttled across to the hole in the ground she'd found after spending most of the previous day moving the stone. It hadn't been easy. It was big and heavy and the only way she could do it was by sitting on the floor and using her arms as anchors behind her against the wall so she could use her legs to push the stone. But she had pushed it, slowly; inch by inch she'd pushed it so that it was wide enough for her to look into. Then pushed it all the way off the raised lip of the hole. When it toppled it cracked in half; the noise had frightened her, but it made pushing the final half off much easier. It left a hole big enough for her to climb into using her hands and feet and bum to scuttle down. It was gravelly and damp at the bottom but it was deep. Too narrow and deep for the dog man, she hoped.

'Where are you going, Blair?' said the man. 'Come on out. I'm going to take you back to your sister and your mummy.'

He clomped down the steps into the basement and Blair made herself as small as she could. She couldn't see him now. She sat down in her hole, knees to her chest, eyes squeezed tight shut, the lantern at her feet filling the space with light. She could see her grubby knees and dirty hands.

'BLAIR!' the man yelled.

She heard that alright. And then he was there, above her, his big face filling the hole opening. 'COME OUT, NOW!'

Blair shook her head.

'Can you even fucking hear me?'

He moved away but then came back and dangled his hand into the hole. Something dropped in. Pink, small. Her hearing aid. She put it in, switched it on. Sound came back.

'Come out of the hole, Blair. People are waiting for you, Kirsty is waiting for you, your mother is waiting for you.'

Blair shook her head.

'I know you're scared. I know it was a shock when I had to take you like I did, but you're safe now. The bad people have gone. We're on a big adventure, you and me. And once we've finished it, you'll be on your way home. Don't you want to see your mum?'

Blair nodded.

'Then come out and we'll go.'

Blair shook her head.

'Come on, you must be hungry. I've got food. Bread and ham and crisps. All up here waiting for you.'

Blair shook her head. She watched his face change then. Like a shadow moving across the sun. It darkened, flushed a deep purple before he leaned back and roared. When he looked back at her, he wasn't smiling. She didn't know what he was thinking but it made him ugly. When he thrust a hand down into the hole, stretching for her, reaching with clawlike fingers, it took her by surprise. She cowered, hands over her face. But he was too big. He could get his head and one arm in the hole but not the rest of him. And even with his long arm he couldn't reach her. He grunted and spat and swore. It went on for what seemed like a very long time. Blair put her hands over her ears and squeezed her eyes shut.

When she took her hands away later after counting to fifty, the noise had stopped. She heard him walking. Back and forth, pacing. It stopped and his face came back into the hole above.

'If you don't come out, I'll put the stone back and you'll rot in there.'

The cry came from somewhere deep inside, but she put her hands over her ears and her head down. She didn't want to hear what the dog man was saying. And inside her she knew it wouldn't work because the stone had broken.

She felt water sprinkle on her head and knees. She looked up. He was there again looking down at her. Looking down and shaking his head.

'Sorry, Blair. I'm sorry. I wouldn't do that. I brought food, and wipes for you to clean yourself. I want you to look nice for when you see your mummy.'

She closed her eyes and put her hands over her ears.

'FUCK!' screamed the dog man. 'I don't have time for this. I don't have fucking time. We have to go now. If we don't go now I'm going to have to leave you here for days. Do you hear? Do you fucking HEAR?'

Blair waited. She heard him stamp back and forth for long minutes. Heard a thump as if he'd hit the wall with his hand. She looked up and saw his bulk above her. Heard the click and saw the flash of a camera. Several times. She listened hard and heard him walking back up the steps. Heard the door opening and shutting and then nothing.

She strained to hear, strained hard and turned the aid up to the top level that sometimes whistled… but not today. And when she listened extra-hard, she heard him breathing. Fast breathing, like he'd been running. She didn't know how long she waited but it ended quickly. His face appeared. Angry and ugly.

'OK, stay there. Stay in your hole. But I will be back with something to prise you out of that well.'

She heard him walk away, up the steps, the creak of the hinges, the door thudding shut. Still she waited and waited and waited, trembling in her dark hiding place. She listened again extra-hard and there was no breathing. Slowly, stiff from sitting with her knees bent, she stood. The walls of the hole – he'd called it a well, hadn't he? – were 6 inches either side of her shoulders. She leaned against it with her back, put her hands behind her and slowly pushed herself up, bracing with her feet, like a caterpillar. She fell back once because she thought she'd heard a noise. The walls were rough and it helped with purchase but the climbing made her legs and arms shake. When she was almost at the top, she knew he wasn't there because he would have grabbed for her by now. With one eye on the trapdoor, she pushed up and out and sat with her legs dangling, looking around at what was left. There was food. Packets of ham and bread and crisps and coke.

She was hungry. She hoped Kirsty would be proud of her for hiding from the man. She hoped her mum wouldn't be too upset. Blair pulled the duvet around her and wondered what day it was back home. Maybe it was still Sunday. Mum made a dinner on Sundays and let her and Kirsty watch films.

*

He sat in the car outside the building containing Blair's cave, heart racing, livid. He thumped the steering wheel with his open palm hard half a dozen times until the pain stopped him.

She'd ruined it.

Ruined everything.

Now, it was too late. Far too bloody late to get her out, drive across the bridge and trek to the venue safely. He needed time to do that. And it would have meant rushing things. And he didn't want to rush things. Not this time. Too much depended on it.

He hit the steering wheel again and glanced at the building. She may be out by now, laughing at him because she'd found the fucking well.

Little bitch.

He'd make her pay. He'd make her pay so much. But he couldn't do it now. He exhaled, shut his eyes and tried to breathe easily, let the anger subside. He fired up the engine, drove out and headed back towards the city, letting the road take him while his mind contemplated and rationalised.

After a couple of miles, he'd calmed down enough to consider his options. He had appetites and sometimes they raged inside him. But he was also a pragmatist. So yes, he'd been thwarted but he also realised he had more time. She was safe. She was secure. So what if she hid in the fucking well? He already knew of a way of getting her out. A simple way. But one that needed a bit of preparation. It was hopeless trying to get it done today. He'd have to wait for another opportunity. He had work commitments after all and it was important he kept to his routine. But with a little bit of tweaking he might manage the end of the week. He would manage it.

Delicious anticipation ran through his veins like a drug, remembering her defiance in the well hole. Spirited, that one.

When he got back to where he lived in a sleepy street in a sleepy suburb, he backed his car in so that the boot faced the garage, got out and opened the garage door before popping the boot.

Inside it was loaded with equipment. In a closed tool box were his cameras, both compact video and digital SLR. They would need to go into the house. But the rest were things he stored in the garage: a roll of plastic sheeting, nylon rope, duct tape, a large rucksack and a smaller toolbox that did contain tools, but not of the kind any sane mechanic would ever have seen or used.

He placed them all carefully on a workbench at the rear of the garage, walked back out and locked the garage door. He removed the camera equipment from the boot, locked the car and entered the house, suddenly realising he was very hungry.

CHAPTER ELEVEN

The office was warm though it was only seven thirty on Monday morning. Anna still thought of it as 'the' office, despite the fact that the name on the door was hers. She had the windows open and the door ajar to try and encourage some air flow. But the atmosphere was sticky. She hoped the morning wouldn't be.

The squad trooped in in turn. Khosa and Holder kept their conversation low, beyond earshot. Anna busied herself with summarising her impressions from her visit to Clevedon until Woakes arrived. He did at a minute after eight. No coffee this time, just him, full of it, all smiles and waves.

Anna stuck her head out. 'A word please, Dave.'

'Said I'd give Forensics a buzz. Are you OK with getting Morton's DNA premiumed? I didn't think you'd want to wait for a slot—'

'Now.'

The smile didn't falter, but it became childlike, inquisitive.

'Shut the door,' Anna said when he was inside.

Woakes sat and adjusted the creases in his suit trousers. 'I waited for you on Saturday. Got a better offer, obviously.' His tone was all cheeky chappy.

For a second Woakes' remark threw Anna completely. She could have smiled, been deferential, joined in the joke, but all she truly wanted to do was give him a slap.

'For God's sake, this is neither the time nor the place,' she said. 'We will meet up—'

'OK—'

Before he could finish, she added, 'With the rest of the team.'

He did something with his mouth and shoulders that might have been a shrug. A 'that's up to you' gesture she didn't like much.

Anna went behind her desk and sat. 'Why did you muscle in on Holder and Khosa?'

Woakes looked surprised. 'Is this about the golf club?'

'Why?' repeated Anna.

'I didn't muscle in. I happened to be there and thought I'd lend a hand.'

'OK. So, if I ask you who it was you were there with and I contact him or her, they'll vouch, will they?'

'Why would you want to do that?'

'Because, sergeant, I haven't worked you out yet, whereas those two out there have worked their arses off on this case. I trusted them to get a job done and now they're pissed off with me because you stuck your nose in and worse, told them I'd sanctioned it.'

'Well…'

'No, not "well". Did you or did you not say that?'

Woakes turned around and looked through the door at Holder. 'Justin been telling stories, has he?'

'He's told me what I wanted to know in response to me asking him for an operational report. Why wouldn't he tell me? It's the truth, isn't it?'

'Listen—'

Anna tilted her head. 'Don't "listen" me, sergeant.'

Woakes dropped his chin and seemed to take stock. 'What I was trying to say to him was that since we got the result, I thought you wouldn't mind.'

'It's not the same thing at all, and you know it.'

Woakes sighed. 'OK. Fair enough. You know your squad but I don't. Not yet. So, I thought I'd go along and keep an eye on things. It just so happens I was in the right spot at the right time and made a call. A good call as it turned out since we got a result. And I don't understand why it is I'm getting grief for it.'

'You're getting grief because I didn't ask you to do that and you made it look like I did. It's not the way we work here. And your brief is to get to grips with the Dawson case. Do I have to remind you that we have a chance of finding some real answers for her family? And last but not least, I *really* don't like being used.'

'K… Got it.'

'Good. Here's the icing on the cake. Peter Morton went AWOL after his shift yesterday. We think it's because you were seen collecting samples at the golf club.'

Woakes sat, sullen and silent.

'I'm waiting, Dave.'

Woakes crossed his legs. 'Looks like I cocked up.'

Anna wrinkled her nose. 'I think what you're trying to say is that you made a big error of judgement which may have lost us the opportunity of apprehending a suspect in a historical rape case.'

'That's a bit harsh, isn't it, Anna—'

'Today, Dave, and until I tell you otherwise, it's Inspector Gwynne or, much as I bloody hate it, ma'am. What bothers me here is your motive. There's no logic to this. You lied to Holder, used me and muscled in on a case for what I have to assume were nothing but self-serving reasons.'

Woakes' face reddened.

'So now two things are going to happen. You are going to go out there and apologise to Justin and Ryia for not trusting them and explain how it was all you and that it had bugger all to do with me. We are going to let them run the rest of it *themselves* unless, and only unless, they want your help.'

Woakes stood, rocking back and forth on the balls of his feet. The smile had gone and his eyes had drifted into a kind of vacant stare.

'The words you're looking for are, "Yes, ma'am".'

He snapped back, nodding. 'Yeah. Yes, of course, ma'am.'

Anna studied him, her frown deepening. She got up and moved to the door. 'Am I going to regret Superintendent Rainsford agreeing to take you on, Dave?'

'No, I uh, I talk a lot, I know. Talk too much and sometimes I overthink stuff and do things maybe I shouldn't. So, I am sorry and I'll put things right with Pinky and Perky.'

Anna sighed. 'It's not who they are.'

'Sorry. With DC Holder and DC Khosa… ma'am.'

'Right. And once you've done that we'll go and meet Hawley. Bath wasn't it, you said?'

She pretended to work while Woakes ate humble pie with the two DCs, anxious to get on with things. As Woakes walked to his desk later, Holder looked across to her and nodded. Small, appreciative. She got nothing from Khosa.

Anna made no further reference in the morning briefing. Though Woakes had badly messed up, they'd wasted enough time already. She addressed them all, standing near the whiteboard.

'Right, let's get things moving. Justin, Ryia, great work in following up on the Morton case. I will get the official sample premiumed today, but it's water under the bridge.'

They both nodded. Anna did not include Woakes in her eye contact. She turned to the images on the whiteboard. 'I want us all to concentrate on Rosie Dawson. Ryia, Justin, let's search for any likely offenders who weren't known at the time of Rosie's abduction but who have come to light subsequently and who might have lived in and around the area.'

Khosa and Holder both nodded.

'We need to look at the military link because of the rucksack and the army connection because of the fatigues. And missing persons under fourteen years of age.'

'Just mispers? Not actual murder victims then, ma'am?' Khosa asked.

Anna nodded. 'As well as, obviously. I keep coming back to the way he disposed of the bones. I've been down to the abduction site. He was careful. Planned everything. He's organised. So why leave the bones in a plastic bag out in the open like that?'

'We got nothing back on the HOLMES search on Down's syndrome, ma'am,' Holder said.

'And I'm waiting for Hi-Tech to get back to me.'

Anna asked Woakes, 'Forensics?'

'We're in the queue.'

No one had any answers. Not yet.

Anna sighed, her frustration still simmering. 'Right, Dave, let's go and see this Hawley.'

In the car on the way to Bath, Woakes drove and they talked business. Saturday's little escapade and the Milk Thistle were put firmly to bed. Anna found out Woakes had been down to Clevedon to the abduction site, too. It brought a welcome smile to her lips.

'What did you think?' Anna said.

'Knew what he was doing. Chose the spot. Might have waited several days for the right moment.'

'Agreed. He's a stalker and a planner.'

'Add in the forensic nous and I'd say we were looking at someone who thinks he's smarter than us.'

Anna glanced across. She knew where Woakes was coming from. The planning and the boiling of the bones as well as the hypochlorite all pointed to a dark intelligence. 'They went over Hawley pretty thoroughly at the time,' she said.

Woakes nodded. 'I'm sure they did. But maybe not thoroughly enough.'

She stomped on the sudden urge she had to laugh. Woakes was an arrogant sod, but she didn't know him well enough to work out if this was mere bravado based on his track record or misplaced confidence.

Anna scanned the traffic on the M4. All these people going to normal jobs, day to day, humdrum, passing their car and not giving it a second glance. None of them, unless they were extremely unlucky, would ever need to be involved with a major crime. And yet she knew, too, that inside one of those vehicles there was a mind capable of the worst kind of horror. Somewhere out there were monsters contemplating perpetrating the most heinous, depraved, unspeakable acts. And yet one of them might walk past you on a street, or overtake you doing 80 on the motorway and you'd have no idea.

As part of her degree, she'd studied physiognomy, the pseudoscience of judging a person's character from their outward appearance. As late as the 1930s people were claiming murderers tended to have straight hair, and that meat-faced mesomorphs were most prone to criminality. All claptrap. There were as many fine-featured thieves as there were troglodytes. And all they knew about Rosie's perpetrator from a physical standpoint was that he was big and strong enough to carry a child.

But the next inevitable stop for this train of thought was Hector Shaw. A perfect case in point. He wasn't an ugly man, and if you looked beyond the physical, there lurked a highly intelligent brain. She could think of nothing that made him stand out as the multiple killer he was. The age gap between them, though never in her experience a barrier from a man's hormone-driven perspective, meant that Anna had never seen Shaw in any way other than a prisoner in standard-issue greys. But now, as her mind played games, she wondered if in another iteration he'd have been easy to interact with. He might have been ordinary, pleasant even, and she might have talked to him if he'd spoken to her, though she was also sure a passing nod might well have sufficed. The fact was he would have appeared normal. Perfectly camouflaged like a screech owl against the bark of a tree, waiting for dark, for the small animals to emerge as prey. He would have seemed unremarkable. There was no warning label stuck to his forehead, though she'd wondered more than once what she might have read had she been able to examine the being beneath. A killer with zero empathy for his victims, manipulative, coldly intelligent with a plasma serotonin level low enough to make him prone to extreme violence. Shaw was the most dangerous being Anna had ever met. And she was not looking forward to seeing him later.

The point was that stereotyping, physical or otherwise, was a dangerous game to play when it came to crime. Especially well-thought-out and clever crime. She hoped Woakes had an open mind. So far, he had done nothing to make her believe that.

Hawley had agreed to meet them in the Bath Hilton on Walcot Street. His choice, and Anna saw why when she walked through the modern entrance. It was big, but not cavernous, and had modern seating in neutral colours offset by orange cushions arranged around tables and little nooks with L-shaped sofas. At a minute after nine thirty in the morning it was empty. They grabbed a table with two chairs set behind a screen and Woakes fetched another chair. A waiter appeared after a few minutes and asked if they wanted coffee. Anna said they'd wait. At ten before the hour, a man appeared in the lobby, looking around expectantly.

'Oy, oy,' said Woakes under his breath before standing up and motioning.

Hawley raised a hand and walked across. Medium height, clean-cut and when he got close enough, wary brown eyes. A worn leather messenger bag hung over one shoulder. Woakes stood and made the introductions but did not offer his hand, and from the way he sat immediately, Hawley didn't expect it.

'Thanks for agreeing to meet with us, Dr Hawley,' Anna said. 'I understand you're coming off shift?'

Hawley nodded.

'Are you back on today?'

'Three days off. Time for some sleep and R and R.'

'Would you like some coffee?' Woakes signalled the circulating waiter, who nodded an acknowledgement.

'No thanks.'

'We're taking a fresh look at the Rosie Dawson case,' Woakes said.

'So you said.' Hawley's eyes remained wary but narrowed through inquisitiveness. 'Have you found any new evidence?'

'I'm not at liberty to say,' Woakes said. 'But we're talking to people who were involved at the time.'

Anna sensed the obvious friction between the two men. Hawley's was borne out of the unpleasant experiences he'd had so far with police over anything and everything to do with Rosie's case. And Woakes' stemmed from his default bluntness. She was quickly realising subtlety was not the sergeant's strong point.

'I wasn't involved,' Hawley said.

'But you were questioned. Extensively.'

'Yes, I was.'

'Could you remind us what your involvement with Rosie was, exactly?'

Hawley smiled and shook his head. He knew Woakes' decision to continue using the word 'involvement' was no accident and was unable to stop a resigned sigh from escaping his lips. 'As I'm sure your records show, four weeks before the abduction, I saw Rosie with her mother as a patient.'

If Hawley was hoping this brief summary would be enough, Woakes' expectant silence told a different story.

'I was working in the A and E at Cheltenham General. They asked me to see Rosie because she felt she had something in her eye.

I examined her, found a small scrap of shell under her lid. I instilled some anaesthetic drops, removed the offending foreign body and that was it. People generally improve instantly when it's subtarsal—'

'Sub what?' Woakes asked. The question was sharp. Woakes didn't like Hawley's confidence, that was obvious.

'Under the lid,' Hawley said. 'It had been a windy day. Rosie and her family had been visiting Sudeley Castle. Sometimes little fragments get caught on the wind. Tiny shell fragments are especially light and can be cup-shaped. They can embed under the lid quite easily. She was a great patient. Better than most adults. She didn't flinch as I put anaesthetic drops in.'

'And then what?'

'And then, as I was writing her up for some antibiotic drops, she walked over to her mum and whispered something in her ear. Mrs Dawson smiled and said Rosie wanted to give me a hug. I stopped writing and before I knew it, Rosie ran across the room, hugged me around the neck and kissed me on the cheek.'

'How did you feel about that?'

'Nothing. Embarrassed if anything. Both the nurse and Mrs Dawson were laughing. Rosie was smiling. It was nothing more than a spontaneous act of gratitude from a little girl. Something she probably did a dozen times a day with her dad or her uncles. I was young. It didn't happen to me often—'

'Often?' Woakes sat forward.

'OK, never. I didn't quite know how to react, but it had happened and everyone was fine with it. I finished writing the prescription and they left. I thought no more about it until a week after Rosie went missing when the police turned up at the hospital wanting to see me.'

'And you understand why?'

'Of course I know why. I let a child hug and kiss me in public.'

'So, it didn't come as a surprise to you when you were questioned?'

Something, a shadow of remembered pain, passed across Hawley's face. 'What do you think?' he said.

Woakes shrugged. 'I think you were probably pretty shocked.'

'That's putting it mildly. I went with them to the station and they held me there for two days. They searched my flat, took my laptop and my girlfriend's. Wanted to see any computer I had access to in work. They did it twice. The first time when she went missing. The second time when they found her remains more than a year later.'

'They wanted to be thorough.'

'That's what they kept saying. They wanted to be thorough. To be sure. That I should realise I was a person of interest and if I had any information it would be better for me if I told them.'

'But you had no information.'

Hawley had a habit of grinding his back teeth. Anna wondered if it only happened in stressful situations.

'Correct. I had no information. I still don't have any information. I have no idea who took Rosie, but it wasn't me. I had a room in the doctor's mess. Luckily, there were CCTV cameras outside the hospital. On the day Rosie was abducted, the cameras showed me entering the hospital accommodation and not leaving. Though, there was a back entrance, but I'd left my phone on and it showed I hadn't gone anywhere. Again, I could have left my phone at home and gone all the way to Clevedon. But I was on an evening shift at seven and that was the clincher, I think. They had no evidence showing me getting out or back into Cheltenham by road or rail. They eliminated me by default. But they took their time.'

Woakes nodded. The waiter arrived, laid out three cups and left a pot, a silver milk jug, sugar and some thin biscuits wrapped in cellophane. Woakes poured out two cups, topped his up with milk and stirred it. 'Sure you don't want any?'

Hawley shook his head. He looked a little sick to Anna. Not the kind of white-faced, sweating look she saw on liars, more the unhappy look of someone traumatised by something in the past, desperately hoping the same thing was not going to happen again.

'The thing is, Dr Hawley,' Anna said, 'time can sometimes help or hinder cases like this. Memories fade. Or sometimes memories surface after they've been buried for long enough.'

Hawley waited, jaw working. 'What do you want from me?'

Woakes spoke again, the bit between his teeth. He picked up his coffee and sipped before saying, casually, 'Do you know that 50% of child abductions are by family members and another 30% are acquaintance abductions? Stranger abductions are pretty rare.'

'I did as a matter of fact. I learned all sorts of things I didn't want to know back then… and since.'

'But you were known to Rosie. She liked you.'

'We'd met once. Twenty minutes for just the once. As doctor and patient.'

'And she hugged you and kissed you.'

'Jesus.' Hawley sat forward, let his head drop.

'You can't deny that.'

When Hawley looked back up again his expression was drawn and sour. 'No, I can't. I didn't then and I can't now. I've explained the circumstances. They were confirmed by the clinic nurse and Rosie's mother.'

Anna said, 'But Rosie told you her grandmother used to pick her up from school and take her to the park, didn't she?'

Hawley nodded, a thin wry smile now on his lips. 'No, she didn't. She was chatty and while I was getting bits and pieces ready, she talked. She told the nurse she'd been to the castle. She told the nurse the name of her dog. She told the nurse she liked going to the park and that her grandmother used to take her every day after school. It wasn't me she told, but of course I heard it all.'

'You were in the room?'

'Yes.'

Woakes put his coffee cup down before asking, 'What did your girlfriend think about it?'

'We split up. That's what she thought about it.'

'You were sharing a flat at the time?'

'Yeah. About to get engaged.'

'Must have been hard to take.'

Hawley's smile was thin and bitter. 'It was and still is. And yes, I did not get the training contract I'd hoped for from the trust I was working for at the time, and yes, it ruined my life. Someone leaked it to the press. Of course, they also published the fact that I was released without charge, but on page eight in one paragraph. The first story was front page news in the local rag, three columns. That sort of dirt sticks. I don't trust the police because, despite everything and for whatever reason, I'm clearly still on your lists as a suspect. I had to take some time off to recover. And now, when I see a kid, I'm paranoid about the same bloody thing happening all over again.' He held up the index finger and thumb of his right hand separated by half an inch. 'My solicitor told me I was this far from ending up on a sex offender list, for Christ's sake. Anything else you want to know, sergeant?'

Woakes didn't bat an eyelid. 'Did you own any other properties at the time?'

'No.'

Anna knew this had gone far enough. 'Dr Hawley, thanks for coming—'

Woakes interrupted her. 'And now? Do you own anything now?'

Hawley blew out air. 'Yes. I inherited a cottage from an aunt.'

'Where's that?'

'Across the channel, a place called Sully in Wales.' He paused and then asked, 'Why would you want to know?'

Yes, thought Anna. *Why?*

'Just curious, Doctor. Or can I call you Ben?'

'I don't want you to call me full stop. Is there anything else?'

'Yeah, you own a computer, right?'

'Of course. Doesn't everyone?'

'Spend much time trawling the internet? Got any favourite sites?'

Hawley blinked, his mouth open. Rightly offended.

Anna took control, 'OK, Dr Hawley. That's all. Thanks for your cooperation. Sure we can't tempt you to coffee?'

Hawley stood, still looking at Woakes with disbelief as he picked up his messenger bag.

Woakes returned the gaze with a smile. 'Yeah, have a coffee. I'm sure we can think of something else to ask you.'

Anna gave him one of her glaring death stares before turning back to Hawley. She stood and offered her hand. 'We appreciate your cooperation,' she said.

Hawley looked at her. Belligerence fought with regret on his face. He nodded, shook briefly, turned away and left.

Woakes waited until he'd gone and said. 'Well?'

'Well what?'

'What do you reckon?'

'I don't reckon anything. He had an alibi. Rosie was an extrovert. Down's patients are often disinhibited. They found nothing to link—'

'His alibi is shit. He knows something,' said Woakes, walking to the door and looking out at Hawley's departing back.

'What?'

'He's hiding something. I'm going to follow him to this cottage.'

'Dave, this is insane. On what are you basing the assumption he's hiding anything?'

Woakes moved his head from side to side, weighing up his thoughts before answering. 'He's reticent and shifty. It's a gut feeling.'

Anna wanted to laugh out loud but then the conversation she'd had with Rainsford on Friday was still fresh in her memory.

Unorthodox was the term they'd bandied about. Woakes was living up to his reputation.

'He has every right to be both. I read the file. His name was leaked and the press got hold of it.'

'So?'

'Hardly surprising he doesn't want to talk to us, then, is it?'

'I think there's more.'

Anna sighed. 'You have nothing to go on.'

'I'm suggesting a recce. See what sort of cottage this is. You'll be OK, right? We can do the Charterhouse visit another time.'

Anna blinked. 'Of course, I mean, let's not let real police work get in the way of your gut instinct.'

'If I'm wrong, we'll go to Charterhouse tomorrow.'

Anna shook her head. 'Is this the sort of bloody bish-bosh policing you did in the Midlands? Intimidate someone and see if they jump?' She wanted to say more, to point out that Hawley didn't look big or strong enough to march out of a park carrying an army backpack full of trussed-up little girl. He'd looked shell-shocked and anxious. But Woakes was already halfway out of the door.

'If I don't go now, I'll lose him.'

So far, she didn't think much of his methods, but Rainsford had said he'd come with a reputation for results and she had another meeting to get to. One she couldn't miss.

Anna sighed. 'Don't do anything stupid.'

'Moi?' Woakes grinned as he trotted out of the hotel in hot pursuit.

CHAPTER TWELVE

Alone in the hotel lobby, Anna poured out what was left of the coffee. She took a mouthful and spat it out. Stone-cold. Like Rosie Dawson's case.

She could have stopped Woakes; of course she could have. But frankly, he was beginning to irritate her. So, for now, a little bit of distance between them would do no harm and there were other things to consider. Charterhouse, as Woakes had said, could wait. But Anna now had no car and she needed to get to Worcester by 2 p.m. She rang Holder.

'Justin, I'm catching a train to Worcester. Can you meet me at the station there?'

A small but perceptible silence followed before Holder said, 'Does that mean what I think it means?'

She didn't answer him directly. She didn't have to. 'I'll let you know what time my train gets in after I board. But you ought to leave now.'

Bath Spa station sat on the river at the southern end of the city. She walked out of the hotel past Waitrose, and then turned south. Bath was a handsome city, there was no doubt about it. The mandatory sandstone helped lend it a consistency sadly lacking in most cities she'd visited. It also helped that you could walk everywhere because it was much smaller than Bristol, so long as you didn't mind tourists blocking the pavements every ten yards by gaping at the architecture.

She stopped in a Pret for something with minimal carbs, bought a paper, caught the 11 a.m. train, found a seat, and let the paper sit unopened on the table while her brain pondered the wisdom of her actions. If you looked at it coldly, there was nothing at all wise about visiting a convicted serial killer in a maximum-security prison. Shaw was complex. The conventional psychiatric assessment of him was that he'd lost control of an already unstable borderline personality type. The trigger: when his daughter committed suicide by throwing herself under a train.

As a GCHQ computer networks expert, Shaw had found out that his daughter had been groomed by an underground group trawling suicide chat rooms, coerced into participating in a sick online game known as the Black Squid in which serial tasks, if completed, ended in a suicide note and death.

It sounded ludicrous, but it targeted vulnerable individuals and was known to be responsible for the deaths of several teenagers, Abbie Shaw's amongst them. Shaw's victims all involved administrators and proponents of this 'game'. He'd also killed his alcoholic wife, whom he blamed indirectly for Abbie's murder. As a result, he was now serving a life sentence with no chance of parole.

Anna's relationship – she snorted when the word popped into her head – with Shaw had also been complex. His daughter, had she lived, would have been about the same age as Anna, something Shaw had pointed out on more than one occasion. Thinking about it always made Anna shudder. Freud would have a field day.

Some years ago, in another life, at a time when she allowed all the shiny things that appeared on her computer screen to distract her, Anna had seen a viral video of a lioness in the wild who allowed a baby baboon – after having killed its mother – to try and suckle it and eventually escape. One of nature's curious quirks. Anna equated Shaw with that lioness. Dangerous and capable of killing at any moment given the chance, but somehow identifying her with something in his life he'd once cared about. But, as with the lioness, she was under no illusion that if circumstances changed, the outcome could be very different. Anna's instinct – not the weird one fed by her dreams, but the good copper's instinct that she shared with Shipwright – was to be highly suspicious of what happened afterwards to the baby baboon.

Whatever it was Shaw saw in her, it was not a relationship she wanted to encourage or foster, but Shaw had revealed more information to Anna about his thoughts and victims in just a few short interviews than he had to anyone else in all the years he'd been in prison. She knew the authorities, Rainsford included, were hoping for more. And so, here she was on a train, a baby baboon stumbling towards a hungry lion, wondering just what Shaw wanted to say to her and knowing that she had to listen, no matter what.

She thought again of Shipwright and what he'd have thought of her analogy. In her head, she imagined his pithy reply.

Come on, Anna. You know I don't do Disney.

It brought a smile to her lips.

Anna watched the fields and towns rush past her window, contemplating the concern she'd heard in Rainsford's voice when Shaw came up. She'd worked hard to get where she was and was grateful to people like Shipwright and Rainsford who believed in her. But the attack on her in Badock's Wood had taken her longer to get over than she thought it would. She was back on the horse, but so far she'd allowed it to do nothing but trot, and seeing Shaw would mean taking some jumps. Resilience was a fine thing, if only they sold it in handy, easy-to-swallow pills at Holland & Barrett.

Anna turned from the window and walked through the carriages to the buffet. She needed a cup of railway tea.

Holder was waiting for her at Worcester station an hour and a half after she left Bath.

'Afternoon, ma'am,' he said as she got into the car. He had the air con blasting out cold air and the radio tuned to a station playing dance anthems.

'How come you're on a train? What's happened to Dave?'

'Following his nose, Justin. We'll see what he sniffs out. My guess it'll be nothing but a waft of hot air, but we shall see.'

Holder nodded and pointed the car north. 'Didn't think we'd be coming back here, ma'am.'

Anna's turn to nod. The last thing she'd said to Shaw when he'd tried to set up another meeting with her was that she was never going to see him again.

'Yes, well, we all live and learn, don't we?'

Holder threw her a glance but said nothing.

Whitmarsh was a category A prison. Britain's prison system was arranged on several criteria including crime severity, sentence length, escape risk and degree of dangerousness to the public. Category A contained the most dangerous prisoners who'd committed the worst crimes. Within its walls there were further risk categories based on likelihood of escape. Shaw remained an exceptional risk category despite his cooperation with Anna. No one wanted him getting out.

Someone had stuck a new air freshener in the stark and familiar interview room at Whitmarsh, with its black plastic and tubular steel furniture. Anna wondered if the grey paint on the walls had a pretentious name, like Drum Dust, or Ostrich's Breath. She'd played a game with Shipwright to come up with a few. Her favourite, by a long way, had been Lifer's Tan. The cheap air freshener failed miserably to mask the aroma of stale sweat and urine that seemed to seep out of the floor. Two uniformed prison officers sat at the rear of the room.

Shaw looked up when Anna entered. He didn't acknowledge Holder's presence and instead sat with his forearms on the Formica-topped table, legs apart on the black plastic chair, his chin low.

'Hello, Anna.'

She sat, not wanting to show him how much her legs were trembling, and placed a digital recorder on the table.

Shaw watched her do it.

'Can we talk about Petran?'

Shaw smiled. 'Straight to the point as always, eh, Anna? How long has it been – six, maybe seven months? I like your hair. The lighter colour is a nice contrast with your youthful face. Are you well, Anna? Fully recovered?'

'Mihai Petran,' Anna said.

Shaw blinked. He did so slowly, carefully. Anna had come to learn that it was a good barometer of mood. Too slow and it meant trouble. When he replied, it was to say only one word: 'Scum.'

Holder said, 'If you weren't his partner in crime, how come his blood and yours turned up on Tanya Cromer's clothes on the night she was raped?'

Shaw turned his gaze on Holder before turning back to Anna. 'Do you have any theories, Anna?'

'Either you and Petran were working together and Tanya fought you both, or you and he fought and your blood ended up on Tanya's clothes.'

Shaw gave nothing away. He turned back to Holder. 'Let's see if the apprentice has done his homework. What do you know about Petran, DC Holder?'

Holder threw Anna a glance. She nodded.

'Petran was in the UK on a work visa but went AWOL after two women reported he'd attempted to sexually assault them.'

'Gold star for you, Justin. Don't mind if I call you Justin, do you, Justin?'

Holder shifted in his chair.

Shaw kept talking. 'Those were just the things he'd been caught doing. Petran was scum and an ignorant prick. He was in chat rooms, looking for info on pubs where he could find underage girls in different towns. He couldn't help himself, and the younger the better. His English was crap. He left a trail that wasn't difficult to follow. I was looking for links to the Black Squid sites. The administrators mainly. But there was some overlap with men targeting vulnerable girls. Then his name came up somewhere else. Another site.'

'What site, Hector?' Anna asked.

Shaw smiled. 'We've got a bit of a way to go before we get there, Anna. He was a busy fucker, though. Nasty bastard. I dragged Petran off Tanya Cromer, though I was too late to stop him assaulting her.' He let his head drop, exhaling. Anna read it as regret. 'I wanted to make sure she was OK but I let him get away. I should have killed the bastard there and then. When I found out Tanya went missing three months later, I knew it must have been Petran. And I was right. He killed her because I ripped off his mask in the fight and the paranoid bastard was scared she might pick him out in an ID parade.' Shaw shook his head. 'It was too dark for her to see. He shouldn't have done that.'

'How do you know he killed her?' Holder asked.

Shaw didn't smile. 'Because he told me, amongst other things. She was just a bit of fun for him. Nothing to do with the Black Squid. But he did show me where he'd buried her, remember? Nice little spot, wasn't it Justin?'

Holder shook his head. 'How do we know it wasn't you who kidnapped her and killed her?'

Shaw's smile was mirthless and transient. A sad ghost of a smile. 'I'm not a rapist, Justin. And Petran wasn't his real name. It was Krastev, Boyen Krastev, Bulgarian origin.'

Holder snorted. 'Jesus. When are you going to give us something real?'

Anna turned to Holder. 'Justin, give Trisha a ring, ask her to find out what she can about a Boyen Krastev.'

Holder looked annoyed, like he wanted to protest.

'Now, please.'

'Yes, ma'am.' Holder got up. Security at Whitmarsh meant that mobiles were left the wrong side of the scanners. He'd need to use a landline. When he'd gone, Anna said, 'What do you want from me, Hector?'

'Inspector Gwynne,' Shaw said with mock indignation.

'You know I can't change anything here. I can't get you any privileges.'

Shaw shook his head. 'All I want is for you to do your job, Anna. Look at me as the oil for your engine.'

'What does that mean?'

'You got Willis, didn't you?' Shaw paused before adding dramatically, 'The Woodsman.'

'He almost killed me.'

Shaw beamed. 'But he didn't, did he? Besides, he'll be inside soon, with all the other monsters.'

His Mancunian accent had a nasal edge as he dragged out the syllables.

Anna said, 'I doubt it'll be here.'

'Nah, his snake barrister will get him into Rampton or Broadmoor for a couple of cushy years, but then he'll come out and join the rest of us somewhere. And then we'll see. Be patient, Anna. Be patient.'

She tried to suppress the little shudder that went through her but failed, shifting in her seat instead in an attempt at concealing it. For someone as astute as Shaw was in reading signals, she might as well have screamed in protest.

For inmates to have influence in other prisons and outside prison with illicit access to phones, even in a maximum-security unit, was not unheard of. And someone as intelligent as Shaw must have known all the angles.

She looked away and then back again. 'So, do you have something else to show me?'

'Just say the word, Anna. It's summer, there's lots of light. We can stay out until it's late.'

A tendril of horror flickered along her nerve endings. She became aware that her fingers were icy cold. She squeezed them together under the table. The pain helped her stay in control.

'Where?'

'Sussex. That gypsy bastard Krastev used to work in a pub over that way. Never been there myself. I'm looking forward to it.'

'Who's there, Hector? Do you have a name?'

'No. But Krastev drew me a map.'

'Why?'

'Because I asked him to. Trouble was, I had paper but no pen. Why is there never a pen when you need it? So, we improvised. I suggested his blood. There was plenty of that.'

Anna took a deep breath in through her nose and let it out slowly. 'Why did Krastev kill this victim in Sussex?'

'Because he was told to by those Black Squid bastards.'

Anna made herself swallow. 'You have an approximate location? Why don't you let me have it?'

Shaw smiled. His teeth were yellowing but still all there. 'You know why. Because I don't have to. And I need to see if Krastev was telling me the truth. I'd be disappointed if he hadn't been. How's work, Anna?'

She didn't answer, kept her eyes on her notebook.

'Have they replaced that ugly sod Shipwright, yet?'

She looked up then. She could have been offended but Shaw's delivery had been almost tender.

'I expect you miss him, eh? He was good for you, Anna, wasn't he?'

Don't, Anna. Don't.

'But you don't need him, Anna. You don't need anyone.'

She closed her notebook and picked up the digital recorder.

'Just say the word, Anna,' Shaw said to her departing back. 'You know where I'll be.'

She found Holder in the reception area.

'Have we finished, ma'am?'

Anna nodded. 'For today.'

'Did he say anything else?'

'We'll swap stories in the car.'

Holder drove. She let him have his droning anthems, low enough so she could tune them out of her own head when she needed to. Shaw was eking out his relationship with her, she knew that. Even so, if what he'd said was true, it was highly significant.

Twenty minutes into their journey home, Trisha rang.

'Hi Trisha, what have you got for us?'

'I ran a check on the European Information System, and Boyen Krastev is a Europol reoffender. Wanted in Belgium, Italy and the Netherlands for abduction, sexual assault and drug-trafficking offences. According to the Border Agency, he has never entered the UK. I've requested more information from the National Unit.'

Anna knew how this worked. She'd been involved in reciprocal information exchanges before. Europol ran the EIS but also had national units facilitating cooperation between its EU partners. In the UK it was the International Crime Bureau that coordinated the service.

'Whereabouts unknown, I presume? They must think he's still at large.'

'Yes. There are warrants out for his arrest.'

She thanked Trisha and pondered this new information. If Petran was Krastev, and they'd need the police in Bulgaria to confirm it, then those warrants should be ripped up. You could not arrest a dead man.

'How come someone like this guy, Petran or Krastev or whoever he is, was let in, ma'am?'

'EU laws for sharing information on criminal records did not come into force until 2012. Petran was a petty criminal. His record would have been deemed of low risk. I suspect Krastev knew this.'

'Do you think Shaw's telling the truth?'

Good question. Great question. More to the point, what the hell did Shaw actually want? Anna'd had enough time to think about that. What Shaw had done, killed at least half a dozen people in the most abhorrent of ways, made him a dangerous psychopath. And he seemed to have no issue with admitting to more murders. What's another sentence to add to life in prison? Was he doing it because he liked her? Or because he trusted her to carry on trying to find the people behind his daughter's suicide? If it was the latter, Shaw had a very roundabout and macabre way of approaching it.

'I do. I think he has an agenda and only he knows what that is, but for now, I'll take what he's prepared to give.'

Back in Portishead, Anna checked in and thanked Trisha for her efficiency with getting information on Krastev so quickly. Trisha held her eyes for a moment longer than was necessary for the exchange. Anna returned a questioning smile.

'How was it, ma'am, seeing him again?'

Trisha was not a warranted officer. She was civilian, a single parent, and the mother of two teenage boys. A dozen years older than Anna, attractive and trim. She brought efficiency and professionalism and like now, a very welcome dollop of emotional intelligence to the squad. She knew more about Holder's and Khosa's personal lives than Anna ever would, because she was an easy person to share those things with. Not a gossip, just a sounding board. Anna, on the other hand, kept her personal life and its details in one of the many compartments in her head marked 'private and confidential – not for public consumption'.

Trisha's question had concern stamped all over it and caught her off guard. Not because she didn't want to answer it, but because it demanded a little bit of self-analysis.

'Always a pleasure,' she said, and winced because it was glib and a lie and there was no hiding the truth from Trisha whose penetrating gaze did not drop. Anna sighed, forcing herself to open the box and look inside. 'The truth? It was very unpleasant,' she said. 'Like handling a pet snake. You know it's dangerous. You know it doesn't have any feelings for you but you kid yourself that the need it has to coil itself around you is affection, when all it craves is warmth. And that warmth could just as easily be a rock in the sun as your shoulders.'

The corners of Trisha's eyes had drawn down and Anna saw muted horror there.

'I don't know how you can face him. After what he tried to do…'

Anna was alarmed to see moisture gathering in Trisha's eyes. It was common knowledge that Shaw was a killer and that his meddling in the Charles Willis case had almost got her killed. It was all in Anna's report. What wasn't in those reports were the personal communications from Shaw that turned up like an unwanted rash. The letter and the card she'd received while in her hospital bed. The occasional untraceable email…

She opted for the emergency escape hatch in the way of humour. 'It's why they pay me such an enormous salary, Trisha.'

A smile, like a tiny fluttering bird, flickered at the edges of Trisha's mouth and the moment faded. Anna could have used the opportunity, if she'd had any sense, to ask Trisha's opinion of Woakes. An off-the-record chat that would not have gone any further, but Khosa chose that moment to bring over a report.

'I found the FLO who looked after Rosie Dawson's family. She's retired, ma'am. At the time of the abduction, Rosie's mother and father were together and there was a sister. The father worked in a local engineering works. There was an uncle who was close but he was thirty miles away that afternoon with a dozen witnesses.'

'We'll need a new FLO,' Anna said.

Any involvement with the family of a victim required the support of a family liaison officer. Someone who provided support when the harsh and difficult questions had been answered and the detectives had all gone. And sometimes, the families would open up and reveal information to the FLO away from the formal interviews. Information which might prove vital.

'I'll sort it, ma'am,' Khosa replied and hesitated.

'What is it, Ryia?'

'I know Sergeant Woakes didn't want us to involve the family yet, but if I ask for a new FLO…'

'Don't worry about upsetting Sergeant Woakes. This is my call. Just do it, Ryia.'

Khosa nodded and turned away, but it left Anna with more of the feeling that Woakes' influence was having a negative effect on her team. A feeling she did not like.

Anna turned back to Trisha but the analyst was absorbed by her screen as usual and the moment evaporated. She went back to her office and busied herself with referring back to Shaw's interview and making notes.

She'd need to brief Rainsford and liaise with Sussex police, chase up whatever they found on Krastev and relay it all to North Wales police. If they got a positive ID for Krastev it might mean they'd want to charge Shaw. Anna pondered how she felt about that. He was already serving an indefinite term. The CPS might not consider it in the public interest given the costs. It could mean Shaw getting away with another murder.

Did it bother her? She didn't think it would bother Shaw. She found herself hoping the CPS might not consider it trial-worthy. Perhaps if they got a formal confession they would avoid trial… It was a nice thought, but even as it occurred to her, the hairs on her arms all stood to attention.

Shaw, for some bizarre reason, had made it clear how he would only talk to Anna about any and all of his crimes. Listening to the details of what he'd done to Krastev was a thought that did not fill her with joyful anticipation. Not if the autopsy report on his injuries was anything to go by.

And she didn't want to be used by Shaw either. But by the same token, what choice did she have? What had happened to his daughter was horrific, but the murders he'd committed in her name were brutal. She thought about how she'd explained her visit to Trisha. The snake analogy.

She felt Shaw's coils tightening around her.

Five o'clock came and went with no sign of Woakes. She phoned him. It went straight to his voicemail again.

'What are you up to, Dave?' she muttered, then grabbed her bag and went home.

CHAPTER THIRTEEN

Inside the shed he used as a workshop, he had a laptop. One that he did not use for work. He fired it up now, having already configured his browser for a proxy server through TOR, The Onion Router, the free software beloved by everyone who believed in online privacy. Whenever he logged on he'd be using an IP address that wasn't his. He'd tried explaining this to someone at work once. The importance of anonymity online so that people didn't know your business. The bloke made a token effort to try and understand, but he knew he couldn't care less. So long as he could WhatsApp his fishing mates and stick a bet on the footie he was happy.

It didn't matter anyway. Other people didn't need to know. In fact, the less other people knew the better. He opened his Chrome browser. From a drawer, he took a small, black plastic oblong and a USB cable. He connected it up to the laptop and opened the SafePocket Chrome app, punched in his PIN and opened his cryptocurrency vault. He had three bitcoins, some Ethereum and Dash. Not enough, but their performance over the last year had been gratifying. He was now convinced, after gambling a few hundred pounds over the last couple of years, investing in this alternative to cash and seeing his profits soar, that this was the way forward.

To the average person, this was all nonsense. Yet the beauty of cryptocurrency was the way it all happened – without regulation and supervision and with no central authority controlling the transactions. A safe and invisible way to move money.

But what he also knew, what he cared about most, was that since cryptocurrency had a value, you could send any amount of money, in cyber form, to anyone in the world at any time as easily as sending an email and without being tracked, without the need for a middle man. For the sort of transactions that interested him, cryptocurrency became a game changer.

On the wall behind him, pinned to a wooden rail, hung a collection of odd and arcane pieces of 'art'. The most recent result of his other preoccupation. Too slow for sport, while his contemporaries were all off playing football or rugby, his mother enrolled him in the church choir. There he'd learned how to sing under the tutelage of the verger, a red-faced frotteur who took every opportunity to be as hands-on as possible. He spent a lot of time helping the younger boys, did the verger.

But amongst his more innocent hobbies was grave rubbing. Using nothing but soap and water, the verger taught him how to wash down the old gravestones, stick butcher paper on their surfaces and use a charcoal block to bring out the carvings. He'd found it instantly calming and fascinating. Especially when some of the younger boys were crying, he would lose himself and try not to think about what was going on a few feet away in the vestry. The younger boys never complained. He had the feeling the verger had coerced them in some way, making them the guilty parties. At least that's what emerged when the authorities had finally investigated. Mercifully, the verger was not attracted to the bigger children, and he'd been big for his age. As a result, the verger left him to his own devices.

Later, the verger was transferred out to a less claustrophobic parish. But the one good thing the old fiddler did was instil in him a love for bringing out the textures and elaborate carvings of gravestones. He loved it for its solitude, its craftsmanship, the sometimes poignant stories he unearthed. He'd begun in local churches, but as soon as he was old enough to drive, his hobby took him far and wide. He especially liked the overgrown graveyards and the forgotten cemeteries in abandoned churches. There he would find little gems. Stories of lives blighted by poverty, sometimes whole families from the last century or before struck down and decimated by disease. In the graveyards he at last found an outlet, a way of suppressing the wanton hunger that haunted his soul. And he was drawn to specific types of gravestones. Ones with *memento mori* in the form of skulls and bones carved into their surfaces. Reminders from the dead of the survivors' own mortality. When all that is left after the flesh has rotted away is the hardened core of our beings. Solid, pure, white. He liked to touch the carved curves of the craniums and run his fingers along the straight long bones wrought with such care. He liked to touch the real thing even more. Dreamed of doing just that.

He turned back to the search engine and typed in another phrase. This time the screen changed and an image appeared. Innocuous. A flower under the title St Nicholas. Slowly, the petals on the flower all fell off to leave a naked stigma, style and ovule. Underneath was a single box with a flashing cursor. He typed in a password and once more the screen changed to a series of security questions. After a couple more layers, he got to a bulletin board on the Bopeep site. Various headlines and threads appeared. Some explicit, some less so, but all buyers and sellers. He chose one called 'fresh daisies'. He typed, 'New bloom available. Anyone have any suggestions?'

Within minutes, he had a dozen answers. He smiled and typed.

This one is special. I will post a verifying image. Thirty-second clips will be available for 0.1 bitcoin. The whole for 1 BTC. Special venue arranged. See here.

A link led to a YouTube video. A famous *Game of Thrones* scene in a dimly lit brothel where the girls, paraded in descending age for the punter's delectation were all dismissed, in turn, as 'too old'.

He sat back and watched the responses flow in. After a while he got bored and typed in a new address. A niche site. The place where he did most of his business now. Where like-minded individuals stumped up the PPV money. Where they'd pay for certain words to be spoken. Pay for close ups of the colour draining from a face with a final breath.

The modus operandi was always his and his alone. But watching him do it could be bought for a price.

He checked the bulletin boards, content in the knowledge that here, despite his own shame at the feelings he'd had for so many years, he shared a sense of belonging. There were no images here. This site was too extreme even for the most hardened of pornographers. He read words and descriptions instead that were almost medieval in their depictions.

He still wondered at a world where technology had enabled him to monetise his sickness. But this was his world.

Soon, he would introduce his new bloom, Blair, to it.

CHAPTER FOURTEEN

Woakes rang at seven thirty. Anna had dawdled in the shower, muzzy from a bad night's sleep in which Shaw's face kept swimming up into her consciousness, making her open her eyes every couple of hours to make sure he hadn't manifested in her bedroom. The three or so hours of the good stuff didn't make up for the bad. Not one bit.

She was out of the shower, her hair still wet, when the phone rang.

'Morning, ma'am.'

'Dave, where are you?'

'At Hawley's place, in the middle of nowhereshire.'

'That won't work with sat nav.'

'Erm… over the bridge. Place called Sully near Penarth. Porlock Avenue. I can walk to the shore and wave to you across the Bristol Channel if you like.'

'Have you been there all night? Where did you sleep?'

'In the car. What does it matter? He's well spooked, is Hawley. At about seven last night he started shipping bin bags out to the front door.'

'I am not going to ask you how you know that.'

'Baa, baa sodding black sheep, ma'am. This morning he's gone out for a run. It's the first chance I've had to take a look and it's all gold. I told you we'd rattle him. I've sent you some snaps. Take a look and I'll ring you back.'

Anna rang off and opened her messages. Woakes had sent three images. The first was of three black refuse bags tied and awaiting collection. The second showed one of the bags opened, full of newspapers and cuttings. The third had the newspapers spread out on the floor. She tapped and enlarged. Three different newspapers, but the same type of headline on each.

POLICE CONTINUE SEARCH FOR MISSING GIRL

HOPE DWINDLES FOR LITTLE KATELYN

MOTHER ASKS FOR PRAYERS FOR HER LITTLE ANGEL

'Shit,' Anna said and rang Woakes back. 'When did he leave?'
'Fifteen minutes ago.'
'Stay there and do not do anything. Understood? I'm on my way.'

Fifteen miles was a damn site longer by road across the Severn Estuary. Anna knew the way. She'd mapped it dozens of times crossing the bridge between the two countries. Still travelled it when she visited Kate and her mother. Penarth had been a destination for her when she was growing up. They'd visit to walk the promenade or get fish and chips on the front and marvel at the huge captains' houses with their rooftop lookouts. But its roots were in the profits of the heavy industry that had ripped the wealth from the valleys in the nineteenth and twentieth centuries. Many of the houses had been built as retirement homes for the coal mine and steel plant owners, and around these bigger properties, the streets had spread and grown as money and people flowed from Cardiff. Its gold-star schools drew the upwardly mobile middle class like a cowpat drew blowflies. Sully she knew only vaguely as a spot along the coast between Penarth and its much brasher neighbour Barry. More retirement homes where you could watch the south westerlies bringing rain up the Channel and wave at the English across the water and know that your weather pain was quickly going to be shared by them.

She took the A4232 off the M4 and headed in towards Llandough and Lavernock Point. Sully was full of three- and four-bedroom detached modern houses and scattered bungalows. Porlock Avenue looked newer than the rest. Red-brick buildings with clay tiled roofs and lots of flowers in baskets and raised beds. The people who lived here had time on their hands, conscious though they might be of it passing too quickly. Woakes met her as she pulled up, and he got into her car. It looked like he'd slept in his suit.

'Is he back yet?'

'Ten minutes ago.'

'Bags still out front?'

Woakes nodded towards the rest of the street. 'They must be expecting a collection.'

'What do you make of it?' Anna asked.

'We've rattled his cage, now we start poking.'

'Didn't you do that yesterday?'

Woakes let out a derisory laugh. 'That was just a measly tremor. He's been collecting newspaper cuttings about missing kids, for Christ's sake. He's continuing the fantasy. It stinks. He stinks.'

Woakes was right. Her antenna was twitching, too, but Woakes' gung-ho approach bothered her almost as much as seeing those cuttings. 'He's done nothing illegal, Dave.'

'Then he's got nothing to worry about, has he?'

Woakes opened the car door but Anna put a hand on his arm. 'We don't know what this is yet, but we need to be careful. I don't like scatterguns, Dave.'

Woakes held both hands up in supplication. 'Fine. I'll play nice.'

He moved to get out again but Anna held him back. 'Make sure you do. The heavy-handed bad cop routine can wear thin very quickly.'

Shipwright had taught Anna a lot. He was old school but his theory about how you dealt with persons of interest had no paragraph entitled rubbing them up the wrong way until they bled.

Anna followed Woakes out and walked to the door of a small 1970s red-brick bungalow. This was not a cottage, as envisioned. No cosy porch. No wild flower garden. Instead, there were white, practical uPVC windows and doors and easy-to-water shrubs in tubs. It looked exactly the sort of place a retired spinster or widow might live with bay trees and chrysanthemums out front. The only incongruity was a newish Audi parked to one side with a surfboard strapped to the roof.

Woakes rang the bell.

Hawley answered dressed in jeans and a T-shirt.

'Dr Hawley,' said Woakes. 'Just a couple more questions, sir. Mind if we come in?'

Hawley didn't move. 'How did you find me?'

'Isn't this where you live?'

'No. I have a place in Bristol. This is my aunt's…' The words tailed off as Hawley did the maths. 'You followed me.'

'All part of the service, sir. Now, can we come in?'

'Why. What do you want to know that I haven't told you already?'

Woakes turned slowly towards the three refuse bags. 'Crows can be a real menace, can't they? I've seen them rip open bags all along a street looking for scraps or shiny things. One of your bags was open earlier this morning. Very interesting collection of cuttings you have, Doc.'

The colour drained from Hawley's face. 'You have no right—'

'No, we don't. So we could do all this back in Bristol, which would properly mess up your day off. Or you can let us in.'

Hawley stood aside.

It wasn't a large bungalow. Two bedrooms, a kitchen and a living room with an extension out into the garden. Hawley led them to the tiny living room dominated by a wall-mounted TV, an Ikea drawer set, a leather sofa and a small kitchen table and chairs in matching smoked glass. On top of the drawer set, a reed diffuser lent the room the aroma of fresh laundry. A gutted laptop sat on the tabletop, its casing open, electronic components scattered in what looked like a haphazard arrangement. A wire led from a small soldering tool to a main plug below.

'Broken computer?' Anna said.

'It's a hobby. I modify, dabble with the mother board, tweak here, add some memory there. Basically bugger up the manufacturer's warranty, that sort of thing.'

'Delicate work.'

Hawley shrugged.

Beyond was the small conservatory with white plastic panels to waist height and glass above showing a view of a postage stamp lawn beyond. In the corner of the lawn stood a sturdy tool shed. Padlocked.

'Nice little bolthole,' Woakes said.

'I'm probably going to sell it.'

'Yeah. I can see that this would be some old dear's idea of heaven. Coffee would be nice.'

Hawley snorted softly. 'Look, I'm happy to answer any questions but I didn't ask you here. I don't intend to make this a social visit.'

Anna watched him, happy to observe his reactions. He was skittish. Woakes was making him nervous. Was it simply that he didn't like people crowding him? God knows she understood that. Her own flat was off limits for all but the inner sanctum of her friends and relatives.

Or are you nervous for another reason altogether, Dr Hawley?

'OK,' said Woakes. 'Tell us about the cuttings.'

'Old stuff,' said Hawley. 'Stuff I was getting rid of.'

'Nothing to do with the fact that we're sniffing around, then?'

'I'm having a clear-out. I want to get this place ready for the market.'

'Sure,' nodded Woakes, his words dripping insincerity all over the beige rug. 'If you're throwing it all away, then you won't mind if we take it?'

'Yes, I would mind. There's personal stuff there too.'

'Yeah?' Woakes asked. 'Never heard of a shredder, Doc?'

'It's still on my property.'

'But if you intended to abandon it, it isn't theft,' Anna said.

Hawley threw her a glance. He looked disappointed in her. She was surprised at how uncomfortable that made her feel.

'Why are you doing this?' Hawley asked.

'Rosie Dawson,' Woakes said. He was standing close to Hawley, the taller of the two, a mirthless smile on his lips that had nothing to do with being pleasant. 'OK, perhaps you didn't take her. But maybe you helped someone else. You had access to all her details. Maybe you flagged her up as a good fit for some pervert who sent you the photos afterwards.' Woakes nodded at the table covered with electronic parts. 'From the look of it, it's obvious you know computers inside out. And we both know that's how it works, don't we, Doc?'

Colour suddenly returned to Hawley's face, a dark stain spreading up from his neck, his eyes glassy, like an animal caught in a trap. 'It's not what happened,' he said.

'No? Then why all the cuttings, eh?' Woakes closed the gap between him and Hawley by half a belligerent step.

'That's none of your business.'

'Of course it's my business.'

'Dave, enough,' Anna said.

Woakes looked at her as if he'd only that instant become aware of her presence. They were in the bungalow at Hawley's invitation. They needed to be careful.

'You're right,' Woakes said, holding up both hands. 'Sorry. It's this case. Kids, you know. Gets to me sometimes.' He sighed. 'Can I use your loo?'

Hawley frowned momentarily as the tension deflated. 'Uh, yeah. In the hall, first left.'

Woakes left. Anna said, 'How long had your aunt lived here?'

'Fifteen years. She died eighteen months ago.'

'You're not in any hurry to sell, then?'

'I thought about doing it up, but then I thought, what for? It'll sell just as well as it is. Heat-efficient, low maintenance, there's a market for that.'

Anna nodded. Though she didn't feel any of it herself, she sensed the appeal. 'It's quiet here.'

Hawley nodded. 'But the neighbours are close. Too close.' He walked into the conservatory and pointed through a window at an identical-looking bungalow 4 metres away over a low fence. 'I love the seaside, but if ever I buy something, it'll be away from the crowds.'

She understood alright.

'Maybe you could—' Her words were cut off by a shout from Woakes.

'Oy, oy! Look what I've found. Jackpot!'

CHAPTER FIFTEEN

Panic flared in Hawley's face a second before he turned and bolted back into the living room and into the little hall beyond. Anna followed, wondering what Woakes was up to now.

Which bit of being careful does he really not understand?

The door to a neat bathroom stood open showing neutral oat-coloured tiles and a chrome shower unit next to the loo. But where all the other doors off the hall had been closed when she'd entered the property, they were open now, too. The nearest to the bathroom revealed a bedroom with a double bed, wardrobe and dressing table, a few clothes scattered untidily. But the next door along had Woakes framed in the doorway, his hunter's eyes sparkling. 'Look what I found,' he said.

'You shouldn't be in there.' Hawley tried to push past him but Woakes put a hand on his chest.

'Sorry, got a bit lost. And I think that the inspector should see this, don't you?'

Hawley dropped his eyes and let out a juddering exhalation.

Anna moved past him into the bedroom. On one wall hung a large framed painting, at least four feet square. On the bed, a similarly sized wooden frame lay flat, it's string dangling, this one face down. It was what had been stuck on the back of the painting that was of interest. A back covered with photographs and cuttings. She instantly recognised some of the names. They'd all appeared in newspapers and on TV over the last six or more years. All the subject of massive police operations and all, without exception, still missing. At the bottom was a photograph of Blair Smeaton.

'You have been a busy boy,' Woakes said.

Hawley protested. 'I'm interested… I—'

Woakes rounded on him. 'Just give us an email list of your special friends, Doc. On your computer maybe? How does it work? Do you meet up with these other nonces in some shithole once they've taken the kids? They got a lockup somewhere? A little cellar where you keep them?'

Something flickered behind Hawley's eyes. A spark of something, horror or anger or both. He lunged at Woakes, pushing him backwards, driving him towards the bed, both falling, struggling, fists flailing towards each other. Anna moved quickly, grabbing Hawley's arm, flexing his wrist into a classic gooseneck hold, pulling him up and mashing his face against a wall while Woakes got up and reached for some handcuffs.

'What are you doing?' Anna asked.

'Restraining this bastard,' Woakes grinned.

'No, you are not. Get out of this room and cool down. Better still, sit in the car and wait for me.'

'What?'

Anna glared at him. 'Do it now, Dave. Don't make me tell you twice.'

Woakes glared back, mouth open, ready to object.

'Do it,' Anna said through gritted teeth. She didn't know what this was yet, but having Woakes in the room was suddenly a liability. She watched the emotions rage on the sergeant's face. Anger, distrust, they were all there. Finally, after several seconds too long, he turned and walked away, slamming the front door in his wake.

'I'm going to let you go now,' Anna said to Hawley.

She did and stood well back, giving him space to recover his dignity and his breath. He turned, panting, his lips thin and angry. 'You have no right. No bloody right.'

'I know.' He was right. If it ever came to it, they'd have all sorts of problems justifying being there because they should not have been searching his property.

Even though Woakes would probably say that the door was open and the painting already on your bed.

Hawley glared.

'And I am sorry for what just happened. There's no excuse.'

'You people.'

'Wait a minute. We're here investigating a serious crime.'

'It's not a crime to keep newspaper cuttings, is it?'

'No, but it raises suspicion.'

Hawley was still trembling from the altercation with Woakes, his face sour and hostile. 'I haven't done anything wrong,' he muttered, jaw clenched.

'OK, I hear that. But it's obvious you've been keeping tabs on things,' she used her hand to indicate the cuttings, 'and I would like to know why that is and what you think you've found, if anything. In my experience, when it comes to cold cases, the best information still comes from those involved from the outset.' She was being deliberately reasonable, still unsure of exactly what was happening here.

Hawley looked out of the window and Anna followed his gaze. Outside the day was shaping up nicely. Overnight rain had given way to blue sky and wispy clouds. A breeze shifted the leaves on a copper beech hedge, making them move up and down as if they were waving.

Gradually, his breathing steadied and Hawley shook his head. 'He had no right to go into that room.'

Anna waited, letting him vent.

'I'll talk to you. But I won't talk to him again, is that understood?'

'Fair enough,' Anna said.

Hawley walked around the bed to the second painting and removed it. He carried the cumbersome frame out to the living room and fetched the one already on the bed. Anna followed to find he'd placed them neatly next to one another, leaning against the wall.

Hawley stood for a moment, assessing his handiwork, and then went to the kitchen. 'Water?'

'Fine,' Anna said, absently.

She heard a tap running, but it was white noise as her eyes tried to assimilate what it was that sat propped against the living room wall in a spinster's bungalow. There were five images in total, three on one board, two on the other, beginning with Rosie and ending with Blair Smeaton. They were reminiscent of the boards Trisha set up for them regularly in Portishead, though much more haphazard in their layout.

Hawley came back into the room with two glasses.

'Can you talk me through this?' Anna asked.

'I didn't want anyone seeing this.' He gestured towards the boards. 'That's why I hide them.'

'Hiding it looks twice as suspicious, you must know that. Why, Dr Hawley?'

'It's Ben.'

'Alright, Ben, why?'

Hawley sighed. 'I suppose I couldn't let it go. I couldn't stop thinking about it, about her… I kept watching the news, reading the papers. Anything to do with missing children. I don't know if that's normal, but when you're caught up in it, trying to understand, you read and research and watch. Sometimes until your blood runs cold. And then, when something else happened, I began to wonder if there might be some sort of link. I tried to look for patterns.'

Anna sat up. Patterns were most often what solved serial cases. Patterns that the perpetrator sometimes did not know he or she followed. She believed in patterns. But she had seen no evidence from the previous HOLMES searches so far that Rosie Dawson's abduction had been replicated in any way.

'And?'

Hawley held both hands up, palms open. 'Some threads, but…' He laughed softly. 'But I don't know if they mean anything.'

'Let me be the judge of that, Ben. Please, tell me.' She wanted him to keep on talking. If this was genuine, she wanted to know. If it wasn't, if he was a narcissist documenting his own sick triumphs, thinking he was better than everyone else, the police especially, this was an opportunity to give him as much rope as he needed.

'I'm not a detective. All I can access are press reports and the internet. But when I was being interviewed, they kept on about the fact that I was in a unique position. I knew where Rosie lived. I knew her family. I knew where she went to school, her background. It was all in the notes, in the history the triage nurses took.' For a moment, Hawley lost himself in the recollection. 'They kept on and on about how many other little girls I'd invited onto my lap in the clinic.' Hawley sighed. 'It's why they kept coming back to me. Me knowing all about Rosie.'

'It would be a natural line to take.'

Hawley nodded. 'So, what you see on the boards is my attempt at trying to rationalise that. These five cases are all girls of a certain age, between ten and twelve. All missing. Rosie you know about; the others are from all over the country. Manchester, Devon, the Midlands and now Scotland.'

'So, what's the pattern?'

Hawley shrugged. 'I thought a lot about what the police were asking me. There is a lot of information on children in hospital notes. From what I learned from snippets in the press, these five kids all had some kind of illness that meant they'd had recent hospital attendances.'

Anna frowned. 'Surely, most kids will have been to hospital for something or other?'

'Not really. GP, yes. Hospital, not so common.'

'What you're saying is that their illnesses are the link?'

'I know how it sounds and it's mad because they all have different conditions. Rosie I saw in A and E, Katelyn Prosser had asthma, I think Lily Callaghan might have been diabetic, Jade Hemmings had eczema. There are probably a load of other kids missing without illnesses. It doesn't make any sense because most of these conditions require different specialist input. Doctors move around, especially when they're training. But I can't think of any one doctor who'd work in all these different specialisms in so many different areas of the country. It doesn't add up. I know that the abductions – where and how they were taken – all have different features, but perhaps that's deliberate. Perhaps the bloke knows to not have a pattern. I don't know.'

It was something of a stretch, Anna had to agree. 'And you do not know any of these victims personally?'

'Of course not.'

Anna stood and used her phone to take photos of the two boards and then wrote down the names in her notebook.

'Do you have anything else?' she asked.

'Is this where you take my laptop?' Hawley remained sitting, looking up at her with that same mistrust.

'Should I?'

'There's nothing on it.'

'Then I don't think it's necessary.'

Hawley nodded. Anna sensed that she'd met with some sort of unspoken approval when he said, 'I do have something else to show you though.'

Hawley reached into a magazine rack at the side of the leather sofa and removed a silver MacBook. He went to the table and fired it up, his fingers quick on the keyboard. His hands looked soft, the fingers long, like a piano player's or a surgeon's. Anna had a thing about hands. She hoped that they were not going to reveal something that would incriminate Hawley here. That there would be no way back from.

'Pick an address,' Hawley said. 'Any one.'

Anna went to the nearest board. Lily Callaghan, eleven years old when she went missing in 2014. She read out the address and Hawley typed it in. Google Maps came up, he used the trackpad to zoom in and flicked to satellite view. Anna stared at a street and watched Hawley pan around, past a front gate and semi-detached house before zooming out to a bird's eye view of the adjoining streets.

'I'm only showing you how easy it is, these days, to find things. I realise you know this, but if I wanted to go to Lily's house I could plan my route long before I ever got there. She was taken from the corner on her way back from a shop to get some milk. As far as I know, the police got no further.'

He was right, of course. Compared to the resources available to her, this was hardly cutting-edge technology but he'd given this a lot of thought. Anna stared at the screen, trying to make her mind up about Hawley. He'd been caught on the hop with his victim boards. Could it be that he was simply stringing her along here? Had he taken Rosie and perhaps all these other girls? Was he playing some sick and twisted game by showing her how? Or had the trauma of being a suspect truly sent him down this path of trying to make sense of what had happened to him and these girls? If he was involved in these other cases, it would not be difficult to find out. But her instinct told her something else and she'd learned to trust that. Hawley was damaged. A distrustful, mistreated animal unsure of whether this hand reaching out towards him was also going to slap him down.

'Ben, I can see that you've spent a lot of time on this.'

Hawley snorted. 'One way of putting it.'

'I don't know how useful any of this is. To us and to you. But I'm going to take all this away with me and see.'

'Are you going to turn up at my door unannounced again?'

Anna smiled. 'No. We have your number. And I'm sorry about Sergeant Woakes. About earlier.'

Hawley stood and shook her outstretched hand. It felt warm and dry in hers. He saw her out.

'We'll be in touch.'

Hawley said, 'I'd rather it be you, not we.'

'OK,' she said, not quite knowing why.

She walked back to her car half-expecting to see Woakes get out of his. But there was no sign of the DS or his vehicle. She rang his number when she hit the M4.

'Where the hell are you?' she asked when he answered. From the background noise, it sounded like he was talking to her from a moving vehicle.

'I'll be back in Portishead in about twenty.'

'Don't you want to talk about what just happened?'

'What did he say?'

'What?'

'Hawley, what did he say? Is he going to complain?'

'Not as far as I know.'

'Didn't think so. He's got too much to hide.'

'You were over the top, Dave.'

'Too bloody right. Sometimes you need to push these bastards. Squeeze them until something pops. Did he pop?'

'He has a theory about Rosie's case being linked to other missing girls.'

Woakes stayed silent.

'Dave?'

'And you believe him?'

'I think it's worth a look. Why, what do you believe?'

'I reckon he's got skin in the game. I reckon he's a nonce and we've caught the bastard out. We could easily get a warrant for his Bristol flat.'

'No. No warrant. I see no reason to go in all guns blazing, and you know you were out of order going into that bedroom.'

'Door was open, ma'am. I was looking for the loo. Innocent mistake. His word against ours.'

'Dave, it's not the way we do things here. Hawley might be useful and you almost destroyed any credibility we might have with him.'

More silence.

'Sergeant, did you hear me?'

'Yes, ma'am.'

Do you though? Do you hear anyone but your own voice?

'Get everyone together for a briefing at midday. Meet me in the car park at ten to.'

Woakes didn't answer.

'Did you hear me, Sergeant?' Anna asked.

'Yes, ma'am.'

Technically, Hawley had assaulted a police officer and Woakes could, if he wanted to, make waves. But there'd be no hiding from the provocation and Hawley had been an easy target. She tried to think about how it had been for him when he'd been under suspicion for Rosie's abduction. An ordeal, no doubt. And the press were worse than sharks when they picked up a chum line like Hawley's. The whole overblown episode had cost him his girlfriend, possibly friends and maybe family, too. She'd seen that happen. A tiny little worm of self-consciousness wriggled away at the back of her head. What was she doing thinking about Hawley and his relationships?

She reached for the radio, found a channel and listened to a politician trying to explain why they still couldn't extradite known criminals back to their country of origin for fear of infringing their human rights.

It was a wonderful world she lived in.

CHAPTER SIXTEEN

Hawley sat alone in the kitchen of his aunt's bungalow waiting for his heart to slow and his mind to settle. The police were long gone but still he couldn't believe how completely, *totally*, bloody stupid he'd been to leave all that stuff in the bin bags. He hadn't thought for one minute that they'd follow him here.

'Shit, shit, shit!' He thumped the table, and something from the disembowelled laptop fell to the floor. He bent and picked it up, threw it down onto the surface again. Hadn't he learned the last time not to trust the police?

Woakes, belligerent and confident, reminded him of the worst of the detectives he'd had to deal with last time. The way they'd assumed he'd had something to hide. Disregarding the fact that he was a professional and that you had to use charm and subterfuge when you dealt with kids as a doctor. How easily they dismissed that as something sleazy. It had made him ill then and he felt sick again now.

The cuttings boards were still leaning against the wall. The inspector, Gwynne, had seemed genuinely interested but he knew part of that was because she only wanted to pour oil over the tsunami that Woakes had threatened to cause. He'd told her everything, knowing how mad it sounded, how desperate and pathetic, because what else could he do? And now they had him down again as a bloody person of interest.

Hawley closed his eyes and let his head fall onto his forearm resting on the table.

Stupid. How could he have been so bloody stupid!

He lifted his head back up, staring out into the conservatory and the garden beyond, remembering the look of hate on Woakes' face and still not understanding how someone who knew nothing at all about him could despise him so for something that'd taken just a minute of his time, once, in a clinic years ago.

Hawley's eyes drifted across to the tool shed in the garden. He'd painted it earlier in the year. Put new locks on the door. He wondered if the police had seen that.

For all he knew they might have someone watching the bungalow and him. Like they did last time. Hawley grimaced; it was starting again. All over again.

But they hadn't asked to look inside the shed.

For that, at least, he was grateful.

CHAPTER SEVENTEEN

Woakes was leaning against his car, arms folded, as Anna pulled in to the car park at HQ. He pushed off and walked towards her when she got out. They stood a few feet apart, out of earshot of anyone.

Anna raised her eyebrows. 'I thought you'd prefer I do this here than upstairs in the office because two bollockings in two days will get people talking.'

He gave her a guarded shrug.

'Tell me you know how wrong what you did was?'

'I told you he was hiding something.' Woakes' tone rang sullen.

'He was. And now he's on the back foot and knows we're looking at him again.'

Woakes let his gaze drop and put his hands in his trouser pockets. His left leg kept jiggling, like a puppet on a string.

'Dave?' Anna insisted.

His head snapped up. 'OK, what I see from this morning is that we got a result. I was right, yeah? I've seen this before working serious crimes, or the human exploitation directorate as the PC brigade insist on calling it. We broke up a gang grooming kids. Nonces are nonces forever. They never stop. And they're all fucking cowards. We squeezed a couple in the Midlands and they started singing. Led us to all sorts.'

Anna's brows lowered. 'Hawley was never a nonce, Dave. He was cleared completely.'

'Then why does he have a list of victims stuck to the back of two landscapes in his bedroom?'

'Definitely the more interesting question and I haven't got an answer for it yet. But it isn't the point. Dave, come on. Your instincts are good, spot on in fact. Hawley may be valuable to us. But your way is not my way. I need you to understand that.'

'We've got the bastard on the ropes, haven't we?'

'Exactly. His defences are up. He knows we're looking. But what I want to know is how familiar he is with Clevedon. Is he a hiker? Someone who can carry a heavy backpack? The sort of thing you learn from subtle interrogation. Do you think he's going to volunteer that sort of intel now?'

Woakes sighed. 'This is the way I function. I need to get stuck in. Ma'am, all I'm trying to do here is be a good copper. OK, I admit I can be a bit… overenthusiastic.'

'Let's hope Rainsford sees it that way.'

Woakes let his head drop. 'Oh for fuck's sake, do you have to—'

Anna snorted. 'Of course I have to. Rainsford's expecting us to close the Morton case. How do you think I can explain us messing up his apprehension, let alone walking all over Hawley for no good reason?'

Woakes' expression hardened. 'I don't think you're being very supportive.'

'Supportive? Is that how you see it? Jesus, Dave, smell the coffee here. All I see is that you've walked in wearing size twenty clown shoes and thrown a grenade into my team. No one gets to do that.'

Woakes shook his head. Small, repetitive movements with his gaze deflected. 'God, they told me you were a frosty…' He caught himself just in time.

'*They*? Just exactly who are *they*, sergeant?'

Woakes' mouth hardened. 'I didn't see you pushing Hawley's buttons. I mean, with all due respect, what did you do? Just sat there, watching him, waiting for inspiration.'

Anna nodded. 'Yes, exactly that. Watching and waiting. You should try it sometime. Because what I saw as I watched and waited was that he lives alone, uses the preparation of the property for sale as an excuse to hide the fact he hasn't been bothered to redecorate, though he lives there most of the time judging by the six-pack of light beer and a couple of bottles of good wine in the fridge. There were no spirits in the drinks cabinet. Probably doesn't trust himself. The mail on the table was addressed to him there. You saw the recipe books and the shopping full of fresh vegetables and some cuts of meat, I take it?'

Woakes stared back at her.

Anna went on. 'All this means that he's self-contained, looks after himself, and can't decide whether to keep his aunt's bungalow or not because it's a safe haven away from his professional life. But you, of course, got all that, too, simply by shaking the tree, yes?'

Woakes responded with a dismissive shrug. 'I spoke to his colleagues in two A and E departments. They think he's weird. He won't see kids. Runs a mile from them.'

'Should it surprise you after what he's been through? He's probably terrified.'

'You saw he had new locks on his garden shed, did you?'

Anna snorted. 'Yes, I did. And he has every right to do that. And we have no right to ask him why.'

'Christ, I can't believe your defending this bloke.'

Anna nodded. 'Believe what you like. But you need to start doing as you're told and learning to be a team player and showing the rest of us, me especially, some *respect*. Second and last warning, Dave. I can always have you working on something else if you'd prefer?'

Woakes said nothing.

'I said is that what you'd prefer?'

'No, ma'am.'

She could have turned away and left him standing there. But she'd learned from Shipwright that a dressing down should be delivered swiftly and decisively. Once done, best forgotten.

'Right, now, let's get this briefing sorted.'

Upstairs, Anna told the squad about their meeting with Hawley, while Woakes sat at the back. But he looked distracted and she surmised he was still smarting like a schoolboy caught smoking in the bathroom. She ignored him and concentrated instead on what she'd learned from Hawley.

'I know how this sounds,' she said after writing the names of Hawley's victim list on the whiteboard, 'but I'm coming at it from two angles. The first is that we've caught Hawley out and he's involved in some way in these five cases. The second is that he's trying to make sense of the distressing experience he had as a suspect. That the original investigators had a point when they focused on him, but they didn't realise at the time what it was exactly. And it's made him believe that perhaps these victims were connected somehow by their medical histories, or the doctors they saw, or the hospitals they visited. Either way, it's worth at least looking and ruling out any connections.'

Holder spoke. 'But if he was involved, why show you all this?'

'He didn't have much choice once Dave accidently discovered his cuttings library on the back of a painting.'

Holder turned to look at Woakes. 'Intuition?'

Woakes didn't answer.

'There is that,' Anna said. 'Or as Hawley's solicitor might interpret it, an illegal search.'

'The obvious thing to do would be to find out if Hawley's ever worked in the places the victims lived,' Khosa said.

'Good idea, Ryia. Let's throw it into the mix. Justin, drag the files up from Hawley's list and find out if and where they were treated. Then ring the hospitals and see if Hawley ever worked there. Where are we with the image?'

Holder shrugged. 'We've had it enlarged and gone over it. There is no branding on the bottles. The clothes Rosie wore were what she was abducted in. She had the vest on under her school uniform. No price tag on the blanket or the bucket. There's nothing there.'

'There must be something,' Anna said.

'I've spoken to someone in Hi-Tech, ma'am. They can get to us tomorrow.'

'No. Not good enough. This is fresh evidence. The only fresh evidence in nine years. We need their input and we need it now.'

Holder nodded. 'I'll ring them again, ma'am. See if they can get someone to us today.'

Anna looked at her watch. 'By close of play today, Justin. OK, Ryia, that gives us three hours to get over to Charterhouse where Rosie's remains were found. Sort out the location and you're driving. Let's say, thirty minutes?'

Khosa nodded.

Anna turned to Trisha. 'I'll dig into Hawley's background.' In her peripheral vision, she saw Woakes sit up. But Anna ignored him. 'Trisha, let's get some fresh search terms into HOLMES. Hospital sex offenders, links to doctors, nurses, etcetera.'

Trisha wrote on her pad. She'd have access to indexers who provided admin support, inputting the various reports their lines of enquiry generated, and extract data from the cross-referencing queries. But Anna knew that Trisha did the interpretation and analysis of what these database searches threw up. She was the receiver. They'd need filtering for relevance and then phone calls to follow up. The end result, if anything of use did appear, would be her well-written summary. It wasn't simply a question of pressing a button.

'Any joy with military links?' Anna asked.

'Not yet, ma'am.'

Finally, she looked at Woakes and the red flush spreading up from his neck. 'Dave, you get on to the SIO involved in the original enquiry.'

'Haven't you asked Ryia to—'

'I'm on it, ma'am,' Khosa said. 'Trisha, did you follow that up?'

Trisha consulted a notepad. 'The original senior investigating officer was a DCI Sutton. He's now in Thames Valley.'

'It'll carry more weight if they know it's a DS who's asking,' Anna said.

Woakes let out a mirthless laugh. 'I thought you wanted me with you at Charterhouse?'

'Getting a handle on the previous investigation is as important. We may be lucky and find one or two people still around. I'll leave that to you.'

Woakes' eyes slid towards the ceiling, but Anna turned back to Trisha. 'And let's set up a board for these four. Nothing elaborate. Dates, places, witness reports. I'll send you the photographs I took.'

'Blair Smeaton's on that list, ma'am,' Holder said.

'I know. Since it's an ongoing, I'll speak to Edinburgh myself, but only if it becomes relevant. It'll be manic up there and I don't want to complicate things unless we get something concrete. For now, this stays on our radar only. Everybody happy?'

Holder, Khosa and Trisha all nodded. Woakes did not.

Anna had barely sat down in her office when Trisha appeared at the door. 'It's about the special constable witness, Kevin Starkey. He left four years ago, but we have a contact number so I've left him a message to ring you.'

'Thanks, Trisha.'

When she didn't turn away immediately, Anna looked up. Trisha was grinning.

'What? Toothpaste on my cheek? Mascara running?'

They both knew the latter was a bloody impossibility as she didn't wear any.

'No,' said Trisha, still smiling. 'It's just good to have you back, Inspector Gwynne.'

Anna nodded. She found compliments difficult, both to give and receive. But this one she acknowledged. There'd been times during the aftermath of Willis's attack when the idea of ever running a team in a full-blown investigation again seemed laugh-able. She'd seen that doubt reflected in the faces of visitors when they'd seen the stitches and the bruises. But she'd not read that doubt in Trisha, nor the rest of the MCRTF.

She'd always be grateful for that. And it did feel good, *really* good, to finally be back in the saddle.

CHAPTER EIGHTEEN

The location where Rosie's remains had been found took them out to a section of the Force's patch Anna was not that familiar with. This neck of the Mendips was all wooded lanes looping up and over hills, past derelict stone buildings and limestone outcrops. A forty-minute drive brought them to the village of Charterhouse. Khosa had a map in a plastic folder and a GPS reference, and once they'd parked in a field study centre, they set off up a side road and across a stile and out into open countryside dotted with little green hillocks.

The day was warm and dry and the ground underfoot rock hard. After ten minutes of walking from where they'd parked, they were alone on a windswept expanse of paths winding between tumbled-down stone walls. To their left a fenced-off area in the distance drew Anna's attention.

'Any idea?' she asked Khosa with a nod towards the fence.

'Mine shafts, ma'am. Lead. This place is pockmarked with them, not to mention the caves and sinkholes.'

'Has a sort of Arthurian feel to it,' Anna said.

'You'd be right there, ma'am. I knew someone in college who came from Taunton. She said the Mendips were nothing but old ghosts and the ruins of cathedrals.'

'What the hell was the killer doing here with Rosie's remains?'

Khosa shrugged and walked on. Ten more minutes and they were at the spot. Merely a point on a path, a slight depression. Khosa took out a photograph from her folder and twisted it this way and that.

'Roman fort to the north, Neolithic settlement to the east. There's a church with a medieval crypt half a mile south… erm. The plastic bag and the bones were found… there.' She pointed to a spot behind the remains of a wall. 'Found by walkers out with a dog who paid a lot more attention to the bag than he normally would, apparently.'

Anna looked around her. There was nothing here.

'Let's walk to the rise.' She pressed on. Fifty yards later they emerged from the sunken part of the path. This point afforded a better view. On both sides, heathland stretched away. Towards a farmhouse on one side and a road on the other. Once more Anna pointed to a fenced-off area, this one much bigger, fifty yards to the right. She stepped off the path onto tussocks and rough ground and walked to the edge of the fence. It marked the boundary of a deep depression perhaps thirty yards in diameter, lined with grass and gorse bushes but with a dark opening right at its centre.

'Sinkhole, ma'am,' said Khosa, joining her. 'It's marked on my map.'

Anna turned, stared back along the way she'd come and retraced her steps. This was a lonely spot on the outskirts of a pretty isolated village. Whoever had brought Rosie's remains here had been hoping not to be disturbed.

At the point where the bag had been left, it would not have been possible to see anyone coming over the ridge until they were fifty yards away.

'Any thoughts, Ryia?'

'None, except this is not a place I'd like to be alone in. Not even in daylight.'

Anna knew what she meant. The place had a desolate feel about it. The sort of place it might be easy to get rid of evidence, perhaps down a sinkhole, if you knew where to find one.

'He wasn't here by accident, that's for sure,' Anna said.

'What do you think happened, ma'am?'

'If he'd wanted Rosie's remains to be found, he's hardly likely to have chosen this place. There are a million better spots that would guarantee discovery within a few minutes of you discarding something. No, he was hoping not to be seen. Perhaps he was on his way to a sinkhole to get rid of the evidence once and for all. Did you say there was a church and a crypt?'

Khosa nodded.

'Maybe he was on his way there. To bury her. Might have been some sort of ritual for him, who knows. But down in that dip you have no line of sight. He might have been preparing, opening the bag and suddenly someone appeared. A dog maybe. What if he panicked and dumped the evidence and made himself scarce?'

Khosa said, 'It fits. But why here?'

'Because he's familiar with the area. He knows about this place. Putting it together with knowing exactly what he was doing in the park in Clevedon when he took Rosie makes him someone with good local knowledge.'

Khosa nodded. 'I suppose that puts the kibosh on your doctor's theory, then. I mean the other girls were taken from all over the place. He wouldn't have local knowledge in those cases.'

Anna nodded. 'There is that.'

Khosa kept looking at her. 'You don't sound convinced.'

Anna shrugged. 'I'm letting it all marinate. Let's see what it turns into.'

When they got back to HQ, Anna noticed the board Trisha had put up with Hawley's list of mispers. Four more images had joined Rosie's. Holder looked pleased with himself.

'I got hold of the FLO that looked after Lily Callaghan's family. She confirmed that Lily had diabetes and was seen sometimes in the paediatric clinic in the Nottingham Children's Hospital. I put a call in to their Human Resources department. They confirmed that Hawley had never been employed there. Lily left a friend's house 50 yards from where she lived. Not seen since.' He tapped a pen towards another image. 'Same story here. Jade Hemmings, eleven. Manchester still have the file open, though it's five years since she went missing. No one saw her. She went to a birthday party in a park on her bike and disappeared. Jade had eczema. She attended the dermatology clinic at the kids' hospital in Manchester. No record of Hawley ever having been near it.'

'Good work, Justin. Any sign of Dave?'

'No, ma'am. He left soon after you did.'

Trisha made them all a cup of tea, and Anna went into her office and turned to the transcripts of Hawley's original interviews.

His story had been consistent. He'd voluntarily allowed them to examine his computers. The browsing history sourced from his internet service provider was unremarkable. They'd found no evidence of anything remotely paedophile-related, which was always a consideration in cases like these. Like 75% of other men in his age group, and 40% of women, he'd visited pornography sites, streamed but not stored downloads. Anna stayed up to speed on all that thanks to regular talks from the internet crime guys. A generation of kids had grown up thinking it was completely normal to watch hardcore sex on their phones. A decade ago it had been much more difficult to find, and internet access was restricted to a single PC in a parent's study. Technology abolished all that. Almost 30% of twelve-year-old boys had seen some sort of pornography. Kids were as likely to find it by accident as deliberately: it had become that ubiquitous. Anna had seen her own fair share and she was no angel. *Fifty Shades* had done a lot to open the lid on that one. Statistically, 'well-endowed stripper' and 'girl on girl' came up tops as the commonest search terms during Prosecco-fuelled hen nights. Hawley's habit, though probably humiliating when confronted with it, did not throw up anything the dirty squad wanted to know about.

There were cuttings in the file, too. Headlines relating to the local press's unsubtle approach to Rosie's death. Though the tabloids had not taken up the story, one local newspaper had been far less reticent.

ROSIE MURDER SUSPECT ARRESTED

A man held by police over the abduction of Rosie Dawson is known to have worked at a local hospital where he regularly came into contact with children. Sources last night confirmed that for the three months leading up to Rosie's abduction, the health professional had worked shifts in the hospital's A and E department. A police source confirmed that he was still being held in connection with the case, so far with no charge.

It read as an innocuous enough statement, laden with innuendo, yet lurid enough to cause Hawley significant personal and professional pain, and for the editor to receive a warning from the Attorney General's office.

There was no figure more reviled than a man who murdered children. The tabloids had a string of words that were a pick-and-mix of revulsion: 'beast', 'paedo', 'monster', 'pervert'. The broadsheets and public broadcasters shied away from the more lurid and prejudicial choice of language; nevertheless, even they had gravitated towards words like 'predator' designed specifically to feed parents' fears. The inevitable press frenzy only fuelled the panic and anger the general public felt.

Luckily for Hawley, his quick release meant that the national newspapers lost interest before his story took hold. The mudslinging had all been local.

Anna frequently pondered this pattern of reporting. The more heinous the crime, the more words were written about it. Murder remained king in the media. No doubt the more serious the crime, the more need there was to inform people, but the resultant skews, for someone in a job like hers, were enormous. And dealing with the press in the heat of such crimes piled on the strain, as she'd learned only too well in previous cases. Common crime was ignored, rare crime given the most attention. It didn't reflect reality. And of course, it was only right and proper that children were warned of stranger danger, yet statistically, the risk of a child drowning in a swimming pool was three times greater than that of being abducted. But drownings were for the sympathy paragraph at the bottom of page four, not a page one headline.

The police had held Hawley for only twenty-four hours both times they'd had him in for questioning, but it was enough for the *Post* to have their little scoop of dirt and splash it over the mid-week edition. He'd been young and unprepared. She wondered how he'd begun to cope with trying to get back to normality after something like that. The truth was he had not, judging by what she read about his stagnating career.

CHAPTER NINETEEN

The technician turned out to be a civilian data forensic investigator who'd been in a meeting talking to someone from Zephyr, the Regional Organised Crime Unit. Anna wasn't sure what she'd expected, but Szandra Varga came as a pleasant surprise. Stocky, dark hair, efficient, she listened carefully as Khosa outlined what she had and then used Khosa's computer to log on while the DC watched.

Five minutes later she was on the Europol website having traced the image from the reference in the Belgian police's email. The dreadful scene appeared again.

'I see,' she said, still typing. Her accent was subtle, somewhere east of France, extending the vowels but not interfering in the slightest with her diction.

'What do you see?' Khosa asked.

'First of all, it's a png file. That means there would be no EXIF data.'

No one spoke. Varga looked up. 'Whoever posted this file made it into a png image.'

Still no one said anything.

'OK,' said Varga, clearly used to technophobes. 'When you take a photo with your phone or a camera, it is usually saved as a jpeg file. Joint photographic experts group. That is a format used to compress digital images. But if you have a GPS-enabled phone or camera, the file will include metadata like coordinates and the unique ID number of the device. Portable network graphics files, png, do not contain this metadata.'

'If it had been a jpeg, we could have found out where it was taken?'

'Possibly,' said Varga.

'So, he's careful.' Khosa nodded.

Woakes appeared and stood behind Holder, looking in over his shoulder at the screen.

'What sort of website would have posted something like this?' Holder asked.

Varga's eyebrows went up. 'Probably a forum or a discussion board. Perhaps a darknet marketplace.'

'Darknet?' Holder asked,

'Also known as the Dark Web, yes.'

'We know of it,' Anna said.

'OK.' Varga's go-to word. She swivelled around in her chair once again to address the squad. 'Strictly speaking, a darknet is any network that needs specific software or tools to access it. It's an encrypted network overlaid onto the normal internet and only accessible to those who have the tools. The Deep Web are the layers of the internet that normal search engines cannot access. It is the internet that is not within reach of most people. Hidden because of restricted access, such as a government site or a paid streaming service. The Dark Web, on the other hand, is a subset of the Deep Web that has been intentionally hidden. To access it you would need to use the darknet and its tools. In all three instances, the term 'dark' applies because it uses encryption to make users anonymous.'

'How does it do that? I mean everyone has an IP address, don't they?' Anna said. 'I mean you log on with your address.'

'You cannot access the Dark Web through Google or Firefox. You need a special browser. A darknet browser such as Tor, The Onion Router, which has layers of privacy features already included. The smarter criminals also use a VPN or virtual private network to connect to public networks. Because of this, the Dark Web naturally attracts drug traffickers, illicit arms sellers and pornographic or paedophile activity. PPV you already know the meaning of. Probably there would be a link associated with the image, many further layers, and then somewhere to access more photographs, or, in this case, video, for a price.'

'What about paying for that? Surely we can trace credit cards?' Woakes asked.

Varga nodded. 'Mostly these days it is cryptocurrency. Bitcoin, litecoin. There is no link to the buyer's or seller's identity. Though that is changing with blockchain evidence. Large amounts do leave a solid trail but small amounts are more difficult to track.'

The silence that followed let Varga know that she'd left her audience way behind.

'I don't really know what a bitcoin is,' Khosa said, with an apologetic grimace.

Varga shrugged. 'All you need to know is that bitcoin has grown exponentially as a currency and there are even bitcoin ATMs. People use it and trade it and it has value, all of which is hidden from normal traceability. Especially on the darknet.'

'I'm still out of my depth.' Holder ran his hands through his hair.

Varga nodded. She'd obviously been here before. 'Bitcoin and other types of cryptocurrencies are decentralised digital currency. They can be transferred from person to person directly. When you have a bank account, the bank controls your money. You have to use them to transfer and withdraw and deposit. That leaves a trail. With cryptocurrencies, there is no need for a bank or clearing house. Bitcoins are made, or mined, by computer activity and have controlled and restricted production to maintain value. They can be used in any country and only you have access to your account. Because of this, cryptocurrency is popular with criminals and in countries where the value of money fluctuates.'

'OK,' said Khosa. 'But I know what a dollar is. I know what a pound is. I just can't see what a bitcoin or a litecoin or whatever you call it is or what it's worth.'

'It's worth what someone is willing to pay for it,' Varga said. 'Think of gold. Does it have any real inherent value other than it is scarce and it shines? It's worth something because someone else covets it. That is the nature of commerce, is it not? And this new cryptocommerce does not store any sensitive or personal data as a bank transaction would.'

'Are these transactions completely untraceable?' Holder said.

'Users have addresses from where they can send and receive. But no names are assigned. Though every transaction is added to a blockchain, a bit like a bank ledger to record the transactions. These confirmations are stored on users' computers. This is called bitcoin mining, and if you are prepared to mine using your computer to process the chain, you can get new bitcoins yourself. Now, because of the great number in circulation, it takes a lot of computer power, and individuals find it difficult to do. But there are also laundry systems that take your digital coins and shuffle them around the many addresses they own and give you back the coins at another address. Then it becomes almost impossible to trace coins.'

'Is that legal?'

'Yes. Governments and banks are way behind when it comes to the dark economy and cryptocurrency.'

'OK,' Holder said. 'I can understand all that, but what can you actually buy?'

Varga turned back to the screen and typed in a search. Up came a site. On it was a list of companies now accepting bitcoin. Flights, jewellery, computers, gift cards, pizza. Most were in the USA. It took a moment for Holder to remember to shut his mouth.

Varga'a knowledge of cryptocurrency and its attraction for criminals was obviously extensive, but they were straying from the evidence. Anna needed to bring them back into focus. 'Szandra, we're interested in the image. Could you find out a bit more for us? Can you date it, for example? Tell us what sort of camera was used? Or when it was posted?'

Szandra shrugged. 'Not always, but we can usually get some information. I can't do it here but I will get back to… Ryia, is it?'

Khosa nodded. She stood to walk Varga out.

Anna said, 'Thanks, Szandra. You've been a great help and I appreciate you have a heavy workload. But I'd also appreciate it if you gave this some urgent attention.'

Varga nodded and smiled. She understood. She'd heard it all before. And Anna sensed that hidden in that sanguine smile was a wariness that held no promises.

'Did any of that help actually help us with Rosie?' Holder asked when Khosa came back into the room.

Anna shrugged, 'Only that we now know he's computer literate and smart at covering his tracks.'

Woakes, who had been quiet throughout the whole of Varga's presentation, finally spoke. 'So he's bright. Like a doctor would be, for instance. And didn't Hawley have his laptop in pieces when we called?'

'He did,' Anna said.

'Therefore it would be a good idea to look at his laptop, wouldn't it?'

'Possibly,' Anna said. 'But this image is years old. We wouldn't get a search warrant based on what we have and I, for one, do not want to start fending off a harassment accusation.'

Woakes leaned forwards, both hands on the desk. 'He might be sitting at home in his little Wendy house right now laughing his tits off.'

Anna thought about reacting but bit her tongue. It was well after five by now. 'Right, let's call it a day. I'm sure we all have homes to go to. We'll pick this up in the morning.'

Anna threw her body around a CrossFit circuit in the gym for an hour after work and let the day's events simmer. They were no nearer to finding out anything else about Rosie Dawson but she'd learned a lot since getting out of her own bed that morning. Mainly that Woakes was a liability and seemed to have brought a lot more baggage with him than anyone had warned her about. In fact, there'd been no warning at all. Rainsford's only handover information had been that Woakes had come to them from Leicester. He hadn't actually said why. And they'd needed the help. Twelve months ago she'd been Woakes, a detective sergeant with a senior detective chief inspector running the team, and Holder as the detective constable beneath her. But DCI Shipwright's ill health had opened the door for her promotion. Woakes was meant to bolster a depleted team. So far, he'd not only forgotten that there was no 'I' in team, he'd added a couple more.

Back in her Horfield flat, Anna ate some pasta and sipped her one glass of wine, pondering if doing this alone every night was the best that life could offer. Kate didn't think so and her mother certainly did not. But did she pine? No. And despite Kate's description of his backside, the thought of Woakes sharing this with her did absolutely nothing to her juices. And then Ben Hawley was there in his T-shirt with that surprised, hurt look on his face. She quashed the thought. There were well-established codes for maintaining professional boundaries and standards when it came to witnesses or victims. Vulnerability was always present and the power imbalance easy to abuse.

But that didn't stop her thinking about Hawley and what he'd been put through. Was that pity or something else altogether? Anna shrugged. He'd had a great deal of time to think about Rosie. Much more time than she or Woakes had. And his theories might all be simply nothing more than wool-gathering, unhealthy preoccupation or, if Woakes was to be believed, the arrogant mind-games of a perpetrator gloating over his triumphs.

Anna became aware of an itch she couldn't reach on the inside of her skull. Like a parasitic worm trying to burrow its way out. She didn't like it, but she'd learned to trust it because it held all the pieces that would make up the pattern that was beginning to form around Rosie's photograph with the PPV caption. They floated in front of her now, those pieces. Disconnected points that somehow remained all part of the same jigsaw:

Rosie's discarded bones on the path in Charterhouse.

The conviction she held that in Rosie's case, the killer had intimate local knowledge.

The certainty, given Varga's assessment, that they were dealing with a skilled, clever predator.

She needed that one extra link, the something that might begin to make the picture whole. But where the hell was it going to come from?

CHAPTER TWENTY

Wednesday morning at HQ and the burrowing worm still gnawed in Anna's head. The visit from Varga the previous afternoon had been interesting but frustratingly unhelpful. Yet, Anna sensed that her input in this case was vital. Unable to quell the urge, she rang Varga's number.

'Inspector Gwynne?' Varga answered immediately. It sounded like she was walking.

'I know I'm pestering but—'

'I am in reception. I will be with you in five minutes. I have news of your image.'

Varga breezed in, sat again at Khosa's desk and got down to it with no fuss. Anna liked that about her. A lot.

'Europol is very efficient. Seized data is an excellent way to generate new leads in any type of internet-related crime. The image you found came from a Belgian investigation which led to forty arrests. The image was buried in a chat room posting. The date of the posting is May 2009. The twenty-fourth to be precise. That is nearly a year after Rosie Dawson went missing.'

No one spoke. Varga told a great story.

'It looks as though the post was deleted, but another user had responded to the post and so the image was preserved on that user's timeline.'

'What did the user say?'

'It is an irrelevance. All that is important is that this other user may have been not as careful as he should have in deleting his posts. The forum was on a site known to be a paedophile haunt. This one was called Littlefeet.'

'Jesus.' Woakes shook his head.

'The bad news is,' Varga continued, 'that the site has long ago been taken down. The urls change all the time. But Littlefeet was not a deep level forum. None of the images from it were classed as severe. Some simple photographs of children. Clothed, taken in play areas or swimming baths with captions from the posters.'

'What are you saying here, Szandra?' Anna said.

'I think that this image is nothing more than an advertisement. A sample to entice people into a deeper layer of the Dark Web. Those that could.'

'Can you get in there?'

'We don't know where there is.'

'What sort of sites are we talking about here?'

Varga held Anna's gaze. 'I am not an expert. I am a technician but my work inevitably brings me into contact. If you want real details you would need to talk to the CAIT in Weston.'

Anna knew about the Child Abuse Investigation Team. But she sensed that Varga was holding back.

'We will, but tell us what you know.'

Varga sighed. 'I work in digital forensics, but we are part of a multidisciplinary team. Operational support, digital investigations and ICAT, the Internet Child Abuse Team. I spend a lot of time with them as colleagues. We all have counselling about the images we see. We talk all the time, obviously. So, I know that even in the depraved world of child pornography there are some rules. Deliberate harm is generally frowned upon, although I realise that those two words are a matter of semantics. We know, though, that despite this, all tastes are catered for.'

Something opened up inside Anna. A dark hole into which her insides seemed to fall. The squad fell silent for several seconds as the impact of Varga's words sank in.

'OK,' said Holder. 'So how does that help us with Rosie Dawson?'

'We can get Szandra to keep looking for photos of Rosie in these chat rooms,' Khosa said. 'There must be others besides Littlefeet.'

'And add in the others from Hawley's list maybe?' Holder offered.

'I can speak to someone in ICAT. But I know they are busy after last week's seizures.' Varga shrugged.

Holder said, 'Yeah, I read about the raids. Ten addresses, wasn't it?'

Varga nodded. 'And a dozen computer hard discs to analyze. I will try but I think it will take some time.'

'How much time?' Anna said and heard the frustration in her own voice.

'Here our local resources are…' Varga's hands fluttered ineffectually.

'Stretched. Yeah, we've heard it all before.' Woakes looked suitably miffed. 'Christ, it's a wonder we catch any of these bastards.'

Varga did not look offended. She had either chosen not to accept the challenge of Woakes' cheap shot, or she hadn't fully understood it. Anna didn't care either way. Varga was good value.

'There are several ways we do catch these… bastards,' Varga said, looking directly at Woakes. 'Seized data, as happened with the Belgian police raid. Following money, real money, credit card records and larger cryptocurrency transactions, we already discussed. Blockchain analysis does exist but only large organisations like the IRS can do this and they are only interested in money laundering. Large amounts. Small transactions remain completely under the radar. Your best option is source information, such as on discussion boards as I have demonstrated.'

Woakes frowned.

Varga said, 'People leave digital breadcrumbs if they are not very, very careful.' She pointed at Rosie's image. 'Like this preserved image in the chat room. And then there is mass surveillance, though intercepted information is not admissible in the UK. And then there are the covert operations. The traps. Pretending to be someone else online is much easier than going undercover. Covert operations are not usually run locally. Usually CEOP—'

'Remind me,' Khosa said.

'The Child Exploitation and Online Protection Command is part of the National Crime Agency. They might be able to help. But you need to remember that the Dark Web is vast and we have no idea what we are looking for.'

'That's not very encouraging, Szandra, but I could listen to you all day,' Holder said.

Varga's eyebrows went up but she looked pleased.

Anna nodded. 'Szandra, this is extremely useful. I'll get a formal action written up for you guys to look at Rosie's image for us. And one of us needs to speak to CAIT.'

'I look forward to it,' Varga said and handed her report over to Anna.

'Bloody geeks,' Woakes said when she'd gone.

'Bloody geeks often get us the answers we need,' Anna replied. She waited for Woakes to come up with the suggestion she expected him to, but all he did was turn back to his screen.

What they had not investigated Hawley for was any evidence of cryptocurrency transactions. Anna felt sure Woakes would suggest this the instant Varga had said it. But clearly it sailed over his head. She filed it away for now and kept staring at the point in space where Woakes' face had just been. The burrowing worm nudged against the inside of her skull. A different idea stimulating it. Their own Hi-Tech squad was stretched and all they had was one image. Searching for more links to Rosie was going to take time. But what about other areas where resources were being thrown at an all-guns-blazing investigation?

Anna went back to her office, an idea taking shape in her head. She got Trisha to put her through to someone on the investigating team in Edinburgh. Police Scotland had different ways of doing things, and Blair Smeaton's abduction, still eminent in the press, would be coordinated by a POLSA, as with every other force in the country. But for what she wanted, Anna decided on the liaison at the National Child Abuse Investigation Unit who'd been drafted in to help the Edinburgh team. A sergeant by the name of Julie Danaher.

'DS Danaher.'

'Hi. This is DI Anna Gwynne with the MCRTF at Avon and Somerset. We're in the middle of reviewing a cold case. The abduction and murder of Rosie Dawson nine years ago. Something's come up which may be of interest to you.'

'Fire away,' said Danaher. It took Anna a moment to work out what was incongruous, but then realised that Danaher had a Northern Irish accent.

In the background, Anna heard Danaher issuing muted orders, her hand over the mouthpiece of her phone, not quite obscuring everything.

'You're busy,' Anna said.

'Mad.'

'OK, I'll be brief. I'm not sure if this is going to be of any help at all, but we've been looking at any links between abductions across the country. Specifically, girls aged between nine and twelve.'

'So have we, ma'am. HOLMES has flagged them up.'

'Then you'll have Rosie included.'

'Probably, ma'am,' Danaher said. She sounded tired. No doubt wondering where all this might be leading.

Anna said, 'We've reopened our case because of some new information. Europol found an image on a site during one of their big raids. Turns out it's an image of Rosie taken while she was in captivity. We've had input from our digital forensic unit and they tell us that the site they found her on was probably linked to other sites where other images might be for sale. I take it you've not found anything?'

'I don't think we've looked. We've been concentrating on searches and physical evidence.'

'Obviously. And I know that would be your priority. But it might be worth your ICAT guys having a peek.'

Danaher sounded surprised. 'OK. But do you honestly think there's a link between your case and ours?'

Anna paused. She still hadn't made her mind up about Hawley. But if there was the smallest chance that he was right and that there was a grain of truth in his theory, then she had a duty to spell it out.

'We're fishing for links, just like you are. Someone has pointed out that in a few cases, the victims all had medical histories. It's pretty thin but—'

Danaher came back right away. 'You can take Blair off that list. She's well. No issues, apart from the hearing problem.'

'Hearing?'

'She wears a hearing aid. Left ear. Recurrent otitis media. It's in every school photograph.'

'And do you have any leads?'

'No.' Danaher's tone stayed flat. 'Brick wall. Family's in pieces as you can imagine. The sister worst of all because she was with her. All we know is that he's white, no distinguishing features and he wore some kind of uniform. Probably nothing official, but enough to fool the girls.'

'CCTV?'

'Partial of a white van. No plates.'

'Age?'

'No go. Hat and sunglasses. The sister got hit by a stun gun and that shook her up. We're still working with her on a description. Accent not local. Height average or above, we think.'

Big enough to carry a small child in a rucksack, then.

'Anything else?' Danaher asked after a few beats of silence.

'No. I only wanted to check if your ICAT were involved and to give you a heads up. It's a stretch, I know, but it might be worth them having a quick trawl through known paedophile forums looking for images.'

'But won't that take forever?' Danaher's voice was weary.

'No. Not if they limit the search parameters to the time since Blair was missing.'

There was a pause as Danaher absorbed this. 'No, of course.' She sounded suddenly awake.

'I'll get Varga's contact details over to you. Let your ICAT people talk to her directly.'

Danaher rang off.

When Anna went back into the squad room, empty apart from Trisha, she asked her to get Varga's contact details up to Sergeant Danaher. It wasn't much, but it was something. If it helped Blair, all well and good. And it didn't do any harm to know that someone else was looking.

CHAPTER TWENTY-ONE

Woakes met with DCI Sutton from Thames Valley Major Crimes Investigation Team at the HQ in Kidlington. Sutton, losing a battle with his sizeable paunch, in short sleeves and tanned from weekend sailing, was affable enough and gave Woakes some tea as they sat in his office: a box decorated with Post-it notes and tacked-up bits of paper bearing flow charts and graphs. He remembered Rosie Dawson alright. Who wouldn't?

Woakes had already spent a fruitless morning talking with the Avon and Somerset CAIT. They knew all about Rosie but had nothing new to contribute, as he knew they wouldn't. There'd been no evidence that Rosie or anyone in the family had any links to pornography but they did provide him with a list of known sex offenders who lived in the area at the time of Rosie's abduction. They also implied that every one of them had been thoroughly looked at.

Sutton, on the other hand, talked about how the investigation had faltered because of lack of evidence, and he walked Woakes through the months after her disappearance up until the bones were found. Though interested to hear that the MCRTF were looking again, he was not optimistic.

'Best of luck. We spent thousands of man hours and came up with bugger all. I can't tell you the number of times I walked through that park in Clevedon. We traced just about every red van in the south-west and came up blank. The post office almost took us to court. We must have spoken to every postie in Bristol with a bloody van. And everyone who bought a decommissioned one and stuck white doors on the back. It was the one definite piece of evidence we had. And now you say they've found images?' Sutton shook his head.

Woakes nodded. 'Looks like he kept her somewhere. A basement most likely.'

Sutton's grizzled face hardened. 'Is Shipwright still running that unit? Ted's a good man.'

Woakes shrugged. 'Nah, it's a DI, me and two DCs. The DI is newly promoted though. Bit of an ice queen, you know.'

Sutton frowned. 'Didn't I read that the squad broke the Woodsman case?'

Woakes ignored that. 'What did you think about the doctor, Hawley?'

Sutton shook his head again. 'After the bones came to light and forensics confirmed who it was, the review team thought it might be a good idea to have another look at him. But he was clean.'

'No suggestion that he might be part of something else?'

'A ring, you mean?' Sutton shook his head. 'Nah, nothing remotely suggesting that. We decided it was a random attack by some desperate bastard with an eye for an opportunity.' Sutton saw the expression on Woakes' face. 'Doesn't help you much, does it?'

'No. But I needed to tick this box by talking to you.'

'Your idea or the DI's?'

'All mine,' said Woakes.

Sutton nodded. 'Sensible. I'd have done the same. She's lucky to have you watching her back.'

CHAPTER TWENTY-TWO

Anna needed to speak to Rainsford. The superintendent had been out at meetings first thing, but she saw him arrive back, striding down the corridor purposefully. She got up and was about to find him when Trisha stopped her with a wave, a phone in her hand.

'Sergeant Danaher, ma'am.'

Anna ducked back into her office and took the call.

'Hi, Julie.'

'Ma'am, my guvnor said to give you a call. We found a photo of Blair.'

A trickle of electricity danced over Anna's scalp. She sat down, made herself concentrate.

Danaher took the silence as her cue to explain. 'Our tech guys did a sweep and found a posted image on a chat site called Pinocchio. We don't know who put the image up or where it came from, but it's on a thread about missing children. A lot of these people pretend to know where these children are, though in fact they get their kicks talking about them. It looks like whoever posted this took the image from some other site.'

Anna waited.

'It has the same caption as the Rosie Dawson image you sent up.'

'PPV?'

'PPV, yeah. I've sent it over via Varga. It should be with you shortly. This was taken when Blair was alive. That's a huge boost to us. My DI says we owe you a night on the town.'

'I'll remember that.'

'The SIO wants to take a look at your case files, ma'am,' Danaher said.

'Absolutely. What's the thinking?'

'A ring possibly. That's his first thought.'

'He's not convinced it's the same perpetrator, then?'

'We're not dismissing it, but the MO in the two cases are so completely different it doesn't add up. Rosie was taken in a park; Blair was abducted into a vehicle with her sister. Admittedly, the locations on the images look similar: concrete floor, plastered walls, but there are differences. Blair seems to be in some sort of hole but Rosie was simply sitting on the floor and there is no hole. Our digital forensic guys tell us these sites often replicate images. Copycats. There's nothing else solid to connect them and we've had to limit our search parameters. Still, the SIO would like to review the file. And our cyber unit are still looking for images. If we find anything else, I'll let you know.'

'I'll get copies up to you right away.'

'If you're ever up at the Fringe, give us a bell.'

Anna woke her computer. The email from Danaher was already there, forwarded on by Varga. She opened it and scanned the message. The image was included as an attachment. Anna watched it develop in front of her eyes, her blood running cold as the screen filled from top to bottom. Blair in some kind of hole in the ground, looking up, her eyes huge and desperate. Underneath, the typed letters PPV and now extra words, a tilt at a more modern world: #crypto, #captured, #pogo. But Anna forced her gaze away from Blair to her surroundings. A grey cement floor, as with Rosie. And, more importantly, in the top right-hand corner of the photograph, at the edge of the frame, the side of a bucket. Black plastic. Just like in Rosie's photograph.

She sat back. Was it the exact same space? It was possible. Very possible. How could Danaher not have seen this? But then Anna saw it from Danaher's angle. Black plastic buckets were ubiquitous, sold in thousands of supermarkets and household goods stores. Even if it was the same bucket, so what? Often, organised rings had a safe house. Somewhere unnoticed where they could secrete and indulge, perpetrate their crimes. A shiver ran through her. It did not bear thinking about. But she had to.

Anna looked out at the daylight beyond the window, giving her thoughts room to move around. Danaher was right: the MO in the Blair case was not the same as what happened to Rosie and not the same as had happened to the others on Hawley's list. But she also knew that sex offenders re-offended. And that put Hawley's theory in a whole new light. Something else Danaher said pushed its way through to the surface. Blair had been alive when the photo was taken.

What if she was *still* alive in the space with the black bucket?

A hundred thoughts cascaded through her brain, all vying for attention. She sat still, letting them settle, waiting for the important ones to float to the top of the pile.

She looked up as Woakes sauntered into the squad room. It annoyed her. He'd become an unnecessary distraction from her process. She saw him ask a question, Khosa answering, Holder not looking up from his PC. Woakes frowning, turning his eyes towards her.

Anna got up and opened her door.

'Dave, a word.'

Woakes walked in, unsmiling, defiant. He sat, so did Anna. But not before closing the door with a touch more force than was necessary. She waited several reasonable seconds for a benefit-of-the-doubt beat. Woakes said nothing.

'Anything useful from the original SIO?'

'Nada.'

Anna nodded. She got up and walked into the squad room. 'Operational briefing, people. Trisha, I've sent you an image. Can you get it printed off for me, please?'

Everyone gathered around the whiteboard. Anna did all the talking. 'I've just had Edinburgh on the phone. They've found an image of Blair Smeaton which bears similarities to the one of Rosie Dawson.'

Trisha came through and handed over a 10 by 6 print. Anna stuck it to the board. 'It has the PPV caption as well.' She tapped the photo. '#crypto we know about; #pogo is anyone's guess. Maybe it's what he calls himself. But here's the thing. The bucket in this corner looks identical to the one in Rosie's image.'

'Oh my God,' Khosa said. 'Does this mean Hawley's right?'

Woakes said, 'Oh, come on. It's a black bucket. There's nothing here to prove Hawley's theory's correct.'

'No, I agree and so do the team up in Edinburgh,' Anna said. But it wasn't what she believed. Her gut was telling her something altogether different, but she let the team air their doubts. She turned to look at the second board, posted with images of Hawley's victim list.

'Edinburgh are also looking at the possibility the images are linked. That we might be looking at a paedophile ring.' She threw it out there, waiting for someone to bite.

'But you don't?' Khosa asked.

Anna paused before saying, 'What if it is the same bucket? The same place. What if it is, despite the different MOs, the same man? Someone who's deliberately chosen to vary his method to confuse us?'

No one spoke.

'Let it simmer while I speak to the super about… things.'

Rainsford was in his show-home office. He looked up and read her expression.

'Problems?'

She told him about the Morton fiasco and then explained about Hawley and didn't pull any punches about whose fault this was.

'I think I need a word with Sergeant Woakes,' Rainsford said.

Anna nodded. 'But there is some good news, sir.'

'Is there?'

She'd un-stuck the images of Rosie and Blair from the white-board and laid them now on Rainsford's desk while she explained the reasoning behind the link between them.

He listened without interruption, his eyes on the prints until she'd finished. When he looked up they were animated. 'This could be a major breakthrough. And not only for your cold case.'

Anna nodded. 'Police Scotland and our people are looking for other images.'

'But there's something else brewing, isn't there?'

Anna smiled. Rainsford could read her like a book.

'Hawley, sir. I can't help thinking he's on to something. He's been very cooperative.'

'Or he's been caught out. How kosher is he?'

Anna shrugged. 'Difficult to say. Either way, sir, I think he may still be useful.'

'What are you suggesting? A warrant? A fresh look at his computers and ISP history?'

'It's a thought. It might come to that. And we need to eliminate him from involvement on the day Blair Smeaton went missing. I can't believe he was anywhere near, and I've a feeling he'd offer us his laptop if we asked for it. But I'd prefer the soft approach for now. If he knows anything, we won't get him to give it up by using thumbscrews the Dave Woakes way. If there is something to Hawley's theory, it's something I need to understand a little better. How would any of these kids' illnesses be of use to a perpetrator?'

Rainsford kept his gaze steady. 'Be careful, Anna. You know how plausible these bastards can be.'

The cursing took her by surprise. Not because of the word itself, but by how heartfelt it had been. She knew instantly what he was alluding to. Both she and Holder had been taken in by Charles

Willis, the Woodsman. He'd been friendly and approachable and had almost ended up killing her.

'Once bitten, sir,' Anna said with an acerbic smile.

Rainsford nodded and sat back, pensive. After a while, he handed the images back to Anna. 'How was your visit to Shaw?'

Anna shrugged. 'I'll have the report on your desk by tomorrow, sir. He's still adamant he didn't attack Tanya Cromer. Claims he fought off Petran and that Petran's real name is Krastev. He's offered to show me another one of Krastev's victims, this time in Sussex.'

Rainsford stayed silent for a moment but then asked, 'Do you want me to set it up?'

Anna nodded. 'I thought we'd get Krastev's ID confirmed first.'

Rainsford nodded. 'Send Woakes in.'

Anna went back to the office. On her way she paused at where Woakes was sitting at his desk.

'Dave, the super wants to see you.'

'Me?'

Anna nodded. Either he was good at feigning surprise, or it was genuine, in which case she was prepared to label him a complete sociopath there and then.

Sighing, he pushed his chair away, grabbed his jacket and headed for Rainsford's office.

Anna waited until he'd left the room before entering her office. Trisha had left a note on her desk.

Witness Kevin Starkey rang, left number. Free now for two hours.

Anna dialled the number.

'Mr Starkey, this is Detective Inspector Gwynne from Avon and Somerset. Thanks for ringing back.'

The slight delay and static hum told her he was in a car. 'Yes, inspector, what can I do for you?'

'I hear you were in the job, once?'

Starkey laughed. 'Long time ago, ma'am. I joined quite late but I've been out of it for four years. We moved and I couldn't spare the sixteen hours a month because of my job and I wouldn't pass the bleep test now unless you stuck a lit firework where the sun doesn't shine.'

'This is about the Rosie Dawson case. I realise it's been a while, but you gave a statement about a van you saw on the day she was abducted. I wanted to check if you'd thought of anything else that might be useful.'

'No, I'm afraid not. I've thought about it a lot, obviously. And I've kept an eye out for that van every time I get in the car. But I gave everything I knew to the team at the time.'

'You were coming off the motorway when you saw the van, am I right?'

'Yeah. Coming of the motorway at the Hither Green round-about. I was on a half shift at the station that evening, six to eleven. My normal employers were good about letting me leave early from work when I had a Specials shift to go to. That gave me time to get home, change into my uniform and get some food. The van had pulled way out over the junction and cars ahead had stopped to let it out, that's why I remembered it. The driver had pulled out at Padmore Road.'

'Heading back towards the roundabout?'

'Yeah, that's it.'

'You don't know if he got on to the motorway?'

'I'd long gone in the other direction by then.'

'And you said,' Anna scanned the report, 'it was a post office van?'

'Yeah. White rear doors but everything else red. Looked like a converted PO van to me. No logo but then they take that off for resale. Definitely a Vauxhall combo though.'

'The other witnesses said they'd seen the abductor get in to a white van.'

'From the back, it would look that way. As I said, my theory is that the van had been pranged and they'd replaced the rear doors. Two hours later I was on the search team. If only I'd known, I'd have looked at the plates.' Starkey sounded genuinely regretful. 'It was unusual, and I've not seen anything like it around these parts or elsewhere. And I drive a lot.'

'Looks like the team spent a lot of time looking for Vauxhall combos afterwards, but they found nothing.'

'I think he went to ground ma'am. There was no CCTV footage but I arrived at exactly the time he would have been at that junction, according to the other witnesses's sightings.'

'Okay. You have our number if you can think of anything else. No matter how small or irrelevant you think it is, okay?'

'So, you're reopening the case, I take it?'

'It never really closed. We're taking a fresh look.'

'Best of luck, ma'am.'

'No thoughts of coming back, Kevin?'

Starkey laughed. 'It's a young man's job. I'm well past it.'

He rang off and Anna put an asterisk next to his name on the file to indicate she'd made contact. Ah well, she'd expected nothing else.

Sighing, she asked Trisha for copies of Blair's image and took it in to her office and placed it next to Rosie's. She stared at them, willing them to give her more information than was obvious from the brutal reality of the girls' prisons. Rainsford was right, it was a breakthrough of sorts, but even so, she felt helpless and lost. Nothing here gave any tangible clue as to where they were taken, and yet there were obvious similarities. There needed to be more. It was rare for a cold case to gather traction so quickly and Anna felt the urge to run with it rather than let it run away from her. But to do so she'd need to take a few risks.

Or one big one.

She hadn't been entirely straight with Rainsford. Trisha had handed her the sheet from Europol on Krastev that morning. It made for unpleasant reading and confirmed what Holder had told her on the way home from visiting Shaw.

Boyen Krastev AKA Mihai Petran
Height: 181 cm
DOB: 30/05/1965
Nationality: Bulgarian
Wanted for Aggravate trafficking in human beings, rape, grievous bodily harm, kidnapping. Forgery of administrative documents, participation in a criminal organisation.

The list of offences read oddly, the charges unfamiliar and a little archaic to Anna. But it was the next paragraph that made her cringe.

While on detention, Krastev failed to turn up to court and his whereabouts after that are unknown.

They now knew to where he'd escaped. And they also knew his whereabouts. The DNA confirmation would take a while but hopefully it was only a question of matching results from Petran with what Europol had on Krastev and, since Petran's body was found on another force's patch, North Wales organised crime unit was doing all that. Trisha, she knew, was keeping tabs on developments.

Anna felt no reason to doubt what Shaw had told her. There could be no reason, either, to delay letting Rainsford arrange for Shaw to take her to Sussex – other than her own reluctance. But an idea had begun tumbling over in her mind; gathering pace with each revolution, an idea which would mean another visit to Shaw before she'd allow him to unearth another of his grisly prizes. And that was definitely something she would not tell Rainsford about yet.

Quickly, she gathered up what was on her desk and left her office.

'I'm off to tie up a few loose ends,' she said to Trisha on her way out. 'Oh, and when he emerges from the super's office, tell Sergeant Woakes he's got the afternoon off.'

Trisha smiled. 'With pleasure ma'am.'

CHAPTER TWENTY-THREE

Blair ate some bread and drank some water. She had no idea what time it was, but she was beginning to feel sleepy. She didn't want to climb back into the hole to sleep, but if the dog man came she might not wake up in time to hide in there. She made herself remember the last time he'd come. The door made a lot of noise and he moved really slowly. She decided there would be time.

She arranged the two duvets into a makeshift bed. One to lie on and one to cover her, though it was warm enough in the cave to lie on top of both. In her bedroom at home, the one she shared with Kirsty, she sometimes slept without a cover in the summer. They'd had bunk beds for ages, but Kirsty'd got a new bed under all her posters on the other side of the room. Blair hadn't minded because she slept on the top bunk now and all her animals slept on the bottom: a purple dolphin called Duane, a fat green snake called Monty, loads of ponies, each with different hair colour, and a brown and white dog mum won in a raffle. Bernard was huge and lovely to cuddle.

And then there was mum… She missed mum. Even when she'd had a bottle of wine that always made her all red in the face, like she'd just run around the estate, she was still mum.

Blair stopped the tears from coming. She didn't believe the dog man anymore. And mum and Kirsty would know by now that he'd taken her. Maybe they were out on the street calling her name. She thought about calling back but her throat was sore from already doing that lots.

Was it Monday? They always had macaroni cheese on Monday. Blair loved the crusty bits of burnt cheese.

She wiped away a silent tear.

She was tired. So tired.

She lay on the duvet, listening and hearing nothing.

Eventually, Blair fell asleep thinking about Bernard.

CHAPTER TWENTY-FOUR

Anna took the fleet car and headed south.

Danaher's call and the image of Blair Smeaton she'd sent was a lit firework in her head. Woakes had been dismissive and his mere presence was proving to be an unwelcome distraction, but Khosa had seen it right away.

'Does this mean Hawley's right?'

Anna had pulled back from accepting that wholeheartedly but Hawley, despite his proven innocence, seemed to be at the centre of everything. Yet Woakes' scepticism stung like a splinter under her nail. She needed to get a better handle on Hawley, satisfy herself he was not a twisted perpetrator leading them up some bramble-strewn garden path. To do that she needed to go back to the victim. Or at least the victim's family.

She found the address in Clevedon, drove to it and sat outside to gather her thoughts. Ever since she'd seen the photograph of Blair Smeaton a knot of dread began tightening inside her. Like some awful virus replicating and growing that she knew she could not shake off. Though she was here to deal with questions surrounding Rosie Dawson's murder, Anna couldn't help but fear for Blair and worry that what had happened nine years before was happening again.

She got out of the car and walked to the front door.

Janice Dawson's house was a tired looking 1970s semi on Kenn Road. There were steps leading up off the pavement guarded by a painted iron gate. Beyond, a concrete path flanked by a gravel garden and some forlorn-looking pot plants in dire need of watering led to the front door. A black bell sat on the frame next to the white-wood effect uPVC front door. She pressed the bell. A minute later, after a couple of muffled and unintelligible shouts, the door opened four inches to reveal a pretty, short girl of perhaps sixteen in a T-shirt and skinny jeans with flip-flops on her feet.

'Hello?' she said.

Anna showed her warrant card. 'Hello. I'm Detective Inspector Gwynne. Is Mrs Dawson in?'

The girl turned and yelled, 'Mum, it's for you,' before turning away from the open door and stomping, with attitude, up the stairs halfway along the hallway. Anna stood alone on the threshold, taking in the interior. Everything looked clean but well used. The laminate flooring was worn, the scuffed and chipped paintwork on the balustrade spoke of a lack of either funds or the will to redecorate. Perhaps both. The patterned rug on the hall floor had a rip in the seam with strings reaching across towards the skirting board, like the black veins of a fungal disease.

A woman appeared and walked towards her. Anna recognised her from Rosie's file. Janice Dawson had not aged gracefully. She wore too-tight jeans and her T-shirt clung unflatteringly, emphasising a midriff bulge. She'd used too much product on her hair and it looked frizzy and dry, and the skin around her mouth and eyes was coarse, perhaps from too many cigarettes or too much alcohol. Her gravelly voice backed up Anna's deductions, sounding, when she spoke, constantly on the edge of a cough.

'Can I help you?'

Anna reiterated her introduction. Janice looked contrite.

'Sorry to keep you on the doorstep.' She turned towards the stairs and said, loudly, 'Some people have no manners.' She turned back, her eyes apologetic. 'She's sixteen and wants to be twenty-three without passing Go. Come in.'

Anna followed into a brightly lit kitchen, passing a half-open door leading into a room with the TV still on and cigarette smoke hanging like smog beneath the ceiling. The kitchen was smoke-free, however. Janice, Anna surmised, kept her tobacco habit confined to the one room at least.

'Mrs Dawson, the family liaison officer will have rung you to explain that we are having another look at Rosie's case.'

Janice nodded. A tight, jerky little movement. 'She did ring. She told me not to expect too much.'

Anna nodded. 'She's right. And I realise how it might be painful to talk about this again.'

Janice had a small tremor and she pressed her hand against the table to control it. 'No. It's not. I talk to her every day. Rosie, I mean. I don't mind taking about her.' She tried smiling but her mouth puckered and tears brimmed on the rims of her lids. 'It's not knowing who did it and why that's painful now.' She wiped the moisture from her eyes with a ruffled tissue, took in a deep breath and let it out again before turning towards the sink. 'Tea?'

They sat at the kitchen table. Anna wondered how long it would be before Janice excused herself to go back into the den for a smoke. Strong tea was the best substitute for now. Anna let hers cool, but Janice sipped at the steaming liquid constantly. Above the fridge was a framed photograph of Rosie. The same one Anna had seen in her file. She may have been missing some baby teeth, but she had a wicked smile.

'Bernice,' asked Anna, flicking her gaze back, 'is she still at school?'

'Yeah. She got some GCSEs but I have no clue what she's going to do with them. And before you ask, her dad ain't here anymore. We broke up three years ago. That hasn't helped. He's moved in with a woman over in Knowle. As you can imagine, Bernice was over the moon when that happened.'

Anna nodded, noting too how Janice seemed less bothered than her daughter about the absence of Janice's father. She'd seen it all before. Family break-ups were common, but in cases involving the loss of a child they seemed almost to be inevitable. She'd read that upwards of 80% of parents simply fell apart from the strain of either trying to pretend life would ever be normal again or wallowing in the guilt and trauma.

'He blamed my mum for it all,' Janice said. 'Said he couldn't stand to look at her. My poor mum. She never forgave herself, but I mean what can you do if someone comes up behind you and knocks you out? Terry, my husband, said she should have done something.' Janice shook her head. 'Truth is, I feel better without him here.'

'What about your mother?'

Janice shook her head. 'Fags got her two years ago, though they called it pneumonia.' She glanced down at her own nicotine-stained fingers. 'And before you ask, I have tried to give up a dozen times. I'm a lost cause.' She attempted a laugh and it spiralled into a hacking cough.

You're committing slow suicide yourself, aren't you, Janice?

'I wanted to talk to you about Rosie's visit to the hospital in Cheltenham.'

Janice's lids spread open in surprise. 'Still on about Dr Hawley? Your lot had a thing about him last time. Don't tell me he's turned out to be a paedo after all?'

'No. But I'm intrigued about your visit. Rosie was no stranger to hospitals, was she?'

'God, no. We spent the first three years at the children's hospital. Rosie needed surgery aged three for an ASD. That's a hole in the heart, but I expect you know that. Common in Down's, they are. Then there was her hernia and the thyroid problem. She had a file as thick as a bible. But that was here in Bristol.'

'Not where you saw Dr Hawley.'

'No. We saw him in Cheltenham. We'd been out to Sudeley Castle for the day. All of us. Terry's from up that way. He loved Sudeley. There's a maze and a big adventure area, so we'd made a day of it. A windy day of it, as I remember.'

'Is that important?'

'It's what Dr Hawley said might have caused her injury. Rosie didn't complain much. She was always so up for everything. But she started rubbing her eye that afternoon and in the car on the way home she said it hurt. She wasn't a crier. We took her to A and E. I sat with her while Bernice and her dad went to get something for us to eat. We promised Rosie a picnic if she was good with the doctor.'

'What was your impression of Hawley?'

'He was young but ever so good with Rosie. Gentle and explained everything. She let him put drops in her eyes, poor little thing. Then she sat on my knee and he put her on this machine to look in her eyes and told her what he was going to do. He took this bit of grit out from under her lid. Marvellous it was and she loved it. Always liked attention did Rosie. While he wrote up his notes she whispered in my ear that she wanted to give him a hug. I didn't think twice about it. I asked if it was alright but before he answered Rosie had run across. He was a bit shocked, to be honest. But he was a sport about it. She gave him one of her big hugs and a kiss on his cheek. Like she did with everyone she loved.'

'He didn't reciprocate?'

Janice frowned. 'He looked terrified. Me and the nurse were laughing and then Rosie started to laugh and I didn't think any more of it. Until the police came and asked me about it. Like you are now.'

Anna nodded.

'You don't think it was him, do you?'

Anna deflected the question. 'Was there anyone else in the various hospitals you saw on a regular basis?'

'Lots of people. Different departments. Specialist nurses or consultants mainly. I gave the whole list to the officers.'

Anna had seen it. The investigating team had been thorough and eliminated each one.

'It wasn't right, what they put Dr Hawley through. The newspapers, I mean. He was only doing his job.'

Anna finished her tea while Janice's tremor got slowly worse. 'Do you think you'll ever find who did this?' she asked, finally.

'We're going to try, Janice.'

'Exactly what they said last time. I want to know. I need to know.'

Anna thought about protesting. She read acceptance in Janice's face and knew, too, that it would be completely wrong to inject a drop of hope into the situation when there was nothing at all to base it on. But those left behind needed closure. Yet Janice looked ill-equipped for 'knowing'. In terms of child abductions where killing was involved, the statistics were harsh, stark and horrific.

Janice said, abruptly, 'He boiled her bones, you know that?'

Anna nodded.

'Cut her up and boiled her bones. I don't…' Janice's voice caught on a sob. 'When I think about what else he did…' Her hand flew to her mouth, her eyes squeezing shut.

For a moment, Anna tried to understand what being told something like that would be like. To have that tiny flame of hope extinguished. To what dark and desperate places your imagination might fly. It wasn't a thing Anna could easily relate to. No one who had not experienced it could. Hearing of her own father's death had been harrowing enough, but no one had then cut him up into little pieces and taken the flesh from his bones. Who could desecrate the flesh of another like that, and, more to the point, why?

'I just wanted to say goodbye to her. That's all,' Janice whispered.

There were no tears left. Janice was at the last stage of her grief. Knowing that Rosie was never coming home but needing that understanding of why, regardless of what horror it might bring. But Anna sensed there was something else even before Janice voiced her thoughts.

'Find him.'

'Mrs Dawson—'

'Janice, please.'

'Janice—'
'That's all I ask.'

Anna took her leave, troubled by the still raw emotions she'd encountered, but relived that Janice Dawson had no doubts over Hawley. She was now convinced more than ever that she needed to do what her instincts told her to, and that Hawley's role in all this was not that of an exposed, manipulative monster, but of a victim who needed closure almost as much as Janice Dawson did.

CHAPTER TWENTY-FIVE

In the car, she dialled Holder's number.

'Justin. I want you and Ryia to go and see Terry Dawson today. It's something we need to do. Lives in Knowle, I think. Trisha will have the address.'

'Anything you want us to ask him especially?'

'No. It sounds like he, of all the family, is the one who's moved on. I also know the original team did a thorough job and he was completely clean. Ask him what he thinks happened that day, his impressions, and then double check with ICAT and the paedophile unit to make sure he hasn't appeared on their radar subsequently. You know the score.'

'Ma'am.'

Another box to tick. But they were all negatives. All leading her nowhere and leaving her flat and empty. It occurred to Anna, as she drove back to Bristol, that disengaging from the team after meeting with Woakes might have appeared, on the surface, a weakness. Might have implied some sort of emotional upset.

God, they told me you were a frosty…

They'd be wrong on two counts. She wasn't unemotional, it was simply easier not to let the damned things in. They took far too much time to analyse. If it meant Woakes perceiving her as frosty, that was his problem, not hers. Perhaps it wasn't one of her strengths, but she had not allowed it to become one of her weaknesses either. She'd long ago given up explaining herself, and the world, according to Anna, fell into those who accepted her and those who didn't. Best to ignore the latter.

No, Woakes had not upset her. Indeed, Anna's disengagement had less to do with the sergeant's maverick approach and odd personality and everything to do with her own methodology. Sometimes she simply needed silence. A little cognitive trick that worked for her but needed far less distraction than the office provided. A chance to let the grey cells put everything in order, apply logic to the abstract. She'd been close to catching Charles Willis before he caught her. But it had been her first case as an inspector and she'd been forced to play it by the book instead of following her own lead. Had she done the latter, she might still have her own spleen and Willis might not have killed two more people.

And as with her runs through Badock's Wood, driving with the radio off allowed ideas to run in the background of her consciousness at a level she was barely aware of. Allowed the pros and cons to lobby and dissect. At some point she'd come to a decision and act on it, right or wrong. Not that she dismissed discussion as a deductive tool, indeed for most of her colleagues it was the blunt instrument of choice, but Anna preferred, at some point in every case, the sharpened spear of being alone.

She allowed herself a small, ironic smile. The silences, the long runs, they were all part of her analytical, introverted character. Yet, as someone who by and large avoided social interaction, she seemed to be running into killers wherever she turned.

She'd talked through the horror of the Woodsman's attack with a counsellor provided by the force. Rainsford, savvy as always, insisted on it. But she'd got a lot more out of talking it through with her old boss Shipwright, who'd been around the block so many times he'd worn a groove in the pavement. He'd recovered well from the heart attack that had triggered his early retirement and was, she knew, more than happy to talk to her about almost anything. His opinions were always worth a listen and inevitably pragmatic. His advice as she lay in the hospital bed, recovering from the stab wounds the Woodsman had inflicted, was to get a dog. A big bugger with teeth.

It was still on her list. But thinking of Shipwright now stimulated a new train of thought.

She dialled his number.

'Anna,' Shipwright said when he picked up. 'Good to hear from you.'

'Busy?'

'Rushed off my feet. Paddling pool emergency. Unless I patch the leak, there are likely to be tears and tantrums in the Shipwright household.'

Ted Shipwright had passed the sixty mark but was on his second marriage with a young family. He'd only decided to call it a day because of his health. Anna missed him a lot.

'What are you up to?' Shipwright asked.

'Oh, you know. Fighting the good fight.'

'You sound a little down, Anna. Rainsford cracking the whip?'

'No. I need a favour, Ted.'

'What can I do?'

'I have a new sergeant. Dave Woakes. Came with gold stars. But he's turning out to be a liability. At East Mids before he came to us. I was wondering if you knew anyone up there?'

Shipwright didn't hesitate. 'Colin Sandwell. He's a DCI in their Special Ops Unit. Can't shut up about Leicester Rugby club, but otherwise he's a good guy. Want me to give him a ring?'

'Would you?'

'No problem, Anna. Woakes, you said?'

'Dave Woakes,' she paused and then added, 'I feel a bit uncomfortable going behind his back like this. Is it the right thing to do?'

'How long has he been on the team?'

'Couple of weeks.'

'Has he upset Justin?'

'Yes. And Ryia.'

'Then you're being a good boss. It's what I would have done. You know them and trust them, don't you?'

'Yes,' Anna said.

'So why compromise the team's ability to function?'

Shipwright was, as always, on the money.

'Give me ten minutes, I'll ring you back.' Shipwright rang off.

CHAPTER TWENTY-SIX

Shipwright kept his promise and rang her as she reached the M5 exit that would take her back into town.

'I spoke to Sandwell about Woakes.'

'And?'

'His reports describe him as enthusiastic, determined and insatiably ambitious.'

'Really?'

'Yes, really. But Sandwell also spoke to his last DI. They did not ask for his reference. If they had it would have been stamped CPT.'

'CPT?'

Anna waited. Shipwright had great timing.

'As in "cannot polish a turd". Woakes, apparently, has issues. Comes across as bright and very enthusiastic. But he's been off on a couple of long breaks with stress. Gets morose and withdrawn and fails to cope. Anger issues, too.'

'Are you saying he's not up to the job?'

'I'm saying that some HR nob had suggested a change of scenery for Woakes so that another force could try and deal with his failings.'

'Do they have a label for these failings?'

'The word paranoid was used. Sandwell shied away from saying "disorder".'

'Bloody hell. How come we've been lumbered with this?'

'Ah, well. That's the thing. He struck lucky with a couple of cases. Blundered in on his own and did the job. That got him a sympathetic hearing with the ACC up there in East Mids. I wouldn't blame Rainsford as he's probably had his ear and several other appendages bent to find room.'

'I knew it. I could smell it.' Anna gripped the steering wheel. 'What am I supposed to do now? Sit back and let him play captain bloody chaos?'

'Keep Rainsford apprised. These things tend to have a way of working themselves out.'

'Is that what you'd do?' Anna asked, fishing.

'Yes, as well as keeping the bugger at arm's length. Find him something he can get his teeth into like a hit and run in Perth.'

'Why Scotland?'

'I meant Western Australia. That's about as far as you could throw him.' Shipwright chuckled.

Anna grinned. 'Don't think Rainsford would stump up the airfare.'

'No, I know. All you can do is be careful.'

She thanked Shipwright and rang off. Not what she'd wanted to hear, but confirmatory nevertheless. She toyed with taking Holder and Khosa into her confidence but decided against it. If Woakes was already paranoid, the last thing she wanted to do was give him more ammunition.

It was well past lunchtime by now. Anna found a Costa and took a flat white and a salad to a table at the rear and set up her MacBook.

The visit to Janice Dawson had made her mind up about Hawley. Woakes' 'shake the tree' approach was all wrong as she guessed it would be; Hawley had nothing to drop.

Anna knew Danaher was working on the images, but she believed what Varga had told her. Further discovery was not totally dependent on resources alone. It needed either luck, as had happened in the discovery of Rosie's photograph, or a trawl of websites that were hidden from plain sight. It would all, in Varga's words, take time.

But the knot of dread in Anna's gut told her that time was something they didn't have when it came to Blair Smeaton. She needed input, a direction, something that might push her towards where to go next in the case. She needed more intel on the image.

And there was one person who knew a lot more about this sort of thing than she did. Than anyone she knew did.

She forked chopped salad into her mouth, logged on to the cafe Wi-Fi and opened a particular folder in her email. Since her run-in with the Woodsman, Anna had received several emails from someone called HuSH.

She'd shown the first couple to Rainsford, who'd enlisted the help of cybercrime to try tracing.

'Unfortunately,' the man had said, 'it's using a pseudonymous remailer. A software programme that anonymises email addresses. The 'nym' server receives the normal email, strips headers and replaces them. The message is then encrypted and sent out through a random three-stage chain to arrive at the server. It is decrypted there and sent to the recipient. This particular one does not allow replies.'

She'd listened, not understanding all the technical terms, but understanding enough to know that she would never want to reply or have these communications traced. She had not shown Rainsford any more of the emails. They were private and she suspected – though he never mentioned his name – from only one possible source.

Hector Shaw.

Each message was brief. Initially they were sympathetic, with Shaw wishing her well after her ordeal, but always spiked with coded messages that he and only he could know anything about from their conversations at Whitmarsh. But it was the one she'd received after her discharge from hospital as she'd recovered at her own flat that she opened now.

Anna, I hope this finds you well and almost ready to return to work. They miss you, I'm sure, and we both know there is much more work to be done. I can find you work, Anna, you know that. Your parents must be very proud that their odd daughter has found a niche in which to flourish. I say parents, though of course only your mother remains alive. Your father would, I'm sure, be delighted with your progress. His death must have come as a great shock. For him to die alone must have hurt you, Anna, given that you were so close. If only your mother could have found it in her heart to let him enjoy those last few weeks under his own roof, it might not have ended so tragically. But then you know your mother. I suspect she is an unforgiving soul. A good trait to have inherited as a police officer, but less attractive when it leads to ending thirty years of marriage. Was she resentful? Were you the cause of that resentment, Anna? Does that thought prevent you from sleeping?

I, on the other hand, sleep soundly every night.

So much to discuss, Anna. I look forward to our next meeting,

HuSH

Anna closed her eyes and breathed deeply. How did he know so much?

But she knew the answer to that one, too. Shaw'd had a hand in the broken jaw which eventually shut her drug-dealing ex up. It was obvious, too, from the email that Shaw had gleaned much from Tim Lambert's outpourings before they were stemmed.

He must have used someone else to send the emails. It had to be through a third party because a category A prisoner like Shaw would have no direct access to the internet or a computer. She could have asked Whitmarsh to investigate, but the truth was that these contained too much information. Why on earth would she want the contents of it to be made public? She'd stored the emails away on her laptop, still wondering how Shaw had managed it without any access to a PC.

But what if he did have computer access?

The thought stuck its head above the parapet. Anna's common sense told her that it was impossible, yet the concept blossomed, not because of what Shaw had done, but because of what he might do. She'd considered proposing it to Rainsford, suggesting giving Shaw supervised access to allow him to help her in her investigation…

The notion fluttered briefly before scattering like charred paper on the wind.

Rainsford would laugh her out of his oh-so-tidy office. But still the thought wafted in and out of her mind, stimulating the wriggly worm to gnaw away at her skull. With that thought came something of a revelation. Disturbing as it was, Anna had begun to trust Shaw. In so far as believing that he would not waste her time or deliberately lie to her anyway. She shook her head as she imagined attempting to explain that concept to Ted Shipwright, whose description of Shaw at their first meeting was 'a card-carrying nutter'.

His objections to what she was proposing echoed in her head in Dolby surround sound.

Giving Shaw access to a computer would never happen; besides, Shaw had not been near a computer for years. Yet the idea wouldn't go away. What might Shaw be able to tell her about the Dark Web that Varga could not know?

Incredibly, she felt tears brimming and she wiped them away, angry that remembering Shaw's email triggered fresh memories of her father's death and its shocking abruptness. It had hit her like a hammer. No one knew how long he'd lain there in his two-bedroom rented flat alone. She'd pushed the coroner for an answer and the pathologist finally suggested no more than eighteen hours. The fact that he hadn't rung anyone or called an ambulance also suggested that it had been sudden and catastrophic. Myocardial infarctions were not always lethal. But one that provoked ventricular arrhythmias and resulted in pump inefficiency could result in no blood to the brain. At least it would be quick and instant.

Every day she hoped that was how it happened. And every day she wished she'd been there to say goodbye. The urge to see him again now was overwhelming.

An hour after leaving Janice Dawson, Anna turned her car around, went back to the M5 and headed first north and then west along the M4. Once more crossing the River Severn as she gave in to her urges.

They'd cremated Tom Gwynne and scattered his ashes in a memorial garden at a crematorium on the edge of the Brecon Beacons near Aberdare. Close to the mountains where he always loved to be. When the local authority remodelled the garden, an opportunity arose for the bereaved to purchase a stone bench and have a plaque incorporated as a *memento mori*. Kate and Anna jumped at the chance. Anna's mother had seen it as an unnecessary expense. Kate and Anna did it anyway.

The crematorium was isolated and in a wild, windswept spot. There were no rules about where crematoria needed to be situated, but if she had a choice, Anna wanted to end up somewhere like this, too. She was not religious and she'd cringed inwardly at her mother's insistence at involving a vicar to preach a eulogy. Neither she nor Kate felt strong enough to take an active part and, numbed by their grief, they'd defaulted and acceded to their mother's wishes, incapable of offering any resistance. If she'd had the time back, she'd have insisted on a humanist service, played her dad's favourite songs and mouthed funny anecdotes about his wicked sense of humour. It was her one everlasting regret. At least, and through nothing more than luck, they'd ended up here: a wide-open space, a place where souls might wander unheeded by the living.

The bench with her dad's inlaid plaque had views over the bleak mountains beyond. Mountains where he'd loved to walk before his shortness of breath slowed him down. Sometimes, on busy days in winter when funerals stacked up, the car parks would fill and the hearses would queue outside the modern, whitewashed building. But on this bright summer's day the place was deserted except for one or two mourners laying flowers.

Anna wasn't a great one for meditation. But what she wanted and usually achieved by sitting on her father's bench was the nearest thing to peace and solitude she knew without the help of an hour's circuit training or a good Sauvignon. What it allowed her to do was open doors in her memory and properly remember her dad. There was no need for the clichéd one-way conversations. All she needed to do was give reign to her imagination. She remembered his love of the absurd, the way he'd pretend not to enjoy board games at Christmas but then get totally involved, the way he'd sit and listen to Led Zeppelin's 'What Is and What Should Never Be' half a dozen times on vinyl just for the guitar solo. She understood that he knew her better than anyone. Had nurtured her, provided wisdom tempered by an astonishing ability not to be judgemental – unlike her.

Sometimes, his tolerance and care, the things that made him such a great teacher, made her wonder how he could possibly be her father. And as she sat on the bench that morning, with Shaw and Woakes and Rosie Dawson battering at the walls of her defences, she remembered one of his phrases. She heard him say it to her as clear as day when she was being sullen or feeling hard done by because of being Anna Gwynne.

'The most fragrant roses grow from the worst-smelling manure, Anna.' And then, being her dad, he'd cap the whole thing by saying, 'Brownie, anyone?'

Smiling stupidly to herself, Anna got up from the bench, turned and ran her fingers over the plaque with her dad's name and the Welsh word for loss and longing for the departed that had no real equivalent in English:

Thomas William Gwynne
Hiraeth

CHAPTER TWENTY-SEVEN

Kevin Starkey pulled in to his drive and parked. He didn't get out immediately, but simply sat there, contemplating. Six thirty on a Wednesday evening and almost another week over. He looked up at the house. A lovely little red-brick semi with bay windows on the edge of town in a great area with good schools. Schools that had given his two a bloody good start in life. Brenda'd insisted they both go to uni. She would, of course, since she wasn't the one paying. He wasn't close with them and they chose to spend holidays with their mother and her lot in Shepton Mallet. He didn't mind. In fact he encouraged it.

This was his house, mortgage all but paid for, would be paid for by the end of this month if all went well.

Starkey let himself in through the front door. He hadn't bothered redecorating since Brenda'd left. Hadn't seen the point. He kept the place clean, lawns mowed. He didn't do much with the neighbours because, thanks to his job, he was hardly ever there.

Except on weekends. And on weekends, he indulged himself. He'd bought a frozen fish lasagne from a fishmonger on Monday and defrosted it the night before. The other half he'd keep for later in the week.

He took himself and his suit jacket upstairs, showered quickly and found some shorts and a T-shirt. It would have been nice to have air con in the house. How many times had he heard that over the last few days as people sweltered in offices and clinics? But twenty-eight degrees was a rarity in the UK and you could count the number of times anyone would need air con in any given year on one hand.

He stared at his face in the bathroom mirror and thought about the phone call he'd taken from the detective inspector. She'd sounded young and efficient. So, they were looking into the death of Rosie Dawson again, were they? Well, what he'd told them all those years ago and repeated today had helped, he had no doubt about that.

He remembered the case very well. The overtime had been brilliant. He'd been involved in door to door and the prolonged painstaking searches of open land. They'd found nothing of course. But his information on the van was vital. It was important then and it remained important now.

Starkey splashed cold water over his face, dried it on a towel and walked back downstairs. He put the lasagne in the microwave and poured himself a glass of wine. He'd finished it before the meal was heated through so poured himself another one. He was big. Always had been. His legs were thick, his neck was thick and he'd had a gut for as long as he could remember, though he had lost a bit of weight. Being tall helped, but everything juddered under his clothes when he moved quickly.

And he did like his beer and wine.

He ate quickly and drank the second glass before he'd finished eating.

After he stacked the dishes in the dishwasher – it only went on twice a week these days – he made a cup of tea and sat down in the lounge to watch the news. He wasn't a great TV watcher, but he didn't mind the odd documentary. True crime and forensics, material that Brenda was never able to stomach. When he'd finished his tea, he took his briefcase and walked out into the garden. The sun was still out, and thankfully the lawn had not grown too much due to the dry weather. He reached his shed – better known as his garden office – unlocked it with the key he left hanging behind the back door and entered.

He'd wired in electricity, and a Wi-Fi repeater meant that he had super-fast Broadband on tap, too. On one wall stood a bench with small items of electronic equipment, shelves of tools and a hobbyist's headband with magnifying lenses. Starkey switched on a DAB radio and found a smooth jazz station. On the workbench were disassembled bits of electronic equipment. Sometimes, if he failed to do the repairs onsite, he'd bring pieces back and have a go so as not to have to send items back to the manufacturers. Especially if they were out of warranty. He had all sorts of equipment supplied by his employer, soldering irons, burrs and tiny saws, specialist glues and a huge illuminated magnifier on a reticulated arm. A fly-tying vice clamped to the bench edge meant that he could anchor delicate and small items to leave his hands free.

Someone had dropped a desk transformer at the job he'd been to that day and now it had stopped charging. He needed to strip it down, see if it was simply a broken connection or if head office would have to replace it. People never looked after their equipment. Still, it kept him in employment. He couldn't complain.

He worked steadily. Removing tiny screws with jeweller's instruments. Soldering, replacing some worn contacts. After half an hour, he replaced the housing, plugged the unit in and ran a diagnostic. Everything worked. He sat back from the bench, put both knuckles into the curve of his back and arched backwards. He needed to start exercising.

From under the bench he retrieved an old laptop. Old only in appearance, since he'd revamped speed and memory through additional hardware. Starkey switched it on. Logged on and opened up Firefox. A newsfeed on the customised page had Blair Smeaton in a headline.

NET WIDENS IN SEARCH FOR MISSING SCHOOLGIRL

That led his thoughts straight back to his conversation with the police and what had made them reopen Rosie Dawson's case.

Another missing girl. Good to know they felt he could contribute. He missed the uniform, of course he did. But he had given it up for good reasons. Even so, he was more than happy to help. More than happy.

Starkey smiled to himself. He wondered if they'd questioned other people. Other witnesses and perhaps the doctor, Hawley, too. God they'd sunk their teeth into him alright.

But it was all so long ago. He didn't envy them. They'd have their work cut out.

CHAPTER TWENTY-EIGHT

Blair had no idea how long she'd been in the cave. One of the torches had stopped working and she'd had to use the bucket. The whole place stank. She almost wished the dog man would come back again and empty it.

Almost.

Then she wished he'd never come back, ever, ever.

She wondered if it was tea-time at home. Spaghetti hoops on buttered toast. That was one of her favourites. Or burger and chips with peas. Or a fish supper with loads of vinegar and a Coke from Carlino's.

Blair squeezed her eyes shut and felt darkness all around her, as if she'd never feel happiness any more, as if it were sucked like smoke from her mouth.

Her throat was sore, too, like it was when she got a cold. She pulled the duvet around her wishing she had Bernard to cuddle. The smell in the cave made her not want to eat any food so she drank some water instead. It helped.

A little.

*

Anna got home and went for a run knowing she'd feel 100% better afterwards. Always did. She showered, put one of her father's old vinyls on the turntable and ate. The Average White Band were telling her to 'walk on by' when her work phone rang.

It wasn't a number she recognised.

She accepted the call. 'Anna Gwynne.'

'Oh, hi. It's Ben Hawley.'

Anna walked out of the kitchen and through the French doors into the tiny garden, away from the music, her mind suddenly fizzing. Hawley, of all people.

'What can I do for you, Ben?'

'I wasn't sure who to ring—'

'Everything OK? You sound distressed.'

'That's because I am. I got back to my digs in Bristol yesterday to find my room broken into and my iPad stolen.'

'Have you reported it?'

She heard him snort. 'What's the point?'

'Let me make a call—'

'Oh please.' His tone was curt. 'We both know what this is, don't we? I mean, if you'd asked I would have gladly let you search the place. There was no need to break the bloody lock and turn the place upside down.'

Suddenly, his brusqueness fell into place. 'You think we did this?'

'Yes, actually, I do.'

'Dr Hawley, Ben, I—' Anna's words hit a wall in the shape of Woakes' sullen face. No, no way, not even Woakes would be that stupid, would he?

Hawley didn't wait for an answer.

'I'd like to think you had nothing to do with it, Inspector, but you're supposed to be the senior detective, aren't you?'

'I am.' There were other things she could have, perhaps *should* have added along the lines of "None of my officers would ever contemplate such a thing", but she held back because, damn it, she wasn't sure.

'Yeah well, I'd like my iPad back please, when you've finished with it. If you want the name of my ISP, you can have that too.'

She wanted to say that anything seized in an illegal search was inadmissible in a court of law, but it sounded too churlish. She should have been angry, raised her voice and shouted him down, but she couldn't. Hawley had been cooperative. But there was one more thing she needed to know. 'Ben, I'm going to ask you something and I want you to be totally honest with me. Don't judge me. This is too important for that sort of bullshit.'

'OK.' Hawley sounded completely nonplussed.

'If we were to drive back to your aunt's bungalow now and I made you open the garden shed, the one with the new locks, would we find something there?'

Hawley didn't answer right away. When he did, his voice was subdued. 'Yes, you would.'

'What would we find, Ben?'

'You'd find a locked box,' he said, his voice croaky. 'A tool box, except there're no tools in it. There's a syringe driver instead. From the old hospital in Didcot, before they abandoned it completely. They had a room full of crap equipment they were throwing out. I was there on the last day and there was no one around. I took a couple of broken syringe drivers.'

'What else is in the box?'

'A couple of bags of saline. Borrowed from another A and E. IV cannulas and two vials of potassium chloride.' He paused and then said, 'It's amazing what you can find in some of these old places. And then there's some stuff I've picked up from overdose patients. The paramedics or sometimes relatives bring stuff in with them. Temazepam, Diazepam, Xanax. On a busy night, you can build up quite a collection.'

Anna nodded, feeling a surge of something, unsure if it was relief or sympathy. 'A suicide kit.'

'Yes,' said Hawley, his voice barely audible. 'I've kept one. Ever since the last time I was questioned. I was in a very dark place. I'm not proud of it. But I stay away from the shed now. I don't want to face what I collected.'

'Understandable.'

'I'm probably breaking all kinds of laws. God knows what the GMC would say. So, there it is. My confession.'

'Thanks for being honest.'

Another beat of silence followed. Eventually, Hawley said, 'I'd still like my iPad back.'

'I'll be in touch,' was all she managed before ringing off.

Woakes! Could Hawley be right? Arm's length, Shipwright had said. She was beginning to think she might be better off with a cattle prod.

She rang Woakes' number, knowing she shouldn't; phone messages left in the heat of the moment had a habit of coming back to bite you if you weren't careful. But she was too angry to let things lie. It went straight to voicemail.

'Dave. Ring me. I've had Ben Hawley on the line. Someone has broken into his apartment and stolen his iPad. He's pissed off and understandably so. We need to talk about this. In the meantime, I am satisfied that Hawley is clean and you are not to go anywhere near him or approach him or his work colleagues? Is that clear? No more bish bloody bosh, Dave.'

She killed the call and almost immediately her phone pinged. A text message from a number she recognised. A DS in North Wales coordinating their investigation into the bodies unearthed by Shaw. Two sentences only, but enough to make her forget Dave Woakes in a heartbeat.

Europol confirm DNA match between Petran and Krastev. Your boy was right, they are one and the same.

Her boy.

That was the trigger she'd been waiting for. Time she paid him another visit.

CHAPTER TWENTY-NINE

She got to Whitmarsh early on Thursday, up with a pink dawn and the promise of more dry weather. On the way, she rang Holder.

'Rosie's father. What did you and Ryia make of him?'

'He's clean, ma'am. Nothing new and the original team went to all sorts of lengths to check his alibi. As for the man himself, I'd say he's never recovered. He's still in counselling with victim support. He was the breadwinner and he's riddled with guilt about not protecting Rosie. Once we got him talking he re-ran the whole day, minute by minute, from when the police turned up on his shift to tell him. He moved out because he needed a little 'distance' to stay sane. His words, ma'am.'

'Computer?'

'Hates them. Doesn't own one. Uses his stepson's.'

'Thanks, Justin. I'll be on the mobile if you need me.'

The call confirmed what she'd expected they'd find. If they were going to get anywhere with Rosie's case, it would be through intelligence around the images. She was sure of it. She rang Whitmarsh from her car to warn them that she was coming. No one objected. If this carried on she might end up with her own spot in the car park.

Shaw was waiting in the interview room, legs crossed at the ankle, his expression giving nothing away. The stench of the air freshener was strong this morning but failed miserably to mask the testosterone stink of sweat that had seeped over the years into the walls and the floor. Anna sat and took out a file.

'Morning, Anna,' Shaw said. 'You're looking better.'

Anna returned his gaze. 'A little stronger every day.'

'Good to hear.'

She took out a file and put it on the table. 'It is Krastev,' she said.

Shaw inclined his head and let it drop a few degrees in acknowledgement. 'Not the sort of person you'd want to take home for tea with your mother, eh, Anna? But then again…'

She ignored the barb. 'North Wales police will want to know how he died.'

Shaw nodded. 'He had a bad accident.'

'Forensics previously confirmed he had bled to death, but you say he was buried alive.'

Shaw nodded again. 'The accident was that he ran into me.' Shaw uncrossed his legs. 'You haven't got your nifty little recorder on, Anna. We both know what that means. Whatever I say here is off the record, right? Which tells me that perhaps you have another agenda.'

Anna smiled. Shaw had seen through her within a minute. The rules with men like Shaw were not to let them inside. Not allow them anything they could try and manipulate you with. But Shaw had already crawled inside Anna's life and there was no taking that back. She knew this was a very dangerous game and she was straying down a path she'd normally have avoided like the black death. Walking along it, moreover, hand in hand with a serial torturer and murderer. But today this was exactly the route she needed to take. Despite everything that had happened in the Willis case, Shaw had been instrumental in helping Anna see the patterns that eventually got Willis caught. Rainsford told her that when his supervisor at GCHQ in Manchester heard what Shaw had done, his initial and bizarre reaction was that Shaw would be difficult to replace. This was a man with expertise who, Anna suspected, was cooperating because he needed and wanted her help.

But cooperation was a two-way street.

'You told me about Abbie and the Black Squid. You told me you'd spent some time on the Dark Web.'

Shaw watched her. 'Too much time,' he said.

Anna nodded. 'There was a case recently in the press. A model who was tricked into a job in Milan and then drugged and abducted for auction on the Dark Web.'

Shaw nodded. 'I read about it.'

'How common is that sort of thing?' She already knew the answer, but she wanted to draw Shaw in with this. See how far he was willing to go.

'That's just the tip of a dirty great iceberg, Anna, as you well know. Illegal arms, hackers for hire who can steal anyone's identity, Nazi sympathiser sites, paedophile forums, and things for sale which should never be saleable. Exotic animals, people, children, weapons, all in the unindexed Deep Web. People were shocked by what happened to the model. Believe me, there are far worse things.'

Anna listened to Shaw's Mancunian drawl listing the horrors and looked up at the guard sitting behind. He heard and saw everything. But the unwritten rule here was that he was the three wise monkeys rolled into one.

See no evil, hear no evil, speak no evil.

'When you say "worse things"… How much worse?'

Shaw's eyes were half-closed. He opened them fully now and leaned forwards. 'Why no minder today, Anna? Why did you come alone?'

Anna kept her eyes on the pad she was writing on. She didn't want Shaw to see her react. 'The others are all busy. We found some images.' She slid out a printed sheet. A photocopy with two images. Rosie Dawson's at the top, Blair Smeaton's beneath.

Shaw looked at the images and frowned. 'Krastev had these?'

She ignored his question. 'Our Hi-Tech people have linked these to some forums. These were adverts. PPV with a promise of more to come. Pinocchio and Littlefeet. Do they mean anything to you?'

'This is not Krastev, is it?' Shaw said, studying the images.

'What about #pogo?'

Shaw looked up then, a sharp movement, his expression unreadable, but Anna sensed something shifting behind his eyes. A flicker of anger? Disgust? 'Anna, what have you got yourself involved in? Is this the case the others are busy with?'

Anna said, 'We know paedophile rings operate on the Dark Web—'

Shaw interrupted her. 'This isn't a ring.'

'What?'

'Do you know what a red room is, Anna?'

'I've read about them.'

'Then you know they're supposed to be an urban legend. Dark Web sites where people use cryptocurrency for pay per view access to live, streaming acts of the worst kind – murder, torture, acts of violence. Otherwise known as Hurtcore sites.'

The guard, the wise monkey, shifted in his seat.

'Is this an advert for a red room? How do you know?'

Shaw shrugged. 'I don't. Not for certain. But #pogo… that's not good. How well do you know your serial killer history, Anna?'

She heard her own heart beating fast, thudding in her ears. 'Not well enough, obviously.'

'No, well, I don't blame you.' Shaw looked at the images again and then said, '#pogo is a reference to John Wayne Gacy. He killed at least thirty young boys in the 1970s, burying the bodies under his house. When he killed, he sometimes dressed up as a clown. Pogo the clown. This hashtag is telling people what your man intends to do. What he's probably done already.'

The room fell into silence. Even the distant prison noises, the slamming doors, the phones, seemed to fade out before fading back into Anna's awareness. She finally found her voice. 'Why do you say this isn't a ring? What makes you so sure?'

'If this is genuine, we're talking about a rogue. One man, if you can call him a man, acting alone. Just like Gacy. The nonces, the real ones, the paedophiles that can't help themselves, they always claim they're misunderstood. That it's love they have to share. Fucking Nabokov.' Shaw's expression was of a man tasting his own bile. 'Most of them don't want to harm their victims. Far from it. They wouldn't sanction this sadistic shit.'

Anna forced herself back to the images. 'There's no reference to Pogo or any clown on Ros— on the first image.'

'How long between?' Shaw asked.

'Nine years.'

Shaw nodded. 'Remember Willis, Anna. Remember how the first time is either an accident or an experiment. But they see what they can get away with. It thrills them. And if it is successful, if they do get away with it, the seed is planted and it always grows. Always.'

Anna exhaled. It made a stuttering noise in her throat. She was getting lessons in serial murder from this man. She forced herself to press on.

'The first time…' She hesitated, but there was now little point in trying to hide anything. 'Rosie Dawson. The evidence suggests a well-prepared abduction. It wasn't spontaneous. He knew the area.'

'And the others? I presume there are others besides Blair Smeaton.'

'How did you know about Blair—'

Shaw's brows lowered a centimetre. 'I read the papers, Anna.'

Anna swallowed. 'There are others. At least three.'

'All in the same area?'

'No. That's the point. None in the same area.'

'So, he chose local to start with. Then he went wide to throw you off the scent. And it looks like it worked. Until now.' Shaw sat back, lifting the images to study them more closely. 'Abbie had a hearing aid for years, just like Blair,' he said suddenly, his voice soft. 'She was always breaking the bastard thing, too.'

Anna was only half-listening. Her mind was weighing up Shaw's analysis. It made perfect sense and reinforced what she'd begun to think herself. That Blair's abduction was not instigated by an organised paedophile ring. What if it was just one careful, sick, clever predator? He'd choose a different place and a different MO every time, knowing that would derail the investigation. And they'd missed linking the cases because they would naturally concentrate on exactly that. The method of abduction.

Shaw put down the sheet and sucked air in through his teeth. 'Jesus, Anna. You know how to choose them. I can't help you here.'

Oh, but you already have.

'But if you want proof of how much a piece of dirt Krastev was, I can give you that. Say the word and we'll go digging.'

Anna's eyes refocused on Shaw. She knew what he was offering here. More buried treasure.

'Come on, Anna. You must have enjoyed having all that praise poured over you after catching Willis?'

'We both know it was more luck than judgement.'

'Yeah, right. But you'd worked it all out by then, hadn't you? You knew he was far too clever for his own fucking good. Most of them are. Maybe your child catcher isn't as bright as he first seems to be. All he's done is evade capture from the police…'

'He's clever enough,' said Anna.

'But not as clever as you, Anna.' Shaw sat forward, his head low. 'We both want the same thing, you and me. We want to be left alone to wander around inside ourselves. But the world won't let us, will it? The world is full of meddling arseholes. Never mind all that "the evil that men do" bullshit. It's arseholes and cockroaches and us.' Shaw laughed. 'Me and you, Anna. We work things out and then do something about it. We either wipe the world's arse or step on the fucking cockroaches.'

He's identifying with me.

'I don't think I'm like you, Hector.'

'Of course, you don't. But it's not a slur. Not in the way you think. Come on, tell me the truth. How many times have you wished they'd all just fuck off?'

It was a good question. An excellent question. One she'd asked herself hundreds of times when some social interaction had grated so badly that all she wanted to do was shut herself away and scream.

'I'm not that egotistical.'

'Ego's got nothing to do with it. It's all about difference, isn't it? You're different, Anna. I know I fucking well am. I pretended I wasn't for a long, long time and look where it got me. Now I don't pretend.'

'But you're in prison.'

Shaw nodded. 'And they locked me away for it. But now I've got you, haven't I?'

His words were almost tender. She wanted to protest but bit it back. There was unfinished business here and she was determined to see it through. Shaw understood like she knew he would.

'We will, of course, look into Krastev's activities. I'll be in touch, Hector.' She got up. Shaw didn't move, but he let his eyes fall to the folded paper before he handed it back.

'You want to catch the Pogo wannabe? Work out how he chooses which flowers to pick.'

CHAPTER THIRTY

Echoes of the interview bounced around inside Anna's head as she drove back towards Bristol. She'd played a dangerous game with Shaw and it had left her drained. She phoned through to Trisha and asked her to punch in some new search terms around 'clown' and 'Gacy' and 'Pogo', trying to find any cases in the HOLMES database with links. She was fishing, she knew. There was no hard evidence backing up her theories and she had no idea if what she'd done would be of any help, yet.

But there was no denying Shaw's 'expertise'.

Around her, the summer's morning opened out into a blurred shimmer of light as she sped back along the motorway, but Anna hardly noticed. Shaw's words preoccupied her.

'You want to catch the Pogo wannabe? Work out how he chooses which flowers to pick.'

Her phone dragged her back to reality.

'Justin, what can I do for you?'

'Superintendent Rainsford was asking for you, ma'am.'

'Tell him I'll be there in half an hour.'

She got back to HQ in Portishead a little before 1 p.m. The office was deserted except for Trisha, who normally brought her own salads, eating at her desk with her earbuds in. The last time Anna'd asked what Trisha was listening to, she'd said it was an investigative journalism podcast about the death of a reclusive eccentric in

Alabama. 'It's amazing stuff,' she'd added. 'Sophisticated and subtle. You should give it a try. I'll send you the link.'

Trisha's passion was why Anna would crawl over glass to keep her on the team.

Khosa and Holder were probably in the restaurant or Costa. There was no sign of Woakes.

Anna went in search of Rainsford. His secretary was also at lunch but she gambled and knocked on his door. He was in, reading through the small mountain of paperwork on his desk, a pair of glasses perched low on his nose.

'Ah, Anna. Just wanted a little chat.'

Anna nodded. Standard opening gambit for a dollop of the serious stuff from RainMan – Holder's irreverent nickname for the superintendent.

'DS Woakes has been in to see me.'

'How was he, sir?'

'Angry, I think. Difficult to say because he spent most of the time in here pacing back and forth. Said it helped him think. I found it incredibly distracting. But the point of his visit was to complain about the way he was being treated.'

'By me, sir?'

'You as his line manager. He says he feels undermined and isolated. Says you've effectively cut him off from the case he was investigating.'

'For his own good, sir. He searched a witness's house without permission and was very aggressive. There were good grounds for harassment—'

'Now Woakes is playing the bullying card. He says you're spreading lies about him. Shifting blame. Excluding him socially.'

'*What?*'

'He says your attitude is affecting his professional performance resulting in low morale.'

'Sir, I don't do social. If I do, it's half an hour at the pub and the team all know it. It's never been a part of the job description.'

'It's a good way to engender loyalty.'

'Agreed, if you're looking for a way to engender loyalty because you haven't got the team's respect. Would you like me to ask my team if they feel the need?' Anna felt the heat rising in her face.

'I know what your team thinks of you, Anna. None of them want to work with anyone else.'

Anna blinked. She hadn't known. 'Sir, if I can speak plainly and off the record, I've learned that Sergeant Woakes had something of a reputation at East Mids. Effectively, he did well on a case through luck and they've taken the opportunity of shoving him up the chain and dumping him on us.'

Rainsford frowned. 'He came with a glowing reference.'

Anna snorted and gave it to Rainsford with both barrels. 'From an ACC. You'll forgive me for saying this, sir, but ACCs are not always the best people to know what an officer is really like. It may be that he was badly advised. I'd like to think so. But the fact is, Woakes is a loose cannon. Sir, I spoke to Dr Hawley yesterday. He rents a room in a house in Bristol. He told me it had been broken into and an iPad stolen and the place turned over. Someone was looking for something. Hawley is convinced it was Woakes.'

'Does he have any proof?'

'No. And he doesn't want it investigated.'

'Then it's his word—'

Anna interrupted him. 'Sir, I've seen Woakes at work. I would not put it past him.'

'We all know it's difficult for someone new to settle in. Is it a question of him being too eager to please?'

'I'm not sure what's going on with him, but this is not a settling in problem. It's more unsettling.'

'He's still on probation here, I told him that. We agreed that if the job didn't suit him we'd discuss other options.'

Anna tried to imagine what job Woakes might be good at and failed.

'Where is he, sir?'

'I've put him in an office down the corridor indexing in HOLMES. He's not happy, but better to have him here on the job with something to do than wandering about, festering.'

Anna sighed.

'I know. It leaves a bad taste, but welcome to my world of inclusivity and political correctness.'

'Sir, he's already messed up the Morton case. What if he does it again? Something important?'

'Then there'll be lots of ammunition for us, won't there.'

She left with her face glowing from grumbling resentment. Everyone knew they needed help and a new sergeant should have been champagne-worthy, but this situation ran the risk of turning into a fiasco. Find something for him to do?

She'd ask traffic if the bike shed needed painting.

CHAPTER THIRTY-ONE

Anna texted Holder and asked him to bring her back a coffee. Rainsford's criticism niggled and bothered her though her mind was buzzing with what Shaw had told her. She needed to assimilate it and decide on an action. Anna punched Gacy's name into a search engine. It did not make for easy reading. When she'd finished, she stood and walked into the squad room to look at the images of the stolen girls. They stared back at her. Lost and silent.

When the DCs returned Anna took the coffee and gave Holder the money for it. Trisha took out her earbuds and they all turned towards the whiteboard.

'First of all, a word about Sergeant Woakes. I don't think we've got off to the best of starts with him, but for now he'll be providing intelligence support, is that clear?'

Oh, wouldn't Rainsford have been proud.

The exchanged glances told Anna it wasn't.

'Is that clear?' she repeated.

'Yes, ma'am.'

'Right. No more distractions.'

Anna stood and contemplated the whiteboards. Blair's image brought the immediacy of her predicament into sharp focus, especially in light of Shaw's explanation of red rooms. Anna dragged her gaze across to Rosie Dawson's photograph. She turned to Khosa. 'Anything new from Varga?'

Khosa opened her notebook. 'She spoke to me this morning, ma'am. Nothing specific, I'm afraid. But Edinburgh did find another image of Blair on UWAntme.co.uk, which is the sister site of an American third-party advertiser. It's the image used on TV and in the press, supplied by Blair's mother.'

'How does that help?'

'It doesn't. Not in terms of Rosie, but the posting was fresh and dated yesterday. UWAntme has sites in over 900 locations across almost 100 countries. They use a data outsourcing company. But it's a free listing for the first week. Varga thinks it might mean the abductor is trying to alert other people, to drum up business. She thinks because of that, Blair might still be alive.'

Drum up business.

A little spasm of anger tightened in Anna's gut.

'What did the advert say?'

Khosa placed a sheet on the whiteboard. Blair Smeaton's school photograph stared back at them. The caption with it said:

Missing awaiting action.
Pinocchio for interested parties #crypto #pogo.

'Pinocchio,' if you remember, ma'am, was the site Edinburgh found Blair's other photograph on.'

Holder stared at the UWAntme ad, his face grim. 'That's sick.'

'Prospects of tracing who placed this?' Anna asked.

Khosa shook her head. 'Varga was not hopeful. If it's the same guy, he will have covered his tracks.'

'Thanks, Ryia.' There wasn't much to be gained from this new intel, except that it reinforced everything she'd learned from Shaw. The anger inside her skipped up a notch.

Khosa, her expression distant and haunted, asked, 'Do you think Blair's still alive, ma'am?'

The question shook Anna.

'I'd really like to think so.'

After a long beat, Holder spoke in a low voice. 'Maybe it would be better if she wasn't.'

Khosa stared at the image as if she was trying to make it talk. 'I wish I knew what #pogo means.'

'I do,' Anna said. 'It's a reference to a serial child killer.'

Her harrowing words brought them all up short. Both Khosa and Holder were staring at her with expressions of dull horror.

'Are you sure about this, ma'am?' Holder asked.

'No, I'm not sure. But I want to be. Rosie has been our priority here and the link to Blair was a bonus. Edinburgh's manpower is naturally focused on finding Blair and currently, they believe the link might implicate a ring. It's a strong theory, and Varga and the cybercrime team in Scotland have come up trumps with finding images. But what if it's worse than that? What if it isn't a ring but just one man? One very troubled and dangerous man who may have learned to monetise his obsession.'

And as the afternoon wore on, she told them about red rooms. She told them about Hurtcore. She told them about Gacy, about Pogo the clown.

'I don't know how closely this man identifies with Pogo. I dread to think. But Gacy's victims were all murdered… eventually. Murdered and then buried. Is this what our perpetrator was trying to do with Rosie's bones in Charterhouse?'

She watched their faces harden, Trisha excusing herself once to go to the bathroom, coming back with red rims around her eyes.

'I'm going to talk to Edinburgh about this now. While I do that I'd like you to look hard at the other cases.'

She walked over to the posted images from Hawley's cuttings. The innocent faces looked back at her. 'Katelyn Prosser, Lily Callaghan and Jade Hemmings. I want to know what happened to them. Get on to Varga and ICAT and ask them if there have been any web images of these girls posted. Focus in on their medical histories, too. See if there is anything that might link them together. I know I've asked you to do this once, but let's do it again. Fresh eyes, different angle. One each. I'll take Katelyn.'

They already had files. Summarised reports from the separate forces involved in the searches and investigations over an eight-year period during which the three girls had gone missing. Anna took Katelyn's file through to her office. But before she began reading, she phoned Danaher again.

'This is becoming a habit,' Danaher said. But there was no trace of irritation this time. Edinburgh were obviously willing to listen to anything Anna had to say.

'Nothing new, it's only some intel on the image you sent us of Blair. What do your people make of #pogo?'

'We've struggled with that one. Of course, there is the crude reference to jumping up and down using a stick. I don't think you need one syllable explanations of what that implies.'

Anna didn't. 'OK. I may have something.' She told Danaher about the Gacy link and elaborated on the red room theory.

'My God, who have you got working on this stuff down there?' Danaher said.

If you only knew.

'It's only a theory, I know. It's not hard evidence, but I thought you ought to throw it into the mix.'

'I'll pass it on, ma'am.'

'How is it going?'

'Slowly. The super in charge is doing a sweep of known offenders. Pulling people in. We've got several raids set for tomorrow. If there is a ring, we'll flush them out.'

Most of them don't want to harm their victims. Far from it. They wouldn't sanction this sadistic shit.

Shaw's words rang in her ears. But she was in no position to criticise Police Scotland. All she had to go by were the thoughts of a known serial killer and her own instinct. She wasn't quite ready to stick her head above the parapet on that one just yet. Anna rang off and turned to Katelyn's file.

In a nod to Hawley's preoccupation with illnesses, Anna noted that Katelyn suffered from asthma and attended the University Hospital in Coventry for years. This was nothing more than a note in the statement from Katelyn's mother, a single parent with mobility issues. Other than a name, there was no suggestion the father had much to do with the family unit. A unit completed by Katelyn's younger brother, Duane, aged five at the time of her disappearance. Duane's father was not involved in looking after the children. He was also not Katelyn's father. An image of Dawn Prosser, Katelyn's mother, accompanied the images of the abduction site and of Katelyn herself. At the time of the abduction in 2010, Dawn had been significantly if not morbidly obese and lived in council accommodation in Coventry's Hillfields estate. As such, Katelyn was expected to do much of the family's shopping. Twice a week, she would walk to a supermarket two streets away. One cold, damp evening in November, she did not return. CCTV showed her crossing a road on the way back to the block where she lived with her mother and brother.

A second camera in the lobby of the tower block had been disabled with some duct tape fifteen minutes before the last sighting. No one made a big deal of it at the time. The local youths considered it fair game and it was a regular occurrence.

But not, as it turned out, this time.

It was assumed Katelyn was abducted as she entered the building, taken downstairs to the basement and removed through a back door. One witness reported seeing some large laundry bags being removed by a man in a hi-vis jacket.

So here was a man capable of carrying large sacs of laundry. Could it be the same man capable of carrying 30-odd kilos in a military rucksack?

It was a tenuous link. But it was a link of sorts.

There were photographs of the lobby, the basement, the three-room flat the Prossers lived in. What stood out from the investigation was the lack of forensic evidence. No signs of a struggle. No blood. A huge manhunt was launched. Much like the one currently being undertaken by Police Scotland. The press was recruited; Katelyn's mother made several appeals. All of them fruitless.

Outside the windows of the MCRTF offices, the sun kept shining, though its drift was ever downwards. In Dawn Prosser's world, Anna suspected that it had never shone as brightly since that November day in 2010.

At five thirty, Trisha brought Anna some tea and excused herself. Anna thanked her for staying on the extra half hour. Outside, Khosa and Holder did not look up from their desks.

Anna busied herself typing up her report on the visit to Janice Dawson in readiness for Trisha to enter it in HOLMES. She should have done it already. A witness assessment, a commentary on Janice's state of mind and emotional state. Something Shipwright insisted on. 'Treat the case like it happened yesterday.'

But there was another report she wouldn't type up. The intel she'd received from Shaw would have to remain unrecorded. That was for her eyes only.

When she'd finished, she sat back in her chair and sighed. She was out of ideas. She remembered she hadn't eaten properly since breakfast. Maybe her brain needed a little sustenance? At six thirty, she got up and walked out into the office.

'Right, come on. Let's have a debrief away from here. I fancy the Lantern. My treat.'

Holder and Khosa stretched in unison. Neither of them objected.

The Lantern was an eighteenth-century riverside pub outside Shirehampton on the banks of the Avon. It was popular, big and had a beer garden, which on a sultry evening in June was a must.

They sat outside. This, Anna could do. A small group, colleagues she trusted, the talk – to begin with anyway – all work.

'Jade disappeared during a friend's party. They'd gone to a park with their bikes. No one missed her for half an hour. By then it was too late,' Holder said.

'And Lily didn't come home from visiting a friend who lived 50 yards away. She was rushing because she was late for her tea. Didn't wait for the friend's mum to chaperone her. Quiet street. No CCTV. Some eye witnesses reported a workman and a workman's van. There was some suggestion of a logo. There'd been a cordoned-off manhole for a day before on that same street. It was still cordoned off at the time she went missing. None of the utility services reported any issues, and the cordon and warning cones had all been stolen from a street half a mile away.'

'It the same story with Katelyn,' Anna said. 'It looks spontaneous enough to suggest stranger abduction but in reality, every one of those could easily have been carefully planned. There's a report of a van in the vicinity. But a different colour to the one in Rosie's case.' Anna toyed with her food as her thoughts tried to mesh. Frustration growled inside her like a hungry animal. She needed to find the thing that would jolt the investigation forward and over this road block.

'It would take an awful lot of knowledge, ma'am,' Khosa said.

She was right. It was asking a great deal of any single theory.

'What about social circumstances? Rosie, we know, had a big family unit.'

Holder shook his head. 'Jade was one of three. Father in prison. Mother holding down a job as a shopworker.'

Khosa put down her fork. 'Lily had one sibling, a sister. Both lived with their father. Her mother had moved to a different town. She had a lot of personal problems. Saw her every other week, but not always.'

Anna pushed her plate away. 'Is that a pattern? They all seem to come from dysfunctional families. Blair included. Her mum is a single parent and they lived in social housing. Could the difficult family dynamics mean they were slightly more vulnerable?'

'That doesn't work for Rosie though, ma'am,' Holder said.

'No,' Anna agreed, but Shaw's words stayed fresh in her head. 'But if Rosie was his first, his trial run, it's possible it wasn't a consideration. He might have been concentrating on other things. Like being certain of the geography, his exit plan. Or maybe he was close enough to them to see the cracks in their relationship already beginning. Her parents weren't with her when she was taken, remember.'

Khosa looked unconvinced. 'OK. But if it was all planned, how could he possibly know this information about the victims unless he knew the families?'

Something in her question struck a chord in Anna. She didn't have the answer, not then, but there was something that chimed.

'Thanks for supper, ma'am,' Holder said.

Anna looked at him, realising she'd been wool-gathering for almost a minute.

'It's a pleasure, Justin. You two both deserve it. Maybe we should be doing a team night out as a regular thing?'

Holder looked aghast. Khosa frowned. 'Us three?'

'Yes. You know, for a meal or a pub thing.'

'Uhh, you turned into a zombie after an hour of the bowls night for the super's birthday, ma'am. It was scary. I don't think you spoke for like, twenty minutes.'

'Didn't I?' Anna knew she had. 'My battery gets drained.'

'You don't need to do that for us, ma'am,' Khosa said. 'That's for needy bosses, not you.'

Anna thought about protesting, but then simply nodded. Her team knew her well. Perhaps too well. She was about to ask Khosa to elaborate on why she thought knowing the family was important when Holder sat up suddenly.

'I don't believe it,' he said, looking beyond Anna and Khosa to the bar entrance.

'What?' Khosa said.

Holder's mouth opened and shut wordlessly before he raised a hand half-heartedly in greeting.

Anna turned to see Dave Woakes standing there, dressed in jeans and T-shirt, drink in hand. 'Evening.'

'What are you doing here?' Anna asked.

'Having a drink. Like you. Supposed to meet up with a couple of the lads after they finish work.'

'What lads?'

'Not here yet. Mind if I join you?'

Anna did, but Woakes was already pulling up a chair.

'How did you know we'd be here?' Anna asked.

'I didn't. Like I said, I'm meeting up with some lads.' He turned to Holder. 'So, Justin, any news on Morton?'

Khosa must have seen Anna's expression because she turned her eyes down towards her drink in a way that suggested she would happily dive into it.

'Erm… no… not yet.'

'You were unlucky there, mate. Still, he's not on Mars, is he?' Woakes let out a chortle.

Anna stared. The man was unbelievable. Brazen was not the word. He must have known Rainsford had spoken to her. Even so, this was pushing his luck. Acting like nothing had happened. A flush bloomed on her neck. She wanted to ask him what the hell he thought he was doing, but this was neither the time nor the place.

He's still on the payroll. Find something for him to do.

'Nice spot,' said Woakes. 'What's the occasion?'

'Late finish,' Anna said. She wasn't going to let Woakes back in. He'd lost her trust.

Woakes nodded, unfazed. Khosa and Holder stared into their drinks.

'Didn't peg you for a pub-goer,' Woakes said, leaning back and fixing Anna, his smile as genuine as a cardboard sword.

'Special occasions only,' Anna said. She got up. There was half an inch of wine left in her glass and she downed it in one swallow.

Khosa watched and followed suit, Holder taking up the rear, but leaving what was left of his beer in his glass.

'Another drink?' Woakes said. 'My shout.'

'We're all driving, Dave,' Anna said. 'Things to do.'

'Yeah, thanks but no thanks, sarge,' Holder added.

Khosa merely shrugged.

Anna stood. 'See you all tomorrow.'

The atmosphere felt strained if not hostile. Woakes stayed seated as the rest of the team all left. He was still sitting there, watching them as they turned the corner form the beer garden to the car park. No one said anything and Anna respected both her DCs for that.

They said their goodbyes and Anna left in her own car, Khosa and Holder sharing a lift. There was no easy way back into town; it was either one stop down the motorway or in along the gorge and across the suspension bridge. But something was bothering Anna and she knew she'd have no peace until she scratched the itch.

She got back to HQ ten minutes later and went up to the office, mulling over Khosa's assessment of the victims. Something in what she said was pulling at her, but despite looking again at the files, it wouldn't gel. After half an hour, she sat back, frustrated and still nursing a dull anger. Seeing Woakes turn up in the pub disturbed her. Confirmed her feelings that he was not the full shilling. Yes, perhaps he was good at his job, though that was open to debate having seen his approach first-hand, but it didn't say anything about his personality.

She went back to her office and mentally replayed her suggestion of an early supper. All she'd done was walked out and said it. Spontaneously. She hadn't emailed or sent messages. Little more than a throwaway remark. She stood in the same position now in her doorway, looking out at the desks, at where Woakes should have been sitting.

She stared, her intuition guiding her towards his desk, the first stirrings of disquiet roiling in her gut. The surface was littered with papers, his computer screen stuck with Post-it notes along the top rim. Telephone numbers, names, to-do lists. She scanned them and found nothing until her eye was caught by a yellow note stuck to the middle of the top edge of his screen. Something about it looked different. The top edge, the one coated with adhesive, was torn, a small section roughly removed. Within that section a green light shone at the centre of the black glass exposed by the tear in the note. She removed the paper and sighed. There, at the top of the screen, a small, green LED light glowed. A mixture of incredulity and anger at her own naivety triggered a mirthless laugh.

He'd been watching them. All this time he'd been absent, Woakes had been watching them. There'd be some software running, a FaceTime or a Skype equivalent, something which allowed him access. That was how he knew about them leaving together. And if she confronted him, he'd plead ignorance, she was sure.

Must have left it on without knowing, ma'am.

Yes, of course, easy mistake.

She grabbed a cardboard folder, emptied its contents and laid its open leaves over the top of the screen, blanking out the camera, fighting the urge she had to throw the screen across the room. More than that, she wished Woakes was there now in front of her. Her mind had already come up with ten different ways of telling him how much of a waste of bloody space he was. Most of them involved words only four letters long.

The guy is a bloody lunatic.

But she knew her anger was merely a smokescreen for the hot embarrassment that was burning her face. Woakes had outsmarted her and that, more than anything else he'd done, irked her immensely.

He was playing games. Watching her, seeing the investigation stall and go nowhere. What else was he laughing at? His conviction that Hawley was somehow involved niggled like a hangnail. Though by now convinced of his innocence, she still felt that Hawley somehow held the key to her understanding.

On impulse, she rang him.

'Inspector, what can I do for you?'

'Dr Hawley, Ben, I need a favour. Are you free tomorrow morning?'

CHAPTER THIRTY-TWO

Anna's dreams were bad.

A darkened room in a ruined house. A cupboard. Empty except for a pinpoint of light far at the back. A voice, further away than was possible in the confines of that space, called to her, rising and falling.

'Help me, Anna. Help me.'

A second light, blinking, remained silent. And further away, like faded stars, she saw others, barely visible, pulsing weakly.

But she couldn't reach into the cupboard. Something, a web, invisible but strong, prevented her from getting so much as a hand across, towards the voice. Above she heard the fluttering of wings. There, a crow sat, settling itself on the edge of a jagged tile that bordered a rent in the building's roof. Its dark, intelligent eyes watched her as it tilted its head from side to side. Only now she noted the ladder and started to climb, up towards the bird and the blue sky above where the clouds crossed at impossible, rampant speeds.

She heard a voice then. Her father's, but not his, not quite his, calling to her, and she glimpsed the shadow of someone moving beyond the bird.

'Come up here, Anna. Come and see what's out here.'

But as she climbed, a tree and its reaching branches grew in towards the hole in the roof, filling it as she ascended, its pungent leaves brushing against her face, its twigs harsh against her skin. She fought and pushed through until the crow took flight, its warning caws caught and scattered by the wind.

A man stood on the edge of the roof looking down into the fields beyond. When she craned her neck, standing on the top rung of the ladder, she saw the field and in it a figure next to a huge cauldron with thick, oily steam billowing up. The figure held something in his hand with which to stir, something white and long with bulbous ends.

At the edge of the roof, the man, her father, stood with his back to her.

'Look, Anna. All you need to do is look.'

She hesitated, crept forwards onto the rickety slates, heard them creak and crack beneath her. The man on the edge had thicker hands, a bigger frame, less hair than her father. She stood, unsure, unsafe as he began to turn and reveal himself for the imposter he was. The imposter who'd enticed her up above the world to see. The same large shape as the figure in the field below…

She half-woke, the face not seen, the last of the dream beating in time with her racing heart. The digital read-out on the bedside clock was her link to reality. 4.57 a.m., grey light leeching into the day.

The man on the roof was who she needed to find. Or was it Shaw leading her on?

There was still time for rest, but peace had flown with the crow. She lay there, half in and half out of consciousness, her mind bouncing like a pinball against the bumpers of worry. Untangled knots of her professional life presented themselves for intrusive inspection. The mock-up model of Rosie Dawson in that rucksack, folded and mute. Woakes, a capricious thorn; Hawley, damaged goods.

She emerged into full awareness as traffic noises began to intrude from the earliest risers. From the park, birds erupted into full song to greet the dawn, a dog somewhere barked at a squirrel or a cat.

When the sun arced around to lance through a gap in the curtains, Anna got up.

CHAPTER THIRTY-THREE

He'd had to work late on Thursday evening. Still, by hanging around he knew he'd create a good impression and that the feedback to head office would be favourable. But today was Friday.

Today he had something very special planned.

He dressed for work as normal. He usually met the neighbours on a school run. They'd expect him to be smart. Suit grey, shirt white, tie plaid, shoes black, polished. He was in no rush. He planned to be in the city by 9 a.m.

Before he left, he went back to his workshop and removed something from a drawer. It had its own space, wrapped in a soft cloth. He placed it on the bench and carefully pulled back the cloth to let it fall open. It revealed a single, startlingly white, bone. A human ulna. The first and only one that he had ever kept. It was beautiful and, under his fingers, smooth yet contoured where the muscles and tendons had once attached so elegantly.

He nodded. This was his affirmation. Slowly, reverently, he wrapped up the bone and placed it back in its drawer.

He drove to a McDonalds, bought coffee and a McMuffin and sat going over everything in his mind. He'd repacked the boot of his car with all the equipment: the nylon rope, duct tape, the large rucksack, placed on one side, careful to leave enough space for something else. He put the roll of plastic sheeting along with the digital SLR in its box and the video equipment on the back seat.

There was half an hour to kill before heading towards his one and only stop in Bristol. One of the guys down the pub had told him about a place he could buy what he wanted.

'Cost you,' he'd said. 'Big market for them in Asia, apparently. Take whatever they can get.'

He was prepared to pay. No pain, no gain, as his dad used to say sometimes. And always when he used his belt.

He had his phone in a holder on the dashboard. He removed it now and smiled as he scrolled through the replies to his posting on the forum. Thirty so far after the image of Blair in her well hole. Two offering 3 bitcoins each for post-mortem images. One asking for something else very specific. That one for 5 bitcoins. There were other boards where a lot of interest had been shown but no actual money offered. There was always a market for images and video and so it paid to advertise. But Bopeepers knew what they wanted and you needed a proven cryptocurrency account to gain access. The administrator demanded a token transfer as proof of wealth. This way everyone knew they were dealing with no time-wasters.

He quickly totted up the pre-orders: 11 bitcoins. At today's valuations that was a great deal of money.

At half eight, he set off, the radio playing a Chris Rea track, 'Sweet Summer Day'. He smiled. He appreciated the poetry of it. It felt like the gods were with him. Above, scattered high clouds in sculpted shapes framed the sky to the east. Behind them the air was clear and crystal.

Commuters choked the roads. He followed the river in, took the feeder road to Small Street in St Phillips. He negotiated Chapel Street, took a few lefts and then a right to a unit next to another breaker's yard. It was little more than a large lock-up, a distribution unit in an industrial block next to a plastics manufacturer. Three vans outside. He parked and went in through the front door. A man in a white coat was busy loading trays of ice-filled palettes onto a dolly ready for transfer to a van.

'Help you?' he asked.

'Yeah. Friend of mine said you might have some eels?'

The man looked over his shoulder at his car. A black Renault Megan. 'Sorry, mate, eels are protected species.'

'Look, I'm not from environmental health or DEFRA or whatever. My dad used to cook eels unskinned. I heard you might have some. I wanted to surprise someone with them. Special occasion.'

'Sometimes we do get some. Accidental, mind. We throw them back as a rule.'

A shrug. 'Oh well. I'd be willing to pay, but…'

He turned for the door.

'Tenner each,' said the man.

He turned back, grinning. 'I'll take two. I've got a bucket.'

'Try roasting them with a bit of garlic and rosemary,' the man said and winked.

He put them in the well of the front seat, lid on so the water wouldn't spill, and the eels couldn't get out. Two of them, writhing and wriggling in the confined space. They'd continue to do that for hours even after you cut their heads off.

One of his father's farming friends once told him of how unscrupulous dealers at horse fairs used to feague the animals to make them look livelier. One method was to put a live eel in them – and not through their mouths. He'd never forgotten that. It wasn't exactly what he had in mind, but their constantly writhing natures, like snakes, made them unattractive creatures. Slithering and slimy.

Not many people liked them close up where they could wriggle and twist against your skin. There was something elemental in that abhorrence. He smiled. Most people would run a mile rather than touch one.

He was counting on that.

CHAPTER THIRTY-FOUR

Anna met Hawley in the car park of the Gordano motorway services at a little after nine on Friday morning. It was already warm and the stagnant air held a ripe aroma of stale food and diesel fumes that made Anna glad she'd already eaten. Hawley had declined her offer of parking at HQ. She hadn't argued the point; he would have to pay once his two free hours of parking in the service station were up.

He was standing in front of the Waitrose sign dressed in skinny chinos, an open-neck shirt and a lightweight jacket. Over his shoulder hung a well-used document bag. He held a takeaway coffee cup in each hand. He looked strong and fit and Anna was left wondering where those two adjectives came from and why they'd sprung into her head.

She pulled up and he got in.

'You know there's a charge here after two hours.'

'I'll pay by phone. How long do you think we'll be?'

'An hour to get there; assume an hour there and another to get back.'

'OK.' He took out his phone and started pressing keys. 'I'll go for four. I can always top up if needed. I got this for you.' He offered her a coffee. 'Flat white. I've got sugar or sweetener if you want it.'

'No, it's fine. And thanks. Never turn down a coffee, that's my motto.'

He'd gone inside and bought from a Costa Express. She was with him on that one.

'Tried McDonald's coffee?'

'Yeah. If I'm travelling, it's the one I go for every time.'

'You're a man after my own heart, as the vicar said to the transplant surgeon.'

Hawley had his coffee cup almost to his lips. He paused and looked at her, his inquisitiveness turning to approval with a little nod. 'That's actually not bad, Inspector,' he said, amused.

Anna frowned, bemused by the fact that she'd dragged up the joke and wondering why she had. 'It's my one joke, I don't know any others.'

'Must be nice when you find an opportunity to use it.'

'Very gratifying. And it's Anna, by the way.'

They were back on the M5 within minutes and heading north.

Hawley sipped his coffee. Eventually, he said, 'Do you mind me asking why it is we're doing this?'

'Your idea that the victims on your list all had significant medical histories intrigues me. I need to know how it might have put them at risk.'

Hawley's response was a sour smile. 'Why, so you can implicate me further?'

'You're not under suspicion, Ben. We're undertaking a review. It's not unusual to revisit the evidence in this way. Believe it or not, you're my expert witness. I thought that if we got a better handle on what exactly happened that day, it might help.'

Hawley turned to look out of the window, reluctant acceptance in his face.

Everything she'd told him was true. That she was hoping for one little nugget of insight or trigger to crank the case forward. This was what investigating was all about. Not car chases or fights, though she'd had a few of those in her time. Mostly it was about patience. Re-examining the obvious to spot anything missed. If there was a link between the abducted children and their medical histories, a link that made them vulnerable, what could it be?

More importantly, how would that information be obtained? If Edinburgh was to be believed, details had been shared between a ring of perpetrators. If on the other hand, as Anna believed, this was the work of one man, then how on earth had he gained access? She needed details, something small but vital that would plug the gap in her understanding.

Taking the road less travelled for no other reason than the wind blows you in that direction.

She'd learned to trust the wind.

'How did you end up working in Cheltenham?' Anna asked.

'What can I tell you that you don't know already?'

'Humour me.'

Hawley shrugged. 'I was twenty-three. Had just finished my first-year foundation house jobs and was wondering what direction to take. It was my second six months in A and E and I was toying with a career in emergency medicine. I knew I'd need to move to a bigger unit, get on to a run-through training programme. I mean it was busy enough, don't get me wrong, but I was still making my mind up then. A district general hospital like Cheltenham was a great introduction. The usual sort of set-up. Walking wounded on one side, the serious stuff on the other. I was getting good at dealing with most things that came through the door and the nurses knew I was good with kids. I'm one of four. I had two sisters younger than me so I wasn't fazed if they cried or whined or screamed.'

'And the day Rosie came in and you were on duty. Were you asked to see her, or was it a random act?'

'I picked up the file... No, I tell a lie, one of the staff nurses gave me the file. The other junior was a locum. Older chap, not brilliant with kids. The consultant was dealing with someone having a fit and the staff grade was sorting out a fracture. So, the staff nurse found me. There was a room for eye casualties. Anything serious and we'd call the ophthalmologists, but they encouraged us to have a look and try and deal with the simple stuff. We had a dark room with a slit lamp—'

'Slit lamp?'

'It's a kind of microscope used for examination. You know, you put your chin on a rest and there's eye pieces for the observer. You've seen one in optometrist shops and every advert for glasses that's ever been.'

Anna pictured it and nodded.

'Anyway, Rosie came in with her mum, clutching her eye. She wouldn't let me examine her easily. She was photophobic from the scratches. Protocol is that you apply anaesthetic for a better look. Somehow, I managed to get her to let me put some drops in. Once they kick in, once the pain has gone, patients will open their eyes and it's much easier.' Hawley sat back, eyes front, remembering. 'She was great. Chatty, cooperative. Some people hate small kids, and Rosie was Down's, so her mental age was a bit less than eleven. In fact, I think it's easier when they're younger. They're less cynical and self-aware.

'I examined her on the slit lamp. The anaesthetic has a dye. It shows up scratches on the cornea. She had scratches on the upper half but no foreign body. In those circumstances, the thing to do is to look under the upper lid. Not easy in Down's because of their lid shape, but Rosie was a trooper. She sat on her mum's knee, I popped her lid over and there it was, the foreign body. I wiped it away, repositioned the lid and it was done.'

'And you'd never seen Rosie before?'

'No.' He looked across at her. 'And I never saw her again.'

'And afterwards?'

'What do you mean?'

'You said that it affected you?'

'You know all about the questioning. They wanted to know where I was on the day Rosie was abducted. I'd been on nights. I was in my room at the doctor's mess alone, asleep. They didn't like that. No witnesses for sleep. Then the press got hold of it.' Hawley's smile was razor-thin and bitter. 'In fact, it wasn't so much the press as your lot. I was taken from a clinic. The officers who came for me made no bones about making sure everyone knew what it was about. That sort of mud sticks. They released me but I was branded. You'd think intelligent people like nurses and doctors and hospital administrators would see beyond the dirt.' Hawley shook his head. 'The next day, someone spray-painted 'paedo' on my car. Day after that the local papers printed a story about a health professional taken in for questioning. It spread like wildfire. I took the decision to leave the department.' He turned away, looked out of his window at the traffic. 'I don't see children anymore. I make sure the departments I go into know that.'

'Was that some sort of prerequisite? A requirement of you continuing to practise?'

'No,' Hawley said, still with his face turned away. 'There were no charges. I wasn't reported to the GMC. Nothing like that. It's self-imposed. Punishment, if you like.'

'Punishment?' Anna tilted her head. It was an odd word to use.

'Yes. Because for some bloody weird reason, your lot has managed to make me feel guilty for what happened. I… I don't trust kids anymore.'

His words were spoken quietly, dejectedly. Anna felt like she ought to say something but failed to find any words that would fit.

They sat in silence for a while until Anna turned the radio back on. After a long contemplative beat, Hawley continued. 'They never found out who spoke to the press. And they stopped short of actually naming me. But there was enough there to make life intolerable. The headline was something like, "Accused doctor in missing schoolgirl case asked to leave department." None of it was true but the police made no attempt to clear my name. They simply made it obvious that I was a person of interest. And clearly I still am.'

'You don't like us much, do you?'

'No.'

'We're not all like—'

'Sergeant Woakes?'

'I was going to say like the people who interviewed you at that time.'

'But Woakes is. And there are still a lot of officers like him out there.'

She thought about protesting but there was an element of truth in what Hawley said. She'd experienced the worst kind of institutionalised bigotry and poor policing when she'd investigated the Woodsman case a few months ago.

'And here we are travelling to Cheltenham,' Hawley continued, 'because you still have that little worry. That grain of doubt I'm somehow involved.'

'I am not Sergeant Woakes,' she said, surprising herself again by the firmness with which she delivered it.

He took his time before responding. 'I'd like to believe that, Inspector. Truly, I would'

'It's Anna.'

'OK, Anna.'

'Then believe it.'

Hawley let a beat go by. 'Is that a Welsh accent I'm hearing, by the way?'

She felt her defences come up. Other people had asked her this question. Men in bars, on courses, people with opinions she didn't want to hear. But this time it was different.

It's called having a normal bloody conversation, Anna.

'It is.'

'Wales is a small country. This is probably the point at which I'm supposed to ask if you knew my aunt in Sully.' He laughed.

'Never been to Sully until three days ago.'

'So, what's your story, Anna?'

'My story is very boring.'

'Not fair. You have my file. You know all about me. This is me wanting a little payback for cooperating.'

'Not much to tell.'

'Oh, I don't believe that, Anna. Not for one minute.'

He was easy to talk to. Damaged, clearly, but still a normal guy. Anna couldn't find a good reason for not opening up.

'What can I tell you? I grew up in a Welsh valley in post-industrial decline. My sister and I were the schoolteacher's daughters. We got some stick for that. My dad insisted we live in the middle of the community. He was principled in that way. Until the burglaries in the street got too much for him to stomach and we moved out to a semi-rural semi-detached.'

'It sounds rough.'

'It was, looking back. But you accepted all the teenage pregnancies and made damned sure one of them wasn't you.'

'Your sister – older or younger?'

'Younger and from a different planet. You'd like her. Pretty, sociable, life and soul.'

Hawley's eyes narrowed. 'Not the same planet as you, is that what you're saying?'

'Definitely not. Let's just say she adapted to the situation better than I did.'

'And why the police? As a career choice, I mean.'

She told him about her three years at Goldsmiths and her criminology degree, and about how the challenge, the constant problem-solving, had appealed to her. He, in turn, told her about his normal upbringing in Devon and his training in London and the many stops and hops a junior doctor had to make before ending up in Bristol. But as they got closer to Cheltenham, conversation died away and he became increasingly subdued.

'Is this the first time you've been back here, Ben?'

'Yes.'

'Everything will have changed.'

'Not everything.'

Anna took the motorway exit. She didn't know it well but she'd visited more than once and was close enough a neighbour of the Gloucestershire constabulary to know what went on under the surface. The plummy, Cheltenham Ladies College, Regency Spa veneer still worked for the busloads of tourists. Over the last twenty years, yummies and yuppies slowly infiltrated the town, piggybacking in on the back of lucrative jobs from the software companies. But with money comes drugs, and the nice middle-class Chelters retirees had a reputation for Nimbyism – the not-in-my-backyard brigade – that bordered sometimes on out-and-out racism.

The centre of town possessed a character all its own. On its periphery, the hospital looked over the college and new bits had been added on to the sandstone facade. She'd rung ahead, and the receptionist in A and E made them wait while she contacted an administrator. Only half the seats in the reception area were occupied. The General, it seemed, was meeting its waiting times target.

The administrator, when she arrived, looked even younger than Holder. She took them through and introduced them to an efficient but harassed-looking charge nurse in navy scrubs who listened to Anna explain what she needed.

'Well, there's never a quiet moment.'

'We'll try not to get in the way,' Anna said.

The charge nurse did not know Hawley and shook his hand when Anna made the introduction.

'Could do with the help once you've finished,' he joked.

Hawley smiled, but Anna sensed the anxiety fluttering beneath the surface.

'You remember the layout?' the charge nurse asked.

Hawley nodded and pointed to a central station with desks and screens separated from the treatment areas by etched glass.

'Computer stations.' He turned to his left. 'Resus and major trauma.' He turned back the other way. 'Treatment cubicles and minor injuries and side rooms.' He smiled and cocked an eyebrow. 'That's it. Now I'm trying to think who's still here? Oh, wait, do you remember Coleen Bridges?'

Hawley nodded, his expression softening. 'Of course.'

'She's a junior sister now and you're in luck. She's on duty. Let me find her.'

The charge nurse disappeared, leaving Anna and Hawley alone while all around them the unit buzzed with noise and people getting on with it.

'You OK?' Anna asked.

'Yeah. Slightly weirded out maybe.'

'This nurse Bridges, are you OK with her?'

'Yes. She was on with me the day I saw Rosie.'

'Ben?' said a voice from behind them.

Anna turned. A thirty-something heavy-set woman, dressed in navy scrubs and with her dark hair piled on the top of her head, walked up to Hawley and gave him a hug. Hawley turned a nice shade of pink and reciprocated.

The charge nurse nodded. 'Right, I'll leave you three to it.'

'My God, Ben, how have you been?' Coleen looked him up and down.

'OK. I'm fine. You?'

'Same old. Can't believe I'm still here, what is it, nearly ten years on? Tried Australia, didn't like it. So back I came. Where are you now?'

'Locum stuff. Bristol mainly.'

Coleen sighed. 'Is this still about…?'

'Yes, it is. Coleen, this is Inspector Gwynne.'

Anna shook Coleen's hand. 'Thanks for sparing us some time.'

'There's never enough of it, so I've stopped beating myself up. I don't get paid for getting an ulcer.'

'Ben has agreed to help me understand what happened the day he saw Rosie Dawson.'

'That's easy. She came in with a sore eye.'

'I'm familiar with all those details. I wanted to get a sense of place. A feel for the day.'

'It was summer. They'd been out for the day as I remember.'

'You had to give a statement, too. I've read it,' Anna said.

Coleen nodded. 'We brought her in to the minor side. Sat her and her mum in a cubicle.' They followed as Coleen walked past someone sitting in a chair, obviously out of breath, along a bank of blue chequered curtains, all drawn. She pulled one back and made a face before closing it again.

'This is the one, I seem to remember. It's occupied, I'm afraid. Hand injury.'

Anna nodded, looking around. 'Once she was in here, she'd be out of sight of everyone in the waiting room?'

'Totally,' Coleen said. 'She was triaged in here. We tried washing out her eye, but she wasn't cooperative enough. So, I called in the cavalry.'

Hawley took over. 'I came over, assessed her, no joy on the exam. I fetched some Oxybuprocaine drops from the eye room.'

'Eye room?'

Coleen walked a few steps further on. Three rooms at the end of the corridor in an L-shaped arrangement. The last one opened into what was nothing more than a large cubicle full of machines. Coleen pressed a switch, and a light box on one wall lit up showing an illuminated set of letters.

'Acuity test,' she said.

'And this is the slit lamp I was taking about,' Hawley said.

In the middle of the room was a table on wheels on which sat a tall, thin, skeletal-looking instrument on one side of which were some eye pieces. Anna nodded and scanned the room. There was another chair and an array of instruments attached to the wall;

she recognised a blood pressure cuff but the other bits slotted into holders meant nothing to her.

Hawley caught her staring. 'Ophthalmoscope, otoscope, electronic thermometer and sphyg,' he said.

'So, once you'd applied the drops to Rosie and they'd worked, you brought her in here?

'Yes,' Hawley said.

'Erm well, no, not actually here. We took her next door, remember?'

Coleen took them to a second room, this one bigger with an adjustable couch, a desk, a couple of chairs and much better lighting. 'Yes. We brought the slit lamp in here because equipment was being serviced in the eye room.'

'OK,' Anna said. 'She came in here, you examined her on her mum's knee. Then on the slit lamp.'

'Yes. Then I sat at that desk.' Hawley pointed. 'Rosie and her mum sat on that chair.' He pointed towards the other corner.

'And you were the only other person in the room the whole time?' Anna asked Coleen.

'All the time.'

'And afterwards?'

'I think we put a pad on Rosie's eye. One with a teddy bear on it,' Coleen said. 'I went back to the station to write everything up.'

'OK,' Anna said. 'Great.' She walked out into the treatment area and looked around, leaving Coleen and Hawley alone to catch up.

She stared out into the treatment area, swarming with staff, at the sitting area beyond rapidly filling with the sick and injured waiting for succour. She knew she was clutching at straws in coming here. But something had pulled her in this direction. Hawley's theory? Hawley himself?

She'd read all the pertinent documents from the previous investigation. They'd taken statements from staff at the hospital to corroborate Hawley's account, Coleen included. And later, they'd requested copies of the CCTV footage that backed up his story of where he was at the time Rosie was abducted. Their interest was not in the hospital; it was in the man who worked there and who'd had such intimate contact with Rosie.

A one-off incident.

There'd been no reason to extend the investigation into the unit or the hospital itself, other than to eliminate any possible known offenders. And that would not have been difficult since all hospital workers would have been run through the Disclosure and Barring Service as a matter of course prior to their employment. So where did you draw the line? You could not interview everyone who'd visited the A and E that day. What about the day-trippers who'd been to Sudeley Castle at the same time that Rosie had visited? Or everyone at the motorway service station the Dawsons stopped off at on their way up from Bristol that morning?

It was simply impossible.

She turned as Hawley came out of the room to join her, his expression unreadable.

'Well?' he asked.

'Say I wanted information on a victim. Address, family history.'

'It'll all be recorded in the notes by the triage nurse.' Hawley pointed towards a set of wall-hung files in vertical slots. Each slot labelled with pathway areas: triage, awaiting X-ray, awaiting doctor, awaiting treatment. 'These days the notes are slimmed down as this is A and E. Basic information. Name, date of birth, address, allergies, history of the illness or trauma. It's a pro-forma document. When I was here nine years ago it was more a free-text system. Everything written by hand. Which is also what you're much more likely to find in the other hospital areas. Files that are an inch thick stuffed with illegible handwriting, social worker's reports, blood results. That sort of thing.'

'So, anyone who wanted information would have to have access to these files, or files like them?'

'Exactly.'

Anna stood and watched the flow of paper that followed, or sometimes arrived before, the patients. All returning to the central hub. 'Do they sometimes get lost?'

'Here, no. These notes never leave the unit. If someone is transferred out, they send copies. It's common to lose them for a few minutes, easy to put down and forget where they are, but they're never lost because they're kept here. Very different from other hospital areas. There, they'd be stored centrally and sent to the appropriate clinic.'

'But they never leave the premises, am I right?'

'Yes, I would say that.'

'If your theory is correct, then it must be someone inside the unit or hospital or clinic who has access to the information. To the files. They couldn't be stealing these notes.'

'Exactly.'

'And what sort of person would have access to all areas?'

'Doctors, of course. And nurses. But as I said, it's impossible to envisage any one member of medical personnel working in all these different hospitals and areas.'

Anna nodded. Another blank wall. They'd cross-referenced all the hospitals on Hawley's list for common personnel and come up with nothing.

Patterns. That was what she was searching for. Some tiny thread that might link things together. There came a point when disparate, unconnected bits of information either remained dried-up fragments swept into a corner or became significant pieces of a mosaic. At that point, what appeared to be coincidences became vital intelligence loaded with damning evidence.

As she looked out into the A and E department in front of her, for now all Anna saw were scraps floating on the wind. She wanted to reach out and grab one, pull it to her, digest it. But they were too high up and way out of reach.

CHAPTER THIRTY-FIVE

That same Friday morning, Kevin Starkey drove around to the south, taking Brunel Way to meet the A370, out towards the Somerset Levels.

At first there was traffic heading out towards the airport, but he soon lost that after Backwell. He drove through Congresbury, the Mendip Hills to the south, the M5 creating an artificial barrier to the west. But he didn't need to go that far. This was the old Easton Road, a busy A road. Some enterprising people had set up off-site parking for the airport along this stretch. But it was too far out to be busy. Old farms had turned into breakers' yards and places where people who believed a wet weekend on a bleak coastline was better than a wet weekend at home could buy caravans. But there were still some residential properties.

Pux Cottage on Wird Lane was one such.

He pulled onto the verge. It was dangerous; double white lines along this stretch meant he was blocking traffic. But the lane gate was tied with rope. Quickly, he got out, untied the rope and swung the gates inwards. He got back in and drove along the pitted stone road into a narrow parking space in front of a dilapidated stone bungalow.

He'd begun the project when Brenda was still living with him. Transforming Dunroamin, she'd called it.

Dunroamin.

Of course, it wasn't really called that, but she'd hated its proper name, Pux Cottage. So, she'd christened it Dunroamin in another attempt at jocularity. A failed attempt.

He'd lived with his parents in this house for nigh on twenty years. His father had died there, the cigarettes and alcohol firmly strangling his coronaries into occlusion. His widowed mother had languished there on the edge of dementia for years afterwards until she went into a home and never came out.

Pux Cottage had been in the family for over 150 years. Starkey didn't think it had been decorated since the day it was built. He'd hated the place. Hated the fact that it was miles from anywhere, hated the way the school bus dropped him right outside and the sneering looks and jibes he'd endured whenever it did. The place looked like it should have been bulldozed when Britain was still at war with Hitler.

Starkey hadn't had the money to start with and there'd been no enthusiasm on his part. Only duty, and the germ of an idea that had grown like Japanese knotweed in his heart. He'd made himself do some work – the plan was to renovate as and when money came in. He'd done exactly that for three months last summer until mid-October when the poor light made it hardly worth his while. The long-term goal was to make it something to post on Airbnb. Something to generate a little income.

And this summer he'd been back to do some maintenance. Essential stuff. Preparatory work.

His father's job as a driver for a produce manufacturer took him all over the south-west in a liveried lorry, and his mother worked for a local farmer preparing meals and cleaning. They hadn't had a telephone until he was seventeen.

When his father finally bought a van to use to sell some produce of his own, they would often wait ten minutes before a gap appeared in traffic allowing them to leave the property. Starkey learned to cycle early, but he chose back ways, around the fields, across to Yatton or Congresbury for a bus to get into the city. And, more importantly, the other direction, to where he'd first seen the Turner girls playing in their garden.

The day that changed his life.

The memory, the humiliation, it all came flooding back as he looked around at the familiar lane and the fields beyond. His mind slid back to a warm summer's evening when the twins brother, Mathew, emerged out of the woods behind him, sixteen years old and bigger than him by a long way. The place the Turner family rented was large, with a big garden bordered by the trees where Starkey hid and watched the girls. He was only a year older than they were and what he longed for then was nothing more than innocent companionship. Someone to play with.

But Mathew Turner had seen him, caught him.

'Sit on the floor, oik,' Mathew had said, spitting with hate, tying Kevin's hands behind his back and binding his feet.

'What are you doing here, you little perve?' he'd demanded.

'Nothing. I-I live—'

'Hear that, girls? He lives.'

'I lu-live near the road. Pux Cottage.'

Kevin heard giggles. The girls, he realised, must have walked down behind him. When he tried to turn, Mathew slapped his face, hard.

'Keep your eyes front, peeper. You're trespassing, do you know that?'

'There's a path in the woods—'

'Shut up.' Mathew poked him with a stick. 'This is our house for the summer and we say it's trespass, got it?'

The stick was hard against Kevin's chest. It hurt.

'What's your name, oik?'

'Ku-Kevin.'

Mathew laughed, circling. 'You look like a Ku-Kevin. Hey Kevin, I don't want you wandering around our property ogling my sisters. That's bad. I think I need to teach you a lesson, right girls?'

He hoped they'd say no. But they didn't. They both answered in unison. Spiteful and loud. 'Yes, teach him a lesson.'

'Let's do what we do to little perverts at school. Bag and snag. What do you say?'

'Bag and snag,' the girls again, not so confident this time.

'What's—' Kevin began, but never finished as Mathew's foot thumped into his back and sent him sprawling face first into the grass. The larger boy straddled him, yanking his waistband, pulling down his trousers and pants to below his knees, revealing his bare bottom. They were all laughing, the girls loud and unsure. Laughing at him half-naked in the grass while his face burned with shame. Across the fields, through his tears, he could see the church and the cemetery surrounding it. The dead would be his only witnesses to this assault. And his God, the one his mother made him worship, stayed dumb and blind to his predicament, heedless of his silent prayers for help.

'Shall I turn him over, girls?'

'No,' they squealed.

'Oh, but we have to. We need to snag a look at his jewels, don't we, oik?'

Kevin, face to the ground, hands tied behind his back, unable to resist as Mathew rolled him over. Kevin tried to bend his body, but Mathew had one knee on his chest and one on his thighs, exposing the younger boy to the world. He looked up through tear-stained eyes at the girls, who were looking down, laughing at him.

'Right, go on you two, go back up, I'll get rid of Kevin here. And say nothing to Mum, yeah? Don't need to make her worry.'

The girls ran away, squealing with laughter. Kevin wanted the world to open up and swallow him.

'Now, it's just you and me, Kev,' said Mathew. 'Let's turn you back over on to your front, shall we?'

Kevin cooperated. Glad of covering himself. But Mathew didn't get up. He sat on Kevin's thighs, one hand on his back. At first, Kevin didn't know what the metallic jangling noise was. But then he realised it was a belt being unbuckled. At first, he thought he was going to be beaten. Twice in his life his father removed his belt for the exact same purpose. But that wasn't why Mathew Turner now loosened his trousers.

Up until the older boy put his knee between his thighs to open them, Kevin had no idea what was happening. But a minute later, he knew. The pain was excruciating. Mathew's breath on his neck, his teeth in his shoulder. He felt it all again now as if it had happened yesterday. The weight of the larger boy, the acceleration. When it was over, Mathew got up, undid the rope and walked away with one last sentence.

'Tell anyone and I'll tell them you took your trousers off in front of two little girls. They'll send you away to pervert school. Don't let me see you around here again, Kevin. You know what will happen if I do.'

A car horn from the road not forty yards away brought Starkey back to the present, nausea from the sickening memory making him breathe through his mouth to control it. He wiped sweat from his face and tried to slow his breathing, staring at the rutted lane, remembering the way rain would fill the deep gouges in the earth for months from October through to May. The pungent smell of sprayed manure from the farms. Remembering the years he'd spent jumping over these puddles and never quite managing to keep his shoes clean so that he'd had to clean and polish them night after long winter's night. How many of those nights had he spent dreaming of getting away, of becoming someone other than the humiliated little boy? He'd lost count, and yet, each one had seemed an eternity.

He'd moved out of Pux Cottage at eighteen and never moved back. Despite the proximity of traffic just yards from the front door, he'd been incredibly isolated in this place, and the incident with the Turners had made him frightened of being out in the fields alone.

He'd watched the cars and buses and lorries from his bedroom longingly, wondering about them, wondered why no one ever stopped. If anyone ever bought the place, it would be to knock it down and perhaps fashion a better entrance, a safer way in and out. But Dunroamin was invisible to the hundreds and thousands of drivers and passengers who drove past and barely caught a glimpse of the grey, drab building behind the overgrown hedge.

Years later, when he became a special constable stationed in Clevedon, he'd seen the terrible things people did to each other for the most banal of reasons, and for the most venal. But he'd been interested in the work. Preoccupied, some might say. He'd *studied* it. Watched the TV documentaries, read the books. Knew more about the psychology of the idiots who stole and hurt and abused other people than most of his colleagues. He knew, too, how most of the time there was no planning in any crime. Miscreants bumbled into it and the police simply stumbled around as well, depending upon the fact that the average criminal was a fool and would make mistakes they would pick up on.

Starkey got out of the car and walked towards the building where his life had begun. Across the patch of rutted ground in front with the fields and hedgerows beyond that had shaped him into the adult that he was. Someone brighter than he appeared. Someone who knew about police work and what the review team in the Rosie Dawson case must be going through, searching for a trail that had long since died.

He hadn't lied to them. He had seen the vehicle that Rosie's abductor had used on the day. Despite that, despite searches and enquiries, they hadn't been able to find it.

But now, on this summer's day nine years later, Special Constable Starkey knew exactly where it was.

CHAPTER THIRTY-SIX

Anna waited outside the entrance for Hawley while he said his goodbyes, trying to beat down her disappointment over not finding anything concrete in the visit. Yes, she was wiser as to the practicalities of how information was gathered and stored and the need for patient confidentiality. And of how fragile that was in such an immense organisation as the NHS. But nothing she'd seen there brought her any closer to knowing what happened to Rosie. Nor had it bought her any respite from the sleep-depriving anxiety of knowing that if she was right, then Blair Smeaton might well, at that very moment, be suffering the same fate as Rosie had suffered. Was Blair going to end up a pile of bones in a plastic bag?

Anna squeezed her eyes shut in an attempt at banishing her thoughts but all that did was send them off in another direction.

As a schoolgirl, she'd watched an enthusiastic science teacher set up an experiment to simulate a cockroach's severed leg with DIY batteries made of a slice of potato between aluminium and copper sheets. The cockroach, the teacher assured the class, would grow a new leg within four months. Sure enough, the tiny voltage produced by the potato batteries caused the cockroach's severed leg to jerk. She remembered how it had polarised her classmates. Some, the usual assembly-fainting crowd, were more concerned for the welfare of the cockroach. Others, full of blasé bravado, wondered out loud if the same thing might work with a rat's leg, or even a human's. Only a handful saw beyond to the incredible eighteenth-century leap in neuroscience the demonstration illustrated.

She'd come here with Hawley to see if there was any electricity left that might jerk the cockroach's leg. She'd hoped there'd be a spark or a bolt that might have brought Rosie's case to life. Pointed her in the direction of what had happened to Jade and Katelyn. Some inkling as to who might still have Blair Smeaton. But there'd been nothing; it remained dead and inanimate. Still cold.

She checked her phone. Nothing from Holder or Khosa other than to confirm Woakes was at work and wading through the paperwork Trisha had furnished. Holder didn't comment on whether or not Woakes was happy about that and Anna surprised herself by not caring. She didn't consider herself vindictive but knew Woakes would be seething. Try as she might, she could find no empathy for him. She had no idea what he wanted and what he was trying to achieve. What she did know was that he had no place on her team. Besides, she was too caught up in her own thoughts and they were sucking all the energy out of her.

Hawley emerged after ten minutes and they walked back to the car together and got in. 'So?' he asked, cutting to the chase. 'Any use?'

'Maybe.'

Something in her tone made him frown. 'At least you now know I was telling the truth, right?'

She didn't answer him directly. She pulled out into traffic and pointed the car back towards the south, weaving through the town towards the motorway. After a while, she asked, 'How about you? Did you find it useful?'

'Cathartic, you mean?' He nodded. 'Yes. Surprisingly, yes. Much more than I expected it to be. Seeing Coleen helped.'

'I'm glad.'

'But it's not why we came here, is it?'

'No. Sometimes it's best to see.'

'Me, you mean?'

Anna shook her head and accelerated through some traffic lights they'd been stalled at. 'We, or at least I, look for unusual things in these cases. Something small that goes unnoticed.'

Hawley sighed. 'Perhaps I've been fooling myself. Perhaps there isn't a link. Is it possible that what happened to Rosie could have been, I don't know, spontaneous? Someone spotting her in the park in Clevedon and acting there and then?'

'No, it wasn't spontaneous. It was too well organised. He'd seen her and targeted her.'

'How do you begin to try and find someone like that?'

'You begin with the small things. Like her visit to you. Her contact with you made you a suspect. A sad reflection on today's society maybe, but still a suspect. And it made you think all this through.'

'But has it been useful, my thinking it through?'

Anna shrugged.

Hawley blew out air and shook his head. 'What a mess, eh? And all because we'd used a different room.'

'What do you mean?'

'I mean that if we'd had our usual examination room available when Rosie walked through the door, none of this would have happened. The eye room had a different kind of desk. U-shaped. It meant the slit lamp was fixed in position. Rosie would not have been able to physically climb up on me. Sod's Law the service engineer chose that day to come.'

Anna threw him a glance and saw him react to whatever expression was in her own face. He looked quizzical, alarmed and genuinely ignorant. He hadn't realised the significance of what he'd said. Hadn't felt the earth shift on its axis.

But Anna had.

A tingle, a static burst, flickered in her head. This was what was bothering her. Something small that goes unnoticed. Not Rosie stolen from her grandmother's arms, not even the prospect of Blair's bones in a plastic bag. What bothered her was something exactly like *this*.

She felt the cockroach's leg quiver and jump as the tingling charge rippled over her skin, electrifying her thoughts, solidifying them into a concrete idea that finally slotted home.

What a fool she'd been. They'd all been. Shaw's voice was instantly in her head.

'Abbie had a hearing aid, like Blair. She was always breaking the bastard thing, too.'

Shaw, seeing beyond the terror of Blair's expression to the truth that they'd all ignored.

She picked up her work phone and speed-dialled Khosa.

'Ma'am?'

'Ryia, I need you to contact the FLO in the Blair Smeaton case. In the image we have of her, the first one of her in the hole, she's wearing a hearing aid.'

'OK...' Khosa sounded confused.

'In the image, it's been repaired. Ask the FLO if it was broken before she was taken.'

'Yes, ma'am.'

'Do it now, Ryia, and ring me back right away.'

Khosa rang off.

Hawley was looking at her, waiting for her to say something. 'You know something, don't you?'

But she didn't answer him. Not yet. She drove, her mind spinning, willing the phone to ring. After four long minutes, it finally did.

'Ryia?'

'Ma'am, Blair's mother has seen the photograph. The FLO said it nearly broke her. But she did comment on the hearing aid. It hadn't looked like that before, with the black tape. She said it must have broken and been repaired. Blair, or someone, must have fixed it.'

Fixed it.

The tingle she'd felt moments before became an electric charge. The cockroach's leg began jerking madly.

'Ma'am?' Khosa's voice on the phone again, breaking the silence, but triggering a memory in Anna of other things the DC had said in the pub the previous evening. What was it?

'But if it was all planned, how could he possibly know this information about the victims unless he knew the families?'

Anna breathed out slowly, trying to remember something else, something Hawley had said. She turned to him.

'When you showed me the cuttings the first time, you said something. Why the original investigators kept coming back to you.'

Hawley frowned and shook his head.

'Think, Ben. It's important.'

'Erm… they asked me how many other little girls I'd invited onto my lap in the clinic.'

'No,' Anna said. 'Not that, something else.'

Hawley shrugged. 'You mean me knowing all about Rosie from the notes? They kept on about it. Like Woakes did.'

The cockroach's leg spasmed.

'Ma'am?' Khosa's voice again, small from the speaker. 'Is there something we should know?'

'Stay ready, Ryia. You and Justin. Do not put down your phone.' Anna killed the call and accelerated to a roundabout with a Travelodge and a KFC. Hawley braced against the dash as she took the curve, doubling back at full speed.

'Have I missed something?' he said as she emerged back onto the dual carriageway, back towards Cheltenham and the hospital at speed.

'Not only you. We all have. Every single one of us.'

CHAPTER THIRTY-SEVEN

Starkey stood in the yard at Pux cottage glancing at the adjacent barn. He walked towards it. Through the gap between the padlocked steel doors of the barn he could see two vehicles. One a large horse transporter, one a van covered in tarpaulin. The cover had slipped a bit, revealing a white Vauxhall Combo. Before turning away he put on a policeman's hat. His old hat from his time on the force. He'd kept it because you never knew when it might come in handy. He walked across to the cottage and unlocked the front door, walked quietly into the house and closed the door behind him.

As soon as he pulled back the bolt securing the basement door the smell hit him. Something scurried away below.

'Blair? Are you there. Are you alright, Blair?'

No answer.

The smell was coming from the bucket. Starkey took it out, poured it into the toilet and flushed it. Went back to the basement.

'Time we left here now, Blair. Time to go,' he said softly.

'No,' she said from the well hole.

Starkey walked across and looked down at her. She was clean. Had looked after herself. 'You need to come out from there, Blair.'

'No. What do you want?'

'I've come to get you. To take you home.'

Blair shook her head.

'Back to your mum and your sister.'

Tears sprang to Blair's eyes and her face crumpled. 'You're lying. You're not a bobby. You're not taking me home.'

'Of course, I am.'

Blair shook her head. 'I don't believe you.'

'Don't you want to go home?'

'Yes.'

'Then it's OK, it's safe. But you need to come out.'

'Bring Kirsty. Then I'll know you're telling the truth.'

'I can't do that, Blair.'

'Then I'm not coming out!'

CHAPTER THIRTY-EIGHT

Anna pulled in to the hospital car park and got out. Hawley followed. She barely noticed.

She hurried back through the entrance, flashed her warrant card at reception and this time was let in without needing the administrator. Coleen Bridges was pushing a cart laden with a dozen or more sealed and packaged items. Anna stopped her.

'I thought you'd gone.'

'I had a fresh thought. I see you're busy, but this is urgent. Five minutes, I promise.'

'Right,' Coleen said.

'I want to go back to the room where Rosie was seen.'

Coleen obliged and they stood once more in the room with the couch.

'But you told me this is not where you would have normally seen her?'

Hawley replied from behind her. 'No, the room next door has, or had, black-out blinds for eye exams. For looking at the back of the eye. But we didn't need that here with Rosie.'

'Because you were examining the front of her eye and the equipment was mobile?'

'That's correct, the slit lamp is on a wheeled adjustable table.'

'But normally you wouldn't move it?'

Coleen shook her head. 'The ophthalmologists go spare. They say rattling it around can dislodge mirrors and lenses.'

'And that day you had to move it because of maintenance?'

'Yes.' Coleen pointed to the wall unit. 'We have people in to service all the bits of equipment we have. That day it was the Rowsys guy. I know because when I went in to put the light on for Rosie to be seen, he had the wall unit in bits on the desk. Has to be done, of course.'

Anna felt the tingle surge.

'He?'

'Sorry?'

'You said, "He had the wall unit in bits."'

'Yes. He's been coming for years and he's as good as gold. Never a bother. Gets on with it and he's quick. But in a unit like this there's never a good time. So, we have to work around him otherwise he'd never finish,' Coleen said brightly, but then her expression became puzzled as she saw the look Anna gave her.

'Do you have a name?'

'Rowsys. That's the com—'

'The man. The one that's as good as gold.'

'Ooh, uh, he was here a few months ago. Big chap. Could do with losing a few pounds. We even offered to take his blood pressure last time. I'm sure we have his card somewhere.'

Anna nodded, her brain fizzing. She forced herself to be calm. 'Can you find it?'

'Sure.' Coleen smiled and walked away.

Anna didn't look at Hawley but she sensed his eyes upon her. Coleen came back with a card. Anna took it, placed it on a desk. She read the name and felt the world tilt once again.

Rowsys-uk
Specialists in on-site calibration and repairs.
Systems engineer: Kevin Starkey

CHAPTER THIRTY-NINE

In the basement of Pux Cottage, Starkey turned away from Blair Smeaton and came back with a bucket. She looked up at him, her eyes huge with fear. She sucked in a great gasp of air, her body quivering, terror turning her eyes into globes of pure fear. Starkey looked down at what was in the bottom and said, 'Eels like well holes, too.'

Blair wailed.

Starkey upended the bucket into the hole. Blair screamed and leaped upwards reflexively as the eels writhed and flexed at her feet, all thoughts of hiding now gone. Starkey grabbed her by the shoulders and had her out in three seconds. Put tape over her mouth and her hands tied within a minute. Her struggles were futile. Five minutes later, he was driving back out onto the main road, music turned up loud in the car so that he didn't have to listen to her moving about in the boot. She'd exhaust herself soon and settle down.

He had a CD in the player. Hits of the 1980s. Frankie Goes to Hollywood kicked in. 'Relax'. Starkey smiled. Yeah that's what he should do: relax. But he couldn't. A crackling inferno of anticipation was raging inside him as he pointed the car north on the motorway. He'd only truly begin to relax when he was over the bridge. He'd keep the music on loud as he paid the toll just in case Blair decided to make some extra noise. Something gnawed at him. A hunger.

Only this hunger, he knew, could not be assuaged by food.

This was a different type of hunger altogether.

His palms were sweating. He half-turned, checking the contents of the back seat. The big, camouflaged backpack was there and he knew he'd put the ropes inside it.

Everything he needed.

Good. Everything was good.

He'd never told anyone about the crime perpetrated upon him by the Turners.

He preferred, instead, to scream it into the faces of his terrified victims as they trembled before him.

Madness' 'Baggy Trousers' began. Starkey knew all the words. He started to sing.

CHAPTER FORTY

Anna's hands were shaking as she took out her phone.

Kevin Starkey. The witness she'd spoken to a few days ago. The special constable who'd seen the red van. Whose useful statement had given them a direction of travel. A direction of travel that deliberately sent the whole investigation the wrong way.

Kevin Starkey. An engineer. A fixer.

Forcing her hand to be as steady as possible, she photographed the card back and front. When she looked back up she was all smiles. 'Right, thanks Coleen, we'll let you get back to work.'

'Don't be a stranger,' she said to Hawley.

He nodded and smiled.

But Anna was already striding out of reception, phone to her ear, and Hawley had to hurry to catch up.

'Do you think—'

She held up her hand to silence him.

'Trisha, I'm sending through a business card for a Kevin Starkey who works for a company called Rowsys... Yes, I know. The same Starkey... Drop everything else and find out from them what he does and where he works. Tell Justin and Ryia I want as much information as I can get about Starkey. I'm on the way back but this is a priority. I want all this yesterday.'

Once again, they got into the car and Anna drove off. She spoke as she drove, not looking directly at Hawley.

'The answer to your question is that this man is known to us. He came forward as a witness. He told us he'd seen a red van at a junction leading to the motorway in Clevedon the afternoon Rosie went missing. Other witnesses said they thought the van had white rear doors.'

Anna's jaw clenched, not wanting to think about the wasted man hours his simple statement and colour change had caused.

Edinburgh's number was in her phone book and she called it up now.

Danaher answered after six long rings.

'Julie, it's DI Gwynne, Avon and Somerset.'

'Hello ma'am. Please tell me you've got some more news for us?'

'You are going to be getting calls from my team over the next half hour. We have a suspect in the frame. A Kevin Starkey. He visits hospitals, repairs equipment. Can you find out which hospitals Blair has been seen at over the last year or so?'

'Of course.'

'My lot are already on the case. They'll liaise. Stay near your phone.'

Hawley was looking at her, blinking, assimilating.

She put him out of his misery. 'We believed him because he was a special constable, one of us. He was part of the crew that searched for Rosie when she was first abducted. He gave up because of his other job. A job servicing instruments and small bits of equipment that might take him to various parts of the country. Blair's hearing aid might have been damaged in the abduction. Someone had to have repaired it. Someone who knew what he was doing. Someone who could watch unobserved, pick a victim, wait for an opportunity to pick up hospital notes that contained all sorts of information.'

How many more hospitals did Starkey visit? Every single one on Hawley's victim list, she'd be willing to bet. And others? How many others where he watched and planned in plain sight?

Hawley sat back as if he'd collapsed, his face bearing a pained expression. Anna could only guess what he must be thinking.

Horror? Relief possibly. Woakes, she knew, would undoubtedly have now tried to winkle out some sort of link between Hawley and Starkey but she knew there would be none. Starkey saw Rosie in Cheltenham's A and E, had accessed her notes while the department ignored him, found out she lived in Clevedon. Lived near him. That might well have been the trigger. He'd started close to home, where he knew the lay of the land, the roads, the nooks and crannies. But then he'd found a way of going wide.

'You want to catch the Pogo wannabe? Work out how he chooses which flowers to pick.'

The calls started coming in before they reached the motorway.

CHAPTER FORTY-ONE

Starkey took the old crossing over the river on the M48. It always pissed him off to pay for the privilege of heading west. There was talk of scrapping the tolls soon. Too late for him. He'd probably paid for at least one of the steel suspension cables by now.

He clutched the steering wheel and let his mind wander along paths no normal people would ever stray down. Anticipation flickered along his spine. You could already use cryptocurrency to pay for flights. After this, he'd take a holiday. He'd already been a couple of times. Knew exactly where he wanted to go, even though the flights were expensive.

Thailand was too hot. Indonesia was by far the best place for now. For what he wanted. Easier pickings on the beaches there. Start in Bali and move on. He had safe addresses, knew from the forums the best spots. Half the population still earned less than $4 a day. What you would get for $10 was simply mind-blowing in the poverty-stricken towns and villages.

Starkey's whole body trembled at the thought of it. But first there was Blair.

He paid the toll, music on loud, nodding at the toll booth operator who took the exact money and opened the barrier. It didn't feel like a different country, not yet. But it was. The river stretched beneath him like a sleeping snake, its surface reflecting the sun in a rippling dazzle before he exited. He came off the M48 and headed north on the A466 towards St Arvans and the Devauden Road running through the Chepstow Park Wood. He pulled in to a spot about halfway along, avoiding the more obvious parking spaces, and got out.

A few miles to the north and east was Tintern with its twelfth-century abbey drawing tourists in like a honeypot. To the east of the abbey on a hill stood the ruined Church of St Mary the Virgin. He'd found several interesting gravestones hidden in the overgrown vegetation there. But more enlightening was the conversation he'd had with a man whose interests, though similar to his, were more inclined towards architecture than the dead. On holiday from Yorkshire, the man, who never introduced himself, bored Starkey with the history of the church and the others nearby. But in amongst the tedious monologue was a snippet that had lodged firmly in Starkey's consciousness.

'I've only today left and it's going to rain this afternoon. I'll not get over to Devauden and St Wystone's. Now that's one I'd like to see. Not easy to find, mind you, what's left of it. I expect you'd find some interesting stones there as well.'

Starkey'd gone the following week. And it had been very difficult to find. A tiny chapel, hidden at the bottom of a valley next to a stream, abandoned and isolated, its graveyard virtually unrecognisable with the stones covered in ivy and hidden by coarse tussocks of grass. He'd spent the afternoon there, uncovering stones, reading dates as far back as the 1700s. But it was when he explored the tiny old building that late winter's day that his world slipped and slid, and everything changed.

Now, at the height of summer, the foliage off the main path was exultant. He had to lean forwards to cope with the weight of the heavy backpack. Occasionally, what was contained within shifted and wriggled. Then he'd wait until it settled and move on. Tall nettles lined the way. The average walker strolling through the thick and matted patches of head-high cow parsley would have no idea what lay beyond. Starkey was careful not to cut a swathe through the vegetation, parting it carefully instead as he pushed his way along, first climbing to a ridge and then descending along a narrow path under the huge trees that had been here for centuries. No road led to the chapel. Whatever might have been here before had long been reclaimed by the forest. An old wooden walkway, rotted and unsafe, indicated the path. But the wet and clay-filled bank had eroded the way, with bramble and fern and blackthorn providing a barrier. Starkey walked through it, feeling the tendrils catch and pull at his clothes, as if they were trying to hold him back from his task. His destiny.

As if.

On the other side of the 4 metres of overgrowth, the path reappeared. There beneath him, hunkering in a dell, stood the chapel, and beyond it a pond, fed by the streams that surged and hissed in the winter but that were little more than trickles now in June.

The path became easier and he picked his way across the uneven ground to the grey stone building and its graveyard beyond, its stones angled and tilted in a way that suggested the dead were desperately trying to push up and out. The walls of the building stood mottled with lichen, a padlocked metal gate across the porch barring entry. There was no view into the interior; the leaded windows caked with years of grime, the lowest lancets boarded with wood. A single diamond in the leaded panels in the southern elevation had been punched out. Someone as tall as Starkey could peer in, but there was nothing to see except an eerie gloom and nothing to smell except musty damp.

He stood for a moment in the shadow of the trees that covered this spot and stopped the sun from ever reaching the stones, listening for a stick cracking underfoot or the chatter of conversation that would indicate other walkers nearby. There was none. The breeze, so welcoming in the sunlight, carried cool air up from the stagnant pond water below, a sickly waft of decay on its breath.

Starkey walked behind the chapel to the north transept, the one closest to the bank. Now, in the summer, another wall of greenery stretched across, preventing the casual walker from circumnavigating the building. But in February, on his day of revelation, all that had died away to reveal what had once been a wall. Its stones, battered by the rain and wind over centuries, collapsed in a heap. Through the gap, which Starkey guessed must once have been a blockaded archway, he glimpsed another building. Smaller, square, still of the same stone. He'd been to enough graveyards to realise that this must be a sacristy or vestry, used to house sacred items, robes or records.

Again, Starkey was careful not to disturb the screen of vegetation too much, not wanting to reveal his presence. He removed gardening gloves from his strapped-on tool belt and teased an opening. Stepping over the tumbled wall, he walked to the east wall and a jumble of stones. Quickly, he removed them, piling them carefully a few feet away until the low access way he'd found that first day was revealed, guarded by a metal grid. He'd placed it there to repel the curious, if anyone had the gumption to remove the stones. So far, no one had.

He slid off the rucksack and put it down. The grill was not attached and he lifted it away easily. From his belt, he took a headlight and slid it onto his forehead before slowly manoeuvring backwards into the sacristy itself. Other than a thin square of light from the access way, inside was cold darkness. Four bare walls and stone floors, unadorned and stripped of all their glory. But this room, this abandoned room, held one secret Starkey had stumbled upon by accident. He shook his head. Being here was no accident. Fate had brought him here. Given him an opportunity to flourish.

He wished he'd known about this place that very first time. The dead and their bones thrilled him. A fitting place in which to maim and kill. Had he known about this place he would not have panicked and left Rosie's bones on the path near Charterhouse. His plan then was to hide her in a crypt. One that he was familiar with. One that was open to the public with its own ossuary behind a flimsy rail that would not have been difficult to remove. A fitting place for Rosie. He had murdered her at Pux Cottage, boiled her clean there too. But when he'd arrived at Charterhouse, workmen were renovating, and the path was unusually busy with a rambling club. They'd surprised him and he'd foolishly thrown her bones into the undergrowth and run. It might have been the end of it. The first and last.

But the pain of the laughter of the Turner girls never left him. And then he'd discovered St Wystone's. This was now his stage. Where he brought them to die. They'd go back to Pux Cottage as corpses. Ready for boiling. Then he'd bring the bones back again to St Wystone's. Cleaned and purified. Their final resting place.

All part of the great ritual.

There'd been snow on the ground the day of his first visit to the chapel, some twenty months after he'd taken Rosie Dawson. None of it lasted in the forest proper, but down in the wooded dell there was enough to stick to his boots and be transferred in, though he'd mashed it to a pulp during his exploration of the tiny room and it quickly liquefied to form a shallow puddle.

Starkey had been on the point of leaving when he noticed the puddle had formed a rivulet, as always following the path of least resistance, towards the south wall, where it disappeared into the space around a large square stone. Intrigued, he'd scraped away the dirt and dust to find that this square stone had no mortar around it. It was three weeks before he returned with tools to lift the flagstone away and find the answer to all his problems.

CHAPTER FORTY-TWO

Anna set her phone in a holder on the dash for the call.

'Trisha, talk to me.'

'Rowsys have three engineers that service the equipment they either sell or lease to hospitals. Kevin Starkey covers the west of the country as far up as Manchester. They have contracts in at least 100 hospitals with dozens of departments in each, apparently.'

'Ma'am,' Holder's voice this time, sounding grim. 'Rowsys have equipment in every hospital on the list Hawley gave us. They're all in Starkey's patch.'

'All except Blair Smeaton,' Anna said.

This time it was Khosa who pushed in, her tone deep and strained. 'Sometimes, when one engineer goes on holiday they cover for each other if there's a call out. Starkey had to go to Edinburgh last month and last week to deal with a problem at the infirmary there.'

Anna squeezed her eyes shut, but it was only momentary, enough to calm the tingling surge that rippled up her spine.

Holder said, 'He's meant to be at a hospital in Swindon today but rang them to say he was unwell.'

Anna nodded. 'We need to find him. Get over to his house. If he's there, bring him in. If he isn't, find out where he is.'

'Should we talk to Edinburgh, ma'am?' Justin asked.

'Danaher's expecting Trisha to call. But they're too far away. This is our patch.'

They all knew there was something left unsaid. Something huge.

It was Khosa who came out with it. 'Do you think he might still have Blair—'

But Anna cut her off. 'We assume he does. Trisha, is the super in?'

'At a meeting in Bath, ma'am.'

'Find him and get him to ring me.'

'Yes, ma'am.'

Static ticked over the line telling her it was still open. Frustration boiled over in Anna and she yelled, 'Why the hell are you still there?'

CHAPTER FORTY-THREE

In the Chepstow Wood, in a dank space on the ground floor of an abandoned room, Starkey retrieved the heavy rucksack, ignoring the muffled noises from within. He reached for the crowbar and slid the sharp end into the gap around a stone in the floor. It came away easily and he levered one edge onto the surrounding flagstones before sliding it across. The gap below exhaled cool, dead air into his face, like the breath of a spectre.

An aluminium ladder led down into a narrow tunnel, no longer than a few feet, leading back towards the chapel, and towards whatever sort of place of worship had been here long before Christians thought it wise to capitalise on a sacred spot. But Starkey was pretty sure it was the Christians who had built this crypt. He switched off his headlight, enjoying the darkness. A darkness so dense it became almost palpable; the quiet so complete, the only sound his own breathing.

He stood that way for a moment, savouring it, sucking it in. Then he flicked on his headlight and reached for the first of several battery-operated lamps he'd left here, quickly entering the crypt and lighting the remaining dozen LED lanterns as he went until he stood at its northern limit, under the transept of the chapel, and looked back.

Though he'd been to this place many times, with the room lit, it never failed to take his breath away, cause his pulse to quicken. Bones, disarticulated, piled in neat rows. Femurs and tibias and fibulas and humeri and serried ranks of ribs along the walls. At the centre were skulls, in a huge pyramid, some polished, some dark-stained, all with empty eye sockets silently acknowledging his presence. Far from being a Hollywood horror film set, Starkey saw it for what it was. A bone crypt. A monument for pilgrims and villagers to pray amongst their ancestors. He'd done his research, and the proximity to Tintern was probably no accident. Some of the dead here might have been plague victims, some soldiers from the wars between the Welsh and English, but all were forgotten now, much as this crypt had been after the reformation.

It didn't matter. This was a find. A real find. If he'd wanted to, he could have reported this forgotten ossuary to the authorities, be lauded and get his name in the papers. But it was the last thing that Starkey craved. In fact, Starkey's cravings, if they ever made the newspapers, would fill the front page.

He'd added to the bone count over the years. When he brought them back they'd be bleached and cleaned of the corrupting flesh that coated them. Pure once more. He mentally ticked off their names as he prepared. Jade, Katelyn, Lily, James, Freddie.

He was about to add one more.

CHAPTER FORTY-FOUR

Holder and Khosa were on their way to the car when they heard a shout behind them.

Holder turned back to see Woakes walking towards them.

'Hold on, hold on. Where are you two off to in such a hurry?'

'Boss wants us on something.'

'Oh yeah? Like what?'

'Sarge, we don't have the time to explain.'

'Really,' Woakes said, and began walking towards the parking spaces. 'You can fill me in on the way.'

Holder hesitated. Woakes fixed him with a challenging glare. 'As far as I know I'm a still a sergeant in this squad and your superior, am I not?'

Khosa and Holder exchanged pained glances. Both of them knew they had no time to argue the point, nor to ring Anna.

'Fuck,' cursed Holder under his breath. But he followed Woakes towards the car with Khosa in tow.

It was a fifteen-minute journey to Starkey's address on the outskirts of Clevedon. Khosa filled Woakes in as best they could. Holder drove, mouth zipped shut. Not that Woakes noticed; he was too busy listening, face shining, eyes alight, up for the chase.

'She's cocked this up,' he said when Khosa finished, his glee evident.

'What do you mean, sarge?' Khosa asked.

'Gwynne. She's cocked this up. It's obvious Starkey and Hawley are in it together. She's taken Hawley up to Cheltenham and shown

him her cards. He might have tipped this turd Starkey off for all
we know.'

'We don't know, though.' Holder shook his head.

Woakes hissed out air. 'Loyalty's one thing, Justin. Blind ignorance is something else altogether.'

Starkey's property was on the northern edge of Clevedon. Neat
lawn, swept drive, net curtains, the works. Holder rang the bell. No
one answered and there was no movement apparent from inside.

'I'll go around the back,' Khosa said and headed towards a
wooden door to the side of the garage.

'We need to get inside,' Holder said.

Woakes turned to him. 'We don't have a warrant.'

'No, but we can go in if we believe Starkey has committed a
serious offence. If we think he's on the property. If someone's life
is in danger.'

Woakes sneered. 'Do we? Think he's on the property, I mean? I
don't. I reckon he's done a bunk thanks to our precious DI.'

'You don't know that, sarge.'

'Don't I? Well you go ahead, Justin. Try and find an open
window. I'll go for a walk and pretend I didn't hear what you just sa—'

'Justin!' Khosa's urgent shout made both men run through the
side gate. 'Inside the shed. Look through the window. On the
back wall.'

Holder joined Khosa and cupped his hands around the glass.
Beneath the window was a bench, neat and clean, a range of small
tools arranged to one side. Holder let his eyes slide to the rear.
The back wall was an art gallery. Large squares of paper stuck up
with thumbtacks, and in the middle, one larger than the others.
A centrepiece.

'What the hell are those?' Holder stood back and Woakes took
his place.

'Paintings, drawings? Who knows.'

'They're weird,' Khosa said.

Holder disappeared for a minute. When he came back he held a small crowbar in his hand and went directly to the shed door.

Khosa looked anxious.

'Someone might be in there. We're justified.'

The padlock securing the door looked strong, but it was only held in place by a few screws and gave after Holder leaned his weight into it. Inside, the place smelled musty with a hint of linseed oil and wax. Holder walked over to the full-length drawing and studied it. The paper must have been 4 feet long and 2 wide, covered with red wax, depicting an ornate arrangement of flowers and leaves arching over a skull with two long femurs crossed beneath it and a hand with its index finger pointing upwards, the carved letters standing out as white.

Hetty Sara Davies

Spinster of this parish.
Servant of the Church.
Daughter of Eisiah and Mary

Nov. 20 1856 – June 18 1891

'What's this, a bloody pirate?' Woakes said

'No. I know what this is,' Khosa said. 'It's a gravestone.'

'Gravestone?' Woakes said. He suddenly sounded a lot more interested

Holder quickly looked around the little room. It looked solid, an MDF floor. No trapdoor.

'What if she's in the house?' Holder said.

'Then we go in,' Woakes said.

'Shouldn't you run that past the boss?'

'Look around you, Justin. I am the fucking boss.'

'Don't we need a warrant, sarge?' Khosa asked.

'Not when we're saving life and limb,' Holder answered her.

'Exactly,' Woakes said, his eyes widening. It was obvious to both DCs that Woakes' confidence had increased with what had been found in the shed. He was a dog with a bone now. 'There could be a hostage in there. Sod protocol.'

'But shouldn't we tell DI Gw—'

Woakes rounded on Khosa and leaned in close, his mouth hard and ugly. 'We don't tell her anything. We go in and search for evidence of an abduction. Got it?'

In the end, Holder went in through a window in the back bedroom. He found a ladder, waved at a curious neighbour who looked about ready to ring a burglary in until Khosa flashed her warrant card, reached in through the gap, lifted the stay and climbed in. Two beds in the room, posters on the walls. A teenagers' room. He called out as he moved swiftly down the stairs and into the kitchen where he opened the back door to let the others in.

They all wore blue gloves.

Inside, the kitchen was clean and tidy. Porridge and Corn Flakes in the cupboard. Half a carton of milk in the fridge next to the bacon, eggs, butter and the remains of a fish pie. A magnet in the shape of a cartoon cow held a bundle of papers, bills mainly, on the door of the fridge.

Khosa walked through to the living room, calling out a name. 'Mr Starkey, it's the police. Mr Starkey?'

There was no reply. Holder stayed downstairs; Khosa and Woakes took the upstairs. On a shelf in the living room, under photographs of two teenage boys were a collection of books and magazines. Old copies of *Homes & Gardens* and on one shelf some older books, *Abandoned Castles (Forgotten Heritage series), Relics of Britain.* One on railways. Nothing in the slightest bit incriminating.

Khosa rejoined Holder in the living room.

'Nothing.' She shook her head.

Woakes had wandered back out into the garden and was looking in the shed.

Holder wasn't sure what Woakes was trying to prove. He should have been taking charge. Instead, though not obviously obstructive, he wasn't exactly putting his back into things, either.

'What's the matter with him? Khosa asked.

'Arrest envy is my guess.'

'Pathetic,' Khosa said and then sighed. 'Maybe he's right. Maybe Hawley did tip Starkey off.'

Holder shook his head. 'No. The boss would never have let that happen.'

'So, what exactly are we looking for here? A hidden panel in the wall? A trapdoor?'

'I don't know.' Holder walked out of the living room and scanned the kitchen again. Khosa followed and reached for the cow magnet on the fridge door. She spread the half-dozen or so scraps of paper it had held on the worktop. Two were garage fuel bills, one a Tesco shopping list. The other three were all invoices from a builder's merchant. Sand, cement, chippings and wood. All bought over the summer. Holder stood next to her, intrigued.

'I haven't seen any sign of any building work, have you?' Khosa said.

Holder shook his head but then went very still, frowning. 'That's because he's not building anything here. Look at the delivery address.'

Khosa peered. 'Pux Cottage, Wird Lane. There's even a post-code.'

Holder said, 'You talked to his employer. Where did they say he should be today, Swindon?'

'Yeah, at the Western Hospital, but Trisha rang them and there's been no sign.'

'Maybe he's at this Pux Cottage?'

Khosa was already punching the postcode into her phone. 'Fifteen minutes by car.'

'You go,' Holder said.

'Go where?' Woakes was standing inside the back door, listening.

'There's a second address, sarge. Somewhere he's been doing building work.'

'Then what are we waiting for?'

Khosa threw Holder a glance, but all he did was shrug.

When they'd gone, Holder went back to the shed and studied the rubbings. There were more in a trunk under some books. Dozens and dozens of them. Some very plain, others intricate and elaborate.

'You have been a busy boy,' whispered Holder.

Twenty-two minutes after she'd left, Khosa rang. Immediately he pressed accept; Holder knew instantly they'd found something.

'Justin? This is it. The bloody jackpot! It's a horror film set. A white van and a horse transporter in the barn. And there's a cellar room. A bloody cellar room where he kept them. And it's the one, Justin. It's the one in Rosie's and Blair's images.' Khosa's voice was high and breathless.

Holder heard doors slamming, crashes and bangs. 'What the hell is going on?'

'Starkey's not here. There's no one here. The house is empty. But Woakes has lost it. He's gone ballistic, tearing the place apart.'

'That's a crime scene, for Christ's sake.'

'I've called it in. There are uniforms and Forensics on the way. But Woakes is threatening to come back and go through the house again.'

'Shit. No. There might be more evidence here. He sounds out of control.'

'What can I do? He's the bloody sergeant.'

'You come. Get in the car and leave him there.'

'But—'

'Leave him, Ryia. Get out of there now.'

Four long seconds of silence followed before Khosa said, 'OK. I'm on my way.'

Holder killed the call. They'd found their monster, but where was he? Where would Starkey have gone?

CHAPTER FORTY-FIVE

Anna took Holder's call when they were ten miles from the M4 junction on the way back to Bristol. They'd lost half an hour at least in the never-ending road works and were crawling along in single lane traffic once again.

'What's happening, Justin?'

'I'm at Starkey's house in Clevedon, ma'am. Nothing here, but you were right. Starkey's our man. He has a cottage out towards Congresbury, too. Ryia's there and there's a soundproofed cellar with evidence of recent occupation.'

Holder's words seemed to make the world zoom out of focus before snapping back again. Anna's foot pressed down on the accelerator unbidden and she eased off, trying to compose herself and concentrate. 'Empty?'

'Yes, ma'am. We missed him.' Anna heard the despondency in Holder's voice.

'What aren't you telling me, Justin?'

'Dave Woakes, ma'am. He insisted on muscling in. I had no choice.'

'Shit. Is he with you now?'

'No ma'am, he's at Starkey's cottage.'

'OK, let him stay there. You've mobilised CSI?'

'Yes, ma'am.'

There was hesitation in Holder's voice.

'What, Justin?'

'Sergeant Woakes. He thinks that Hawley warned Starkey.'

Anna looked across at Hawley. He looked back at her, shaking his head. 'Rubbish. I've been with him all day,' Anna said. 'Woakes is wrong. Forget it, Justin. Come on, I need you snappy. Is there anything there that might indicate to us where Starkey has gone?'

'He's into graveyards, ma'am.'

'What?'

'He has a shed full of gravestone rubbings. Most of them have skulls and bones. It's weird.'

'*Memento mori*,' Anna said.

'Yeah, exactly what Trisha said when she looked them up.'

'That's not much use.'

'No, ma'am. But there was a bone, too. In a drawer. I think it's human.'

'*Shit.* OK, so Rowsys think he's off sick?'

'Yes, ma'am."

'Right. Get on to them. Tell them to text Starkey on his work phone, if he has one. Not phone him, text him. Some pretext. Something about where he was the day before. Another equipment malfunction. See if he responds. Do it now, Justin.'

Anna kept driving, not looking at Hawley. Aware only that her passenger was sitting tense and rigid in his seat and knew she was feeling much the same way.

CHAPTER FORTY-SIX

Starkey uncovered the small pile of kit he'd stored from previous visits. Clear plastic sheeting, a couple of cheap duvets, plastic garden ties, box cutters and rope. All in preparation for what was to come. The excitement churned inside him.

Almost there. With trembling hands, he unfolded the sheeting and began cutting it to size to line the floor.

So much easier for cleaning up.

He laid out the duvet, placed the ties and rope near the entrance to the chamber, checked the box of AA batteries for the lights.

He took his time, savouring it all. Though it was cool in the crypt, he was sweating, a foetid body odour leaking out from his armpits that he knew had the tinge of lust about it. He stood, the stacked bones almost at hip level, and fetched some water. He drank thirstily, leaning with one hand against the wall, desperately trying to distract himself from the anticipation coursing through his veins. He drank the whole bottle and waited for the moment to subside. He'd have to watch that, control the urges, otherwise…

Finally, satisfied, he retraced his steps up and out of the crypt to suck in some fresh air.

Soon there would be more bones to add to the hallowed pile.

Small bones.

Exhilaration gushed up from deep in his gut, transporting him from this mundane world to the one he dreamed of. The one where he was king, where no one laughed at his obscene nakedness anymore. Where he could inflict the humiliations he'd suffered onto someone else.

The buzz of his phone in his pocket threw him. Just the one vibration. A text.

He fished it out and read the message from Sheryl, the service coordinator.

Can you contact the Musgrove Park Hospital haematology dept ASAP? Calibration needed on two refrigerators.

Starkey sighed. There was no peace. He texted back.

Will do.

But not yet. Now he had other things to occupy him.

CHAPTER FORTY-SEVEN

Holder rang back exactly seven minutes after she'd issued instructions.

'He's responded, ma'am.'

Anna squeezed her eyes shut and blew out air. 'Right, it means he's still got his phone on. Ring the super. He'll authorise contacting the phone network's SPOC team. Let's find out where Starkey really is.'

Hawley looked confused.

'Single point of contact,' said Anna by way of explanation. 'It's a designated team that works with the service providers to obtain live data on the location of a phone. The providers have staff who can respond to this sort of thing where sensitive enquiries for high-risk cases are concerned. They can tell us which towers and masts he's connected to. But it all comes at a cost. That's why we need it signed off.'

Traffic was stop start. She watched a huge transporter half a mile away easing around a bend. A brake light blinked off in front of her. She drove on thirty yards and then came to another exasperating halt.

Ten minutes later, Holder came back on the line again.

'Ma'am, we have him located in the Chepstow Park Wood area.'

'Chepstow?' Anna glanced to her right at the flat farmland leading towards the estuary. Beyond that was the Welsh border. Chepstow was only twelve miles from where she was now.

'Send me the location. I can be on the M48 in five minutes if these sodding roadworks ever come to an end. Chepstow in twenty. Have you any idea where he is exactly?'

'We're working on it.'

'Contact Gwent Police. Let them know what's happening. What's Starkey driving?'

'Black Renault Megane, ma'am. I'll text you the number plate.'

When he'd rung off, Hawley spoke.

'This Starkey, do you think he killed Rosie?'

'I don't know for sure, but probably, yes.'

Hawley nodded.

'I can drop you off at the services,' Anna said.

Hawley seemed not to hear. 'I've wondered a lot about what I would do if I ever met the bloke who did all this. Partly because of what it did to me. But he's done a lot worse to those kids, hasn't he?'

'Yes.'

Hawley's face hardened. 'Don't waste any time dropping me off.'

Anna didn't argue. He was right. There was no time to waste. At last three lanes opened up and she manoeuvred out to overtake the slower traffic.

It took her eighteen minutes to get to St Arvans. It took her another ten criss-crossing the access roads until, with Hawley's help, they found the Megane parked discreetly off the road in one of the half-hidden car parks. She parked next to it and called Holder.

'I've found the car. It's a forestry car park a mile along the Devauden Road and half a mile in. I'll send you a pin.'

'I'll do it,' said Hawley. 'What's Holder's number?'

Anna put Holder on speaker and he read off his number.

'So, what now, Justin? He could be anywhere.'

'I know, ma'am. Ryia's got some ideas and we're waiting for Trisha to get back to us. We've got some help coming from Gwent, too. They're getting their chopper up.'

'Good,' Anna said. 'But I'm not going to sit here like a lemon. If he's here, I want to find him. Get back to me as soon as you hear anything.' Anna got out of the car and walked around Starkey's

Renault, looking in through the windows. It was clean. Cleaner than any of her cars had ever been. Hawley got out too, looking around.

'Have you ever been here before?' Anna asked.

'Never.'

It was a Friday, a warm summer's early afternoon. The forest looked cool and inviting. But Anna shivered at the thought of what might be going on somewhere in amongst all this cover, under these silently watching trees. Frustration gnawed at her.

'Come on, Trisha, come on,' she muttered. When her phone rang twenty seconds later, it came as no surprise. She knew there was no telepathic link between her and the analyst sitting back in their office in Portishead. It merely felt that way sometimes.

'Speak to me, Trisha.'

'Ryia sent me some details of a gravestone, ma'am.'

'She did?' A hundred questions formed in Anna's head.

'Yes, ma'am. From the birth and death date, I've been able to find some burial records. It shows that this grave is in St Wystone's. It's in the Chepstow Woods, ma'am. I'm sending you a map and coordinates now.'

'Trisha, you're amazing.'

'Be careful, ma'am.'

Anna waited while a PDF downloaded. She opened it onto a section of OS map. It took her a while to find the car park and Devauden Road. Hawley stood back, watching.

'St Wystone's chapel,' she said, nodding in the direction of the surrounding forest. 'In there. You stay here, tell whoever comes where I've gone.'

'Can you read maps?'

'Not my strongest point,' Anna confessed. She kept looking towards the great sprawl of hillside and greenery, her sense of urgency now diamond-tipped.

'Can I?' He held out his hand.

She thrust her phone towards him. He opened his up and scrolled to the compass, turning in a full circle before facing the corner of the parking area where a trail disappeared into the foliage. 'It's east and then north.' He pointed towards the trail head. 'That's our best bet.'

'Our best bet?'

'This place is a rat's nest. Best to navigate by GPS. From your map, it doesn't look like there's an established trail.'

'No. You stay here. We don't know what Starkey's capable of.'

'What if he has Blair?'

His words caught her off guard. 'What if he does?'

'Then you might need me. I'm a medic, don't forget.'

She wanted to object but his words struck home. He was right. God knew what was waiting for them along this trail, and Hawley's skills might well be needed. She hurried back to her car, popped the boot and took out a canister of PAVA spray, a telescopic baton and cuffs, and stuffed them into a small rucksack before slinging it over her shoulders. She turned back to Hawley.

'Right, let's go. Gwent Police are sending some air support as well as bodies on the ground. But if this guy does have Blair and she's alive, I wouldn't be able to live with myself if we didn't move now.'

CHAPTER FORTY-EIGHT

Anna took the lead. Though the foliage surrounding them afforded little or no view of their surroundings, it did appear that someone had been there before them. The nettles and ferns were not broken, but they leaned forwards, pushed there by something large that had passed that way. Twice Hawley called her back and made her backtrack, unhappy with the way she'd taken. They talked little, Anna preferring to listen for any extraneous sounds while Hawley concentrated, issuing instructions only where a turn was needed. The stillness struck her as almost supernatural. As if they'd walked into a place that was out of normal time and untouched by the elements. She wasn't dressed for hiking; she'd dressed for visiting a Cheltenham hospital. Sweat made her white shirt cling to her back under her backpack, and her shoes were already pinching.

After twenty-five minutes along a winding trail, they emerged into a sunken track with the remnants of old walls dripping with moss either side. Anna waited for Hawley, who pointed to the map.

'I think we're here,' he whispered. 'The chapel is supposed to be over that ridge to our left.'

'Who on earth would want to build a place of worship out here?'

Hawley shrugged. 'I have no idea. But maybe it's been dedicated to someone or something. And we're in Wales, now, too. Sometimes, nonconformists had to meet in remote places before it became more acceptable to worship their form of Christianity.'

'Worship? I'd call this place godforsaken.'

'We're looking for a path to our left.' Hawley walked on. They found it after another 50 yards, ascending through the forest where it briefly emerged at the top of a rise before descending again quickly into a dell. Hawley pointed down towards the remnants of a wooden walkway leading to the overgrown building, and beyond that, a dark pond covered by green algae.

Everything was quiet. Nothing moved. It was warm as they emerged from under the canopy of trees but as they descended, the temperature began to drop. Even in summer, because of the height of the ridge, not much sun penetrated such a desolate spot.

When they reached the rotten walkway, half-submerged by rockfall, Anna called a halt.

'Is that it?' she asked.

'According to the map, yes. Not much of it left, is there?'

'Enough, I suspect.'

They were no more than fifty yards from the ruins. Anna checked her phone. One bar. The signal had slowly diminished with every few yards of descent along the ridge.

Anna grabbed Hawley's arm. 'Ben, you need to stay here. I'm going over to take a look but I need you to be here in case the chopper comes over. If Justin's done what I've asked him to, all hell will be breaking loose soon. But they need to know where we are.'

'Are you sure you don't want me—'

'Perfectly sure.'

She left him out in the open and walked the remaining few yards, alert for any sound or movement but hearing and seeing none. She circled the building, registering the intact padlock on the door and the impenetrable foliage. She peered inside, noting the murky leaded lights in the windows, smelling the mushroom damp from the interior.

Below her, the pond was an inky, motionless slick and she wrinkled her nose at its stagnant stench. She might have missed the gap in the surrounding wall were it not for a single broken branch of fern hanging, like a fractured limb, damaged by whatever had passed through that gap. Beckoning.

Anna moved quickly but cautiously. Stood on the pile of broken stones in the remains of an archway and saw the smaller building beyond. She took in the low hole in the wall, the removed metal grill lying to one side, and knew by the sudden juddering charge that shot through her arms and legs that this was the right place.

She stepped lightly over the stones and leaned down to look in through the hole in the wall and the flagstone floor. Artificial light spilled out from a large opening. She stepped inside warily, walked across and peered down.

Battery-operated lanterns, plastic sheeting on the floor, bones, hundreds of them, stacked and arranged neatly. She rocked back on her heels, sucking in air and blowing it out, knowing she was staring through a doorway into hell.

Something, a muffled noise, drew her attention. She looked up, into the dark corner of the ruined building, not seeing it clearly but aware of something moving. Anna got up and peered into the murk. Nothing but a shape, leaning against the wall. A large, oblong rucksack in grey and green camouflage.

'Blair?' said Anna. 'Blair, is that you?'

The muffled sounds and movements increased in intensity. Another charge of adrenaline zipped through her and she quickly moved across.

'It's OK, Blair, it's OK, I'm here to help. To get you out.'

The noise that came back to her through the bag was impossible to make out, but Anna knew it was desperation. Someone terrified and gagged. She fumbled with toggles and zips, preoccupied and desperate. But her need to do something, to ease the suffering, was her undoing.

For a big man, Starkey moved quickly. Anna felt hands grab her from behind. Felt herself lifted up and carried, feet flailing, clear off the floor, towards the opening. She struggled, kicking, hearing heavy breathing behind her, smelling sour breath and worse. She tried to find purchase on the lip of the opening, but something kicked at her knees and then she was tumbling through, ten feet to the floor beneath, landing heavily, trying to roll.

Above her, she heard scraping. The noise of a metal ladder being dragged up and then the scraping of stone on stone.

She looked up to see the gap narrowing. Someone was shutting off the entrance.

'No,' she screamed. 'Kevin, stop this!'

She heard a grunt; another foot of gap disappeared.

'Kevin…'

But it wasn't her pleading that stopped Starkey from shutting her in completely. It was the clatter of blades chopping through the air as a helicopter passed low overhead.

CHAPTER FORTY-NINE

Hawley looked up, waving his arms madly as the helicopter flew over. He didn't know if he'd been seen, but the chopper slowed and banked in the air a mile away, looking like it was going to make another pass. Then a movement in his peripheral vision drew his attention and made him look down beyond the chapel ruins. There he saw a man in combat trousers and a brown T-shirt carrying a huge rucksack, heading towards the bottom of the dell. Moving steadily and unerringly towards the pond a few hundred yards beyond.

Where the hell was Anna?

'Oy!' called Hawley. 'You there!'

The figure ignored him and continued, descending through the bracken determinedly.

'Hey, hang on a minute.' Hawley started moving down off the path but then hesitated. It crossed his mind for a fraction of a second that this might simply be someone on army manoeuvres yomping through the forest.

But even the army didn't have backpacks that heavy. With a rush of horror, Hawley knew who this man was. Knew what was in that backpack.

He moved, picking up the pace, wading through the ferns and small trees at an angle to intercept the man twenty yards from the water's edge.

He kept calling out, 'Starkey, Kevin Starkey, listen to me.'

But there was no let-up in pace. Hawley emerged into a partial clearing a few yards from Starkey, who didn't miss a step. Instead, he suddenly veered towards Hawley and swung a very large and vicious-looking knife in his direction. Hawley danced back with no more than a few inches between the knife's tip and his chest.

'It's over,' said Hawley. 'They know you're here. The helicopter's seen us.'

Starkey said nothing. He half-turned, the knife outstretched towards Hawley, his back to the water. But still he took steps backwards, closing in on the pond, his eyes wild, his face unreadable.

'Is she in there? Is she in there, you fuck?' Hawley yelled. He looked at the ground, saw what he wanted and picked up a fist-sized stone. He ran forwards and threw it, hitting Starkey in the chest. The big man roared and lunged towards Hawley. But he was too slow and weighed down by the backpack.

'Let her go, you bastard,' Hawley spat and threw another rock. This close it was difficult to miss, and it hit Starkey's shoulder, making him spin and wince with pain. The edge of the pond was a reed-filled swamp. Starkey went down on one knee and shrugged off one shoulder strap, leaning back so the other one came free.

'Give it up. Give her up. There's no way out for you,' Hawley pleaded.

Starkey spoke for the first time, and his words, growled out like an angry dog, drilled into Hawley's brain to lodge there forever.

'It's not yours. It's mine. My bones to wash clean.'

Hawley let him have another rock, this one finding its mark on Starkey's neck. But now the backpack was off, Starkey got to his feet quickly and took four large steps forward, causing Hawley to dance away again. But Starkey's move was only so that he could gain some room. The moment Hawley backed away, Starkey turned back and grasped the backpack with a hand on both sides, stepped into the pond, wading quickly up to his thighs.

'No. No. You sick bastard!' yelled Hawley.

With a grunt, Starkey threw the heavy pack out into the dark water before turning back to face Hawley with a dreadful grin.

In the crypt Anna stared about her, taking in the cameras, the lights and the tools of Starkey's terrifying trade with a shiver of disgust, looking for anything to use. In the end, she resorted to grabbing as many of the larger, stronger-looking bones and laying them in a rough cross-hatch pattern on the floor. She knew she was desecrating the crypt and what was probably a crime scene, but there was no choice. She worked until she had a pile about a foot tall in the tunnel under the opening, grabbed one of the duvets and threw it over the top. Gingerly, she stepped up, hearing cracks as some of the old calcified bones gave under her weight, praying that they might hold long enough for one jump. She threw up the backpack and, swaying, flexed her knees. Reaching up, she leaped, fingers extended towards the lip of the flagstones. They found their mark and she used the momentum to pull, flexing her elbows, feeling her jacket snag on the edge of the partially replaced stone lid, pushing through the restraint, hearing material tear as first her chest and then her hips appeared at the rim and she fell forwards, scrambling through, her hands covered in dirt and debris, her muscles trembling from the effort.

Anna paused only to pick up her backpack and stumbled towards the opening. Outside, the brightness of the day took her by surprise after the cold darkness of the crypt. She ran back towards Hawley and saw immediately he wasn't there. His shouts drew her attention and she looked down in time to see Starkey propelling a heavy backpack into the water of the pond below.

Something broke inside Anna then. Gave like a taut string finally yielding to the pressure of an impossibly heavy load. There was no time to consider words like depravity or evil. They were hopelessly inadequate to describe the numb drumming in her ears.

All she knew in that moment was that her body became galvanised by purpose. She had time to hear Hawley swear and move towards Starkey in the water before she began to run.

Hawley had no thoughts other than to get to the rucksack, already three-quarters submerged in the water. Starkey was coming at him, his expression fixed, eyes now wild with an obscene purpose no sane person would ever understand. Hawley moved forwards, reaching down, grabbing whatever he could, aware of the knife in Starkey's hand, driven by the sight of the backpack sinking ever lower in the water. Starkey roared and lunged; Hawley spun and threw mud and dirt into the man's face. It slowed Starkey, caused him to hesitate and splutter, a big hand coming up to wipe, allowing Hawley to run past into the water. He felt the sharp stab in his shoulder, felt the resistance of bone as the blade slid, but continued on, reaching for the straps, ducking sideways in an attempt to get away from Starkey and pull the rucksack out.

Weighed down by its contents and water, Hawley needed both hands to haul, feet sinking and slipping into the silt below, groaning, teeth grinding with effort, the backpack at last now more out of the water than in. He turned in time to see Starkey looming above him, only barely able to turn away from the downward thrust of the knife. But this time there was real pain as the blade cut through the muscles of his forearm. Hawley fell, hitting the shallow water, knowing he needed to get up, knowing Starkey was above him now and that the next strike of the knife might be to chest or neck or head. He turned, spluttering, helpless on his back, looking up at the monstrous shadow above him, hearing only the *whump, whump, whump* of the helicopter blades as it hovered above them.

CHAPTER FIFTY

Anna deployed her ASP and the telescopic baton felt reassuringly solid in her hand. She ran into the water, the splashes loud, her knees high, wanting him to know she was there. It worked. The noise made Starkey hesitate and turn. But Anna had the advantage of momentum.

Move fast, hit hard. That was what her instructors always told her.

There was no hesitation as she put all her weight behind a single blow to the outside of Starkey's thigh. He buckled and she knew the pain would be immense. There was a problem in using the lower extremities as targets because it left you open to blows from the upper limbs. But she had surprise and shock and the water on her side. Starkey's arm holding the knife dropped, and Anna brought the baton back on the counter-swing and hit him above the elbow.

His hand jerked open, spilling the knife into the water.

Starkey howled with pain. He was on his knees. Anna held the PAVA canister in her other hand and, from a metre, sprayed it into Starkey's face. Pelargonic acid vannillylamide was what most UK forces had gone over to using. Naturally occurring and closely related to the irritant in chilli peppers, it incapacitated through severe pain for up to an hour. Anna's aim was good and Starkey got some in both eyes. He screamed, both hands balled to his orbits as he flopped and flailed.

Anna stood back. Starkey was stumbling out of the water, whimpering, unable to see.

'Get on the floor,' she ordered.

He didn't comply.

'On the floor.' She went behind him and kicked at his knees. He stumbled and she booted his back so that he fell forwards.

'Hands behind you. Put your hands behind you.'

Still he didn't comply. She knelt on his back, using the baton against the back of his neck. 'Put your hands behind you, NOW.'

Weakly, Starkey shifted his arms and she had the rigid cuffs on him within seconds. His feet were still in the water. It wouldn't take much to kick him around so his face was in an inch of mud. She could use her foot then. Press his nose and mouth into the filth. Use the Velcro straps to restrain his legs. She wondered how long it might take for the bastard to drown.

Janice Dawson's ragged, broken voice reached out to her.

'*He boiled her bones, you know that?*'

She thought about it then. Wondered how it might have been if the helicopter had not been hovering. Some – colleagues who had to deal with filth like Starkey and the aftermath, the press, the horror etched in the faces of the relatives – might have accepted pressing his face into the choking mud as a blessing, a mercy killing. A way of ridding the world of a blight. But Anna was a hunter, not an executioner. Neither the judge nor the jury. And the force would see it as cold-blooded murder. It would mean a criminal conduct dismissal and a trial. Common sense held sway.

But it took a hefty dollop of self-persuasion and a pinch of self-preservation. Instead, Anna contented herself with imagining it and committing the crime in her mind. That way it was over and done within seconds.

She surprised herself by feeling no remorse. No burning need to chastise herself.

Shaw would have been proud.

Anna turned away. Starkey was no longer her priority. She turned back to Hawley, who was already getting to his feet and yanking on the rucksack once more. They dragged it out, over the mud and through the reeds and the pond scum, both of them panting with effort, Hawley falling to his knees frantically, his arm slick with his own blood mingled with the filthy silt, searching for the zipper, tearing it open, ripping back the cover.

She was in there. Trussed up like a piece of meat. Duct tape over her mouth, around her arms, around her knees and her torso. Anna held the rucksack while Hawley yanked her out by the shoulders. Blair wasn't moving. She was inanimate flesh. Drowned in three feet of water.

'No. No. No,' said Hawley, laying her on her side. Anna fumbled at the tape. But Hawley was reaching for something in his pocket and pulled out keys. Or something that looked like a key, but which he unfolded to reveal a small, thin blade that sliced through the tape around Blair's mouth, her arms and her legs and torso.

Behind them, Starkey was moaning.

Hawley pulled away the tape over Blair's mouth and flipped her over onto her back before he pinched her nose, ready to apply mouth to mouth. But he was shaking, staring at her, and Anna saw that he was terrified. This was what Starkey, and the police's handling of Rosie Dawson' murder had done to him. Paralysed him with doubt and fear, even when it came to a matter of life and death.

Anna walked across and put a hand on his shoulder. 'Ben. It's OK. It's OK to do this. You have to.'

Hawley turned his face up to the sky and screamed in frustration.

'Ben,' Anna said firmly. 'Help her.'

Hawley looked at her, squeezed his eyes shut once and then bent his head to blow air into Blair's throat. Five quick breaths followed by chest compressions, rapidly, twice per second. Then he listened, ear close to her heart. Unsatisfied, he gave her two more breaths and repeated the compressions. Thirty times. After the third set of rescue breaths, as he listened again for any hint of respiration, Blair coughed, threw up two lots of dirty water and moaned. Hawley pushed her onto her side and leaned in close to her.

'It's OK, Blair, everything is OK. Just breathe, lovely. Breathe.'

Anna exhaled one long, tremulous sigh. Something dense and brittle that had been wrapped around her throat cracked. She knew her mouth was trembling, felt the tears come and did nothing to stop them. She fell to her knees in the mud, arms loose in front of her, letting the adrenaline leech away. She reached out and touched Hawley, smiling in approval and gratitude. He returned it briefly before he turned back to his patient, stroking her hair, talking to her. Blair's face was turned towards Anna. Frightened, confused, her flesh pale, her eyes blinking and staring back. But staring back alive.

It was ten seconds before Anna could get back to her feet.

She walked over to where Starkey was lying, face down in the mud. She wasn't thinking about Shaw anymore. She was thinking of Shipwright. What he would have done. She leaned over and said, 'Kevin Starkey, I am arresting you for the abduction and attempted murder of Blair Smeaton. You do not have to say anything. But it may harm your defence if you do not mention when questioned something which you later rely on in court. Anything you do say may be given in evidence.'

Starkey said only one word. With his face turned, it emerged distorted and alien, more like a gruff bark. But Anna heard it well enough.

'Bitch.'

'Too bloody right,' she said in reply.

Within twenty minutes, the dell surrounding St Wystone's was teeming with police. Because of the terrain, they airlifted Blair out and, having seen Hawley's wounds, Anna insisted he go too. In truth, they'd had no choice because Blair wouldn't let Hawley's hand go no matter how much the paramedics asked her to.

As the casualties took off in the air ambulance and before she spoke to the DI from Gwent Police who was coordinating their response, Anna knew she needed to make one call. She took out her phone, found the number on speed dial and walked back up the slope to the ruins, where she stood looking down at the foetid water that Starkey had tried to use with such murderous intent and pressed the call button.

'Danaher,' said the answering voice.

'Julie, it's Anna Gwynne. We've found her and she's alive.'

Two long seconds of inhaled breath led to the noises of a chair scraping quickly across a hard floor, the muffled sound of a hand being placed roughly over a receiver and a disembodied series of incoherent shouts.

'Ma'am, I've put you on speaker,' Danaher again, urgency and bewilderment lifting her voice. 'Could you repeat what you said?'

'I'm in a forest in Wales watching an air ambulance on its way to hospital. In it is Blair Smeaton and she is very much alive.'

Anna would later swear she heard the roar of triumph erupting from Edinburgh even without a phone.

CHAPTER FIFTY-ONE

They took Blair to the children's hospital in Bristol and Hawley to the infirmary. He needed transfusions and sutures, and they kept him in for five days for fear of infection from the stagnant pond water. Blair went back to Edinburgh, to Kirsty, her mother and Bernard after a week.

The press had a field day. Photographs of Blair with her mother and sister made the front pages for weeks, Mrs Smeaton either beaming or in tears in equal measure. The image showed a fridge stocked with lollipops so that Blair and Kirsty never had to walk to the shop for one again.

A search of Starkey's workshop threw up a thumb drive whose contents were never revealed in any detail to the relatives. It was clear he'd used St Wystone's as his killing field. Some of the videos seemed to concentrate on the terror he tried to induce in his victims before and during. Harrowing images linking him to all the abductions and murders of the missing children Hawley tied together with his theory. There were photographs of all his victims, including those he'd used as adverts on the Littlefeet, Pinocchio and UWAntme sites. The stored passwords led to his own Dark Web PPV page. But even Varga did not get access to that. They had specialists trained for that sort of thing. It was not a job anyone did for very long.

It would take weeks if not months to sift through the bone repository. But already they'd found some that were younger, fresher, whiter than the others. Identifications would follow. Lily

Callaghan and Jade Hemmings and Katelyn Prosser, names Anna was by now terribly familiar with, were only three amongst many.

They also found a cryptocurrency hard drive, a wallet which Starkey refused to provide the password for. Despite every effort on the part of the Hi-Tech unit, it remained unopenable. Varga explained to Anna that it was designed to be impenetrable. She also surmised that due to what they found on his laptop, and how many years he'd been using the Dark Web, it would probably be brimming with bitcoins.

In his role as a maintenance engineer for Rowsys, Starkey accessed a huge range of areas not usually available to the public. Hard-pressed NHS clinics where notes would often be left in preparation, or in piles awaiting pick-up, and all the victims had been seen in hospital in the six months leading up to their abductions at a time when Starkey was present. He'd kept a low profile. He must have fitted in. A ghost. Or perhaps more a spectre that watched and waited, read through files and made notes of his own, deciding which of his victims might be the most vulnerable, the most accessible.

Choosing which of his flowers to pick.

A week after Anna and Hawley confronted Starkey, on a dull afternoon with clouds building in the west, Anna met with Rainsford. The meeting had a very different feel to it from the last time they'd met for a Friday afternoon conflab. Last time, they'd talked about Woakes, his gung-ho approach and the risk he posed in future investigations. From the look on Rainsford's face, he was sharing that memory with her now. Holder and Khosa had once again acquitted themselves brilliantly, but Woakes' frantic search of Pux Cottage had been the final straw in terms of his probation.

'I'm sorry about Dave,' Rainsford said.

'You weren't to know, sir.'

'No, but I still should have.'

Anna nodded. 'The CSC at Pux Cottage went apeshit when she saw what he'd done.' She'd heard that had the crime scene coordinator been armed, Woakes would not have made it back to HQ. 'But I've heard he's avoided disciplinary procedures.'

Rainsford's mouth twisted into a grimace. 'He has. It's all HR bullshit. But the good news is he's dropped the bullying accusation.'

'Sir, please don't tell me it's a trade-off. Dave is a liability. The bullying stuff was complete crap—'

Rainsford's expression told Anna she didn't need to convince him, and she shut up. No need to vent here. She'd done that enough already.

'I know that's what you think has happened, but I don't buy it. I think he's had time to think things through. I suspect his ego won't let him admit how much grief you gave him.'

'Because I'm a woman?'

'Probably. Dave Woakes thinks he can do most things better than everyone else. He has delegation issues. We decided, by mutual consent, that his probationary period would end here.'

'Did you suggest a change of career?' Anna asked. 'Any vacancies in the reptile house at the zoo?'

Rainsford smiled. 'As you know, Inspector, we are committed to working with our officers and giving them every opportunity to improve.' The mock officiousness in Rainsford's voice almost made her smile.

'That makes me feel so much better,' Anna lied.

'He's gone back to East Mids. I've suggested a psychological assessment and retraining. Do I think it's likely? No. Dave is one of those people who will never quite fit in. He's a behavioural analyst's dream.'

'So long as they dream somewhere else.'

'Amen to that, Anna.'

'What about Starkey, sir?'

Rainsford shook his head.

'Is he talking?'

'Not much. His lawyers have him gagged while the psychiatrists do their assessments.'

Anna didn't envy them that task.

'The ACC wants to shake your hand again, Anna.'

'Do I have to?'

'You know you do.'

'But it's cold and clammy.'

'You make him sound like one of the undead.'

Anna shrugged and raised one eyebrow. 'You know I'd much rather get back to work.'

'We still need to find someone instead of Woakes. The squad needs a bit of beef.'

'We'll manage—'

'Yes, I've seen how you manage. You'll manage better with help. Don't worry, I'll let you vet him or her next time. I promise.'

CHAPTER FIFTY-TWO

The team held a semi-official celebration at the Lantern the day Blair was released from hospital, and afterwards, Khosa dropped Anna off at her Horfield flat. By the time she got there, the day had all but gone, and over in the park nearby, dogs were being walked and kids were still skateboarding against the backdrop of a red-and-orange flamed sunset. She poured herself a glass of cold water, turned up London Grammar on her iPhone and went out into the garden. Warmth and light had nudged her pots into life, and purple lavender and dark and velvety silver-veined heuchera mingled with ferns and hostas around the tiny corner of the outdoors she'd tamed for herself.

On the little table, next to the iced water, she placed both phones. The one that rang and interrupted the music was her personal iPhone. She scanned the number. A mobile, not one she recognised. She toyed with declining it but something made her press accept.

'Hi, it's me, Ben. Am I disturbing you?'

She'd seen Hawley a couple of times since they'd confronted Starkey at St Wystone's. Both times in the hospital when she'd visited Blair. He'd been interviewed, of course, but Rainsford insisted someone else did that since both Hawley and Anna were material witnesses in the case.

'No, not at all. I'm in my garden. Relaxing.'

'Ah, right.'

The slight delay and the background hiss and hum of traffic told her he was in a car, his voice hesitant and nervous.

'It's hot,' he said.

She played the game. Waiting for him to get to the point. 'It is.'

'I've done a shift at Gloucester Royal. I'm on the way home. Rang on the off chance that you might fancy a drink?'

She'd only had a spritzer at the Lantern, not wanting to sacrifice the evening with too much early alcohol. No one tried to cajole her into acting otherwise. They knew her too well. It was simply Anna staying in control. But now, with Hawley on the other end of the phone, she wondered if something else had made her hold back. An intangible premonition.

Did she? Did she want a drink? The garden was quiet. Idyllic. It would mean changing and a shower because she still had her work stink on her.

Kate, imagined as a little devil on her shoulder, was screaming in her ear. *Of course you bloody do!*

But could she be bothered? Did she want to be bothered?

The answer, when it emerged from her mouth, came as a surprise. 'Yes, I'd love a drink. You know the Welly?'

'In Horfield? Yes. I'm in Patchway. Say fifteen minutes?'

She finished her water, showered, found some jeans and a clean top. The Wellington was a Victorian pub with a bright interior and leaded lights. It retained a community feel and pulled in a rugby crowd in the winter. But this evening, people were eating and drinking outside, enjoying the weather.

The patio was busy, so Hawley'd found a table in an alcove with a nice breeze blowing through from the wide-open window. He looked much better than the last time she'd seen him with a drip in his arm and bandages on his shoulder, pale from loss of blood and sporting three days of stubble. Now he was tanned and lean, his hair cut and his jaw shaven. He stood as she entered, grinned, walked out from the leather-backed bench he'd been sitting on. Anna returned the smile.

'You look well,' she said.

'So do you. What can I get you?'

She glanced at the half-pint on the table in front of him. 'They do a reasonable Sauvignon. The New Zealand.'

She watched him go to the bar and order. He wore a white shirt and chinos. Filled them both well. Kate would approve.

When he'd come back and sat, he held up his glass. 'So, cheers,' he said.

They clinked glasses. 'Are you celebrating?' Anna asked.

'In a way. The fact you agreed to meet me. That's worth a shout.'

Anna laughed.

'Wow,' said Hawley. 'You should definitely do that more often.'

'I haven't had many good reasons to laugh lately.'

Hawley nodded. 'Yeah. I wasn't sure how to play this.'

'What?'

'Well, I've been wanting to talk to you about… him. But I wasn't sure we were allowed to.'

Anna shrugged. 'Of course we can talk. You've given your statement, I've given mine.'

'Plus, you're a little bit scary.'

Anna said nothing and let her eyebrows do the talking.

'You know what I mean,' Hawley said quickly.

'Not entirely.'

'You're a detective inspector to begin with. So, there's always the worry that you're… detecting, watching, deducting.'

'Why should that worry you?'

'You know why.'

Anna conceded with an exhalation. 'Fair enough. In your case. But no one needs to be worried about me… detecting, unless they've got good reason to.'

'And then there's the way you look.'

This time Anna did frown. 'How do I look?'

'Up there. In a definitely-out-of-my-league kind of way.'

'Seems like you scare easily, Ben.'

'Maybe.' Hawley's gaze dropped before it fixed her again, this time earnestly. 'So, was it him? Did he kill all those girls?'

Anna took a sip of wine. 'Yes, he did. Saw them in the hospitals he was servicing. Targeted them. Followed them, sometimes for months I would guess. He had an ideal opportunity. On the road. His job often making him stay away from his home. With Rosie, he chose her because she was local to where he lived. It offered more opportunity for planning. He misled us into believing we were looking for someone with a red van. But it was a white van he'd used. His van.'

'Jesus.'

'Worse is that he was one of us. A special constable. So that lent an added degree of credence to his evidence.'

Hawley sent her a pained look of disbelief. 'Does anyone know why?'

'I expect the forensic psychiatrists will have a go. Your guess is as good as mine.' She wasn't going to tell him about the PPV images and the sordid, dreadful business Starkey was advertising. Red rooms didn't need to be for public consumption, though Hawley was hardly 'the public'. She made the judgement call. What she did tell him about was Starkey's parents' cottage and what they'd found there. He deserved that. In return, Hawley explained how he'd been asked to go to Edinburgh to see Blair and her family and how he'd turned down at least four offers from the press to tell his 'story'.

'You're not tempted? Clear your name?'

Hawley shrugged. 'I might go to Edinburgh. I've never been to the Fringe. I thought I might call in on Blair while I'm there, combine the trip. They want to make me a meal, Blair's mum and her sister. I think it's important for them. It's the least I could do. But as for the press, I don't want to go anywhere near them. I know the truth and your lot do now. That's what's important.' His mouth trembled slightly when he said this and she sensed the emotion behind it. 'How is Sergeant Woakes, by the way?'

'A long way from here.'

'Good.'

They talked. About the case, about work. And talking to Hawley was, to her amazement, easy. He listened and had something intelligent to say about almost everything. More than once his easy humour made her laugh, something he seemed to enjoy doing. And she enjoyed letting him. By the time they'd finished their drinks it was dark outside. Not fully, but the odd twilight that lingers so deliciously in summer.

'Do you want me to walk you back?' Hawley asked as they exited. 'I don't mean to be patronising. I mean, I know I don't need to walk you anywhere. I've seen you in action.'

Anna laughed. It was getting to be a habit. 'There's no need. There are lots of people about and I'm just around the corner near the common.'

They stood next to Hawley's Audi. There were revellers around, happy, relaxed from a good meal and a few drinks. Anna sensed this was something both she and Hawley had a shared enjoyment of. Pub dinners and hot lazy evenings were a universe away from their working lives – his with the travails of the sick and injured, hers with the monsters and the scum.

Hawley reached for his keys but hesitated. 'Anna, I don't know what the rules are on this, but I had a good time this evening so would it be OK if we did this again? If you wanted to, that is.'

'I'm not investigating you anymore, Ben. There are no rules.'

'So, could I give you a ring maybe? I promise I won't grill you next time.'

Anna tilted her head. 'I thought you were scared of me, Dr Hawley.'

'Not anymore. Besides, I'm all for confronting one's fears.'

Hawley opened the passenger car door and from the seat took out a black plastic case with a yellow lid and silvered snap-locks. He handed it to Anna. She stared at it until the penny dropped.

'Your tool box?' was what Anna said. *Your suicide kit,* was what she thought.

Hawley nodded. 'I thought maybe you should take it. Not to use, to get rid of, I mean.'

Anna took the case. 'I'll put it in lost and found. No one will ever find it there. No one ever finds anything there.'

'Thanks.'

'And, yes, why don't you give me a ring. I'd like that,' she said, and it came out easy and honest. 'And if you do decide to go to Edinburgh, let me know. There are some other people up there besides Blair who'd like to say thank you.'

'You should come with me,' said Hawley. He leaned forwards and kissed her on the cheek; his smile, when he pulled back, mischievous, the invitation open and playful.

Nothing more was said and he got into his car and drove off. She watched him leave and turned back towards her flat. Halfway there she touched the spot where his lips had been and felt a warm and pleasant echo. Maybe she would text Kate and tell her she'd been out for a drink with someone. No, she'd keep it for Sunday lunchtime in case her sister's screams woke up the kids.

There were people on the summer city streets, lights on in people's houses. But in a Scottish city many miles away, Blair Smeaton would sleep soundly that night clutching her stuffed dog, with her sister's arm loosely about her and her mother awake from the fourth week of cigarette and alcohol cold-turkey.

When Rainsford had told Anna she was up for a commendation for apprehending Starkey, she'd replied it was Hawley who should have got a medal.

Anna slid the key into her front door and opened it. From the way Ben had looked at her that evening after the kiss, maybe he thought he already had.

CHAPTER FIFTY-THREE

TWO MONTHS LATER

The site known as Chailey Common was but a stone's throw from the grandeur of Sheffield Park in Sussex. Yet this heathland was always meant for common use as opposed to private ownership. The police used the cricket club car park for the ground-probing radar equipment to be brought in. They'd also commandeered the car park on Warr's Hill; that was where the cadaver dog team had encamped.

It was mid-afternoon and a dull day in mid-August, but still humid and warm. Anna suspected rain was on the way and with it a change of air. She, for one, was looking forward to it. Sussex Police were providing support on the ground, but Avon and Somerset, at the behest of Superintendent Rainsford, had provided transport for Shaw. The private companies contracted for prison escort and custody services to and from courts were not geared up for a category A prisoner like him. He was way above their pay grade.

Unlike the last time Anna had accompanied him to an abandoned asylum in North Wales, Shaw admitted he was less sure of exactly where his 'treasure' was buried though he'd guided them to Red House Common unerringly.

'I'll know it when I see it,' he'd said.

Anna knew Shaw was motivated as much by an opportunity to be out of his prison environment as his 'desire' to help the police.

Or more specifically, help Anna. There'd been no discussion. That was the deal. He insisted on leading them to the site, flatly refusing to give directions. He either came with them on what he euphemistically called a 'day out' or they could all stay home and watch *Countdown*.

This time Anna had brought Khosa with her, justifying it as good experience, but also wanting to keep Holder away from the worst of Shaw's barbs. The curious thing about the multiple murderer was his politeness when it came to young women. Women, Anna suspected, who reminded him of his own daughter.

Shaw, handcuffed and flanked on either side by two armed officers, led them towards a windmill, but when they arrived he ignored it and scanned his surroundings until he spied a memorial stone placed to commemorate two people whose work paved the way for the reconstitution of the nature reserve. When Shaw saw it, he stopped, turned and smiled at Anna.

'Tell them to grid the field west of here.'

'Who is here, Hector?' Anna asked.

'Let's find him first, shall we?'

'Do you have a name?'

'No. Krastev wasn't capable of proper speech by the time he gave this place up. But this is it. By the windmill, near the stone.'

Anna gave the search teams their instructions. Shaw watched in his prison kit, a thin sheen of sweat on his shaven head. Khosa stood some way off. Anna hadn't asked her to, but she suspected the DC had no intention of getting any closer to Shaw than she absolutely had to. And he, so far, had ignored her. She was extraneous, not part of his script.

'Right,' she said when the dogs began, 'we'll see what shows up. But is there anything else you can tell me?'

Shaw turned his gaze upon her. The evening was full of normal, earthy smells and sounds. The whine of machines from the farms, the smell of cut grass, the buzz of insects. But Anna knew the flaring of Shaw's nostrils was for her. She'd tried to remember not to put any perfume on that morning, but she'd forgotten in the ritual of preparation – though she only ever used something very light for work. Hours had passed but clearly it still lingered. She was annoyed with herself for giving Shaw this satisfaction of being able to smell her. But it was too late now.

'Hector. What did Krastev say exactly?'

'The Black Squid used Krastev as a verifier sometimes. Where the victims could not verify themselves. Like this one who was ordered to take a bottle of sleeping pills and then be buried alive. Krastev said he'd done as instructed. Buried the boy, photographed it as it was done, sent the images to the administrator.'

'Is this what he did with Tanya Cromer?'

'No. Tanya had nothing to do with the Black Squid. She was for Krastev's own… enjoyment. Off plan. But we both know she ended up being his downfall.'

The noise of the cadaver dog reached them across the common. A black Lab named Sinbad. Anna saw his handler put a heavy collar on him, indicating to the dog a search was imminent.

'Did he tell you about any other Black Squid victims?' Anna asked.

Shaw nodded.

'So why did you choose here?'

Shaw smiled. Out of the corner of her eye, Anna saw Khosa flinch.

'It's beautiful here. It's a long way from Whitmarsh prison. It's a summer's evening.' He gave her one of his slow blinks. She'd seen that before. Sometimes it was a warning; other times she'd read it as a mark of a patient, canted humour.

'None of those are the real reasons though, are they?'

Shaw tilted his head. 'I want you to see that I can be helpful, Anna. I get the feeling you still don't trust me. Even after my help with that child-murdering bastard, Starkey.'

He was absolutely correct on that score. She didn't trust him. Not fully. She glanced at the armed policeman cradling his automatic weapon. He returned a wary smile of confirmation. Next to the monument, Sinbad was covering the ground quickly, tail up, nose down.

Anna considered Shaw's statement. Trust was an odd word to use, but he'd used it before. He'd shown no remorse for his crimes and had cultivated their relationship because he wanted her to trust him. At least when it came to revealing his 'treasures'. Yet she still wasn't sure exactly why. Outside the confines of the prison, he was more open, more willing to talk to her. And he wanted her to know that. Apart from Tanya Cromer, whom, she was now convinced, he tried to save, the 'buried treasure' Shaw was revealing to them was linked to Black Squid. All victims in some shape or form of the nameless, faceless murderous puppeteer who tricked and manipulated his victims into horrible deaths, aided and abetted by Krastev.

Shaw's motivation was vendetta-fuelled and, she suspected, had a lot more mileage left.

Sinbad had covered a 20-metre-square area when he suddenly started pawing at the ground. He ran from left to right but came back to a spot adjacent to a fence bordering a residential property and barked. His handler came over and threw him a ball. His reward for finding the treasure. Anna'd read that a cadaver dog could find a human tooth buried 12 feet under the earth.

The GPR team came in with their mobile detector. Ten minutes later, Anna got the nod to say they'd found something.

Anna spoke to a DI Becker from Sussex Police, a rangy murder squad veteran with cheekbones pocked from old acne scars. This was his case now. She brought him over to speak to Shaw, who, once the presence of a body was confirmed, had been taken back to the transport vehicle where he stood, flanked by the uniforms.

Becker asked, 'DI Gwynne tells me you know who did this?'

Shaw, eyes down, looked slowly up into Becker's face. 'It's a drainage ditch. The man who buried the boy knew they were doing ground works. He didn't even need to dig the hole himself.'

'You seem to know a lot,' Becker said.

Shaw gave him one of his slow blinks. Anna was suddenly glad of the handcuffs and the armed escort.

'I've given the details to Inspector Gwynne,' Shaw said.

'Would you be prepared to give us a statement?'

'Only to Inspector Gwynne.'

Becker sighed and turned to Anna. 'Looks like we'll both be visiting Hector at his, then.'

'No,' Shaw said. 'Don't bother. I will only speak to her. You ask me through her. But she will be busy. Inspector Gwynne is going to have her own case to investigate.'

Both police officers exchanged glances before turning to Shaw.

'What do you mean, Hector?' Anna asked.

'I think it's time I showed you one closer to home. Krastev was reluctant to tell me about it. He needed a lot of, how should I put it, persuading. And there's something about it that smells bad. He kept saying 'chudovishtna kushta'. I had to look it up. It means monster house.'

'That doesn't help.'

'No?' Shaw tilted his head. 'Somewhere you keep the mad and the very, very bad, I'd guess.' He breathed in slowly through his nose, eyes shut. Anna hoped he was taking in the country air, but she suspected it was mainly her that he was attempting to ingest.

His veiled references were beginning to irritate her. He'd already dragged her off to an abandoned asylum where Krastev had been buried. And a small but cynical part of her still wondered if this was merely some kind of sick and elaborate game he was playing.

The monster house.

Had Krastev really said that or was this another bigoted reference to the mentally ill from Shaw himself? His smugness was beginning to annoy her.

'What if I said no, Hector. What if I said I wasn't interested in any more liaisons. Either tell me now what you know or go back to your cell and rot.'

The silence that followed seemed to have its own heartbeat. Finally, Shaw looked up and spoke, his tone even and soft.

'Now why would you want to take that attitude, Inspector? I thought we had an understanding.'

'The only thing I understand is that you're feeding us tidbits instead of letting us have the whole takeaway.'

'Quid Pro Quo, Anna.'

'Days out, you mean?' Anna shook her head. 'Come on Hector.'

'I'm giving you a chance to progress your career, Anna. You should be grateful.'

'Grateful.' Anna nodded. 'I see. Well, dealing with the aftermath of another body should see us through another few months, so I'll be tied up for a while.'

'Time is not on my side, you know that.'

She paused then, assimilating his words. It was a strange thing to say. Shaw was only in his fifties. 'I'm not going to try and understand what that means. But I've got lots of time. So how about I find someone else to walk in Abbie's shoes for you instead of me.' She knew she was goading. Any mention of Abbie Shaw was like lighting blue touchpaper.

'You aren't Abbie and I would be grateful if you did not use her name in an attempt at scoring points off me.'

'But isn't that exactly what you're trying to do every single time you take us out to a body? I'm sure she'd be very proud.'

Becker, who'd watched the exchange, said, 'And there is a lot to be proud of, isn't there, Hector?'

Shaw had been cooperation epitomised. Quiet, wary almost. That went some way to explain why they were all so unprepared for what happened next. Shaw let his eyes drop and, in one lunge, charged at Becker. The detective was caught totally off balance. He fell. Shaw, hands cuffed behind him, fell too. But there was nothing accidental about the way he collapsed on top of Becker, his face reaching up towards the detective's throat. If it hadn't been for the escort's quick reactions, Anna had no doubt that Shaw would have bitten. She'd seen him bite before. Seen a trainee psychiatrist lose an ear in the process.

They bundled Shaw into the cage in the rear of the van. Once he was up he offered very little resistance. All he did in the time it took to put him in and slam the doors shut was glare at Anna. And in that look there was warning.

They drove Shaw away. Becker, though unharmed, looked very shaken as he patted dirt from his suit. Anna took the opportunity to apologise again.

'Don't,' Becker said. 'You should never try and make pets of wild animals, my old gran used to say. But it's a result, isn't it? The body I mean. What I still don't get is why Shaw's being so cooperative after all these years.'

'Who knows,' Khosa said.

Anna kept her head down, massaging the stresses of the day out of her neck with one hand. It hid her face and, she hoped, the guilty expression she wore. She had her own theories but they weren't for sharing here.

She studied her colleagues. Becker had been in the game a long time, but, like most other police officers she knew, had never come across something like Shaw before. Khosa was still sharp and keen, but Anna noticed how she'd kept her distance. She wouldn't blame her for that because it was a shared wariness. The type of fascination you had with a caged animal that, though it was confined, instinct told you not to get too close to.

They talked through the case. Jurisdiction here devolved to Sussex, but Krastev was a link not be ignored and Anna had already briefed them about Shaw's daughter and her tragic suicide.

'What else do you think he has to show you, Anna? And where?' Becker asked. If the bodies Shaw had revealed so far were anything to go by, they could be spread far and wide.

Anna found no answer to give.

The journey home seemed endless and Anna, choosing to drive, spent most of it pondering Becker's questions. The ones she had declined to answer. She thought about the cadaver dog, Sinbad. Clever, loyal, accepting and no bloody small talk. Everything she wanted in a companion.

The sun was a dangerously brilliant orb in her line of sight as she headed directly west in the car with Khosa busy texting her brother beside her. The DC had been subdued since witnessing Shaw's violent reaction, but all it had done was reinforce her determination to keep as far away from the man as possible. Both Khosa and Holder had been on a high for the last few days. Spanish police had picked up Morton and they'd both gone to the airport for the handover a couple of days ago.

They'd brought her back a mug with 'World's Best Boss' written on it.

Hawley would be waiting for Anna at the end of her journey that evening. She comforted herself with the thought as she drove, a wry smile on her face, occasionally lowering the window and letting the breeze wash away the sticky smell of coffee and Khosa's mints steeped in her nose.

But it failed to blow away the thoughts of Shaw that stubbornly kept reasserting themselves.

He'd promised to show her something else and had shown no inclination, now that he had Anna involved, to let her go. His preoccupation with her had everything to do with his belief that he'd found in her an instrument of justice for the crimes perpetrated against him, and his own. It was not a very comfortable feeling.

But the Black Squid and the men who persisted in peddling it were a real phenomenon.

She thought about Shaw festering in his prison cell for all those years, ruminating on those he had been unable to impart his 'justice' upon. He had waited, a patient hunter, for the right prey to enter his domain before reaching out and dragging her into his psychological lair. But should she consider herself the prey here? She suspected Shaw considered her an ally and their relationship a symbiotic one. Despite the heat, Anna suddenly shivered, her heart thumping. That was an equally uncomfortable thought.

Shaw's conversations were as seductive as they were terrifying. She had turned to him twice in order to try and understand the way killers thought and acted. She'd caught Willis first and then Starkey, and Shaw's dispassionate appraisal provided vital insight in both cases.

Shipwright, her old mentor, would have created merry hell had he known. And Anna knew the game she was playing was a dangerous one. But Shaw had somehow managed to align his agenda with hers and she could not, in all consciousness, step away from the lion's cage.

To do so meant letting bodies lie in shallow graves undiscovered, allowing relatives to hope where there was none, and turning away from the chance to hunt monsters.

A LETTER FROM DYLAN

Once again, a huge thank you for choosing to read *Blood Runs Cold*. If you enjoyed it, and want to keep up-to-date with all my latest releases, please sign up at the following link. Your email address will never be shared and you can unsubscribe at any time.

www.bookouture.com/dylan-young

In the next book, the 'buried treasure' Shaw reveals to Anna is right on her doorstep. Another body, another cold case, another Black Squid victim, or is it?

Anna must disentangle the lies and horrifying secrets from a murky past to reveal the truth before more innocents fall prey. But Hector Shaw has ideas of his own…

I hope you loved *Blood Runs Cold*, and if you did I would be very grateful if you could write a review. I'd love to hear what you think, and it makes such a difference helping new readers to discover one of my books for the first time.

I love hearing from my readers – you can get in touch on my Facebook page, through Twitter, Goodreads or my website.

Thanks,
Dylan

dyoungwrites

@dyoungwrites

www.dylanyoungauthor.com/

ACKNOWLEDGEMENTS

Thanks to all the team at Bookouture who do so much to make stories into novels. Special mention goes to Jennifer Hunt and Deandra Lupu for their always constructive comments and guidance. I am also grateful to Rebecca Bradley and Steve Slater for their generous help with the technical side of modern policing.